STARS *in the* NIGHT

STARS *in the* NIGHT

CARA C. PUTMAN

summerside
PRESS™

Summerside Press™
Minneapolis 55438
www.summersidepress.com

Stars in the Night
© 2010 by Cara Putman

ISBN 978-1-60936-011-5

Scripture references are from the following sources:
The Holy Bible, King James Version (KJV).

All characters are fictional. Any resemblances to
actual people are purely coincidental.

Cover design by Chris Gilbert | www.studiogearbox.com.

Interior design by Müllerhaus Publishing Group |
www.mullerhaus.net.

*Summerside Press™ is an inspirational publisher offering fresh,
irresistible books to uplift the heart and engage the mind.*

Printed in USA.

DEDICATION

Colleen, thank you for believing in me from the moment Eric
told you I wanted to be a writer. My life is so much richer
because you've believed in, encouraged, and pushed me.

AUTHOR'S NOTE

I have long loved the World War II time period. Since discovering it in its richness as a teenager, I've often thought I would have made a better teen in the '30s and '40s than in the '80s and '90s.

I love my movies in black and white. I love my music with swing and soul. And I love the heart of a generation that united to fight a common enemy in ways that I hope we would today. That love for the history and time tugged me to this story. I'd been blessed to write two series set on the home front. At the end of those, I began to pray about where I should go next.

Hollywood seemed logical. You've got glamour. You've got glitz. You've got movie stars who stayed and movie stars who put careers on hold to enlist. From Ronald Reagan to Jimmy Stewart to Clark Gable, many stars sought a role in uniform. But not everyone could. Some were exempt because of health. Some were exempt because of age. And others were the wrong sex. Yet as in so many parts of the country, many wanted to find a way to serve the cause.

The Hollywood Victory Caravan was part of that effort. The real caravan traveled by train from Los Angeles to Washington, D.C., where they opened at the White House. The true caravan was packed with stars, a veritable who's who of Hollywood—Bing Crosby. Claudette Colbert. Desi Arnaz. Laurel and Hardy. Groucho Marx. Add in a couple dozen and you have the group that crossed the northern United States and stopped in cities like Chicago and Minneapolis to entertain crowds and, more important...sell war bonds. The trip was highly successful.

My mind began to spin with ideas. What if there were a second caravan? And what if it ended up having the flair of The Orient Express? What if people died and you had to suspect people you would never in a million years have believed capable of murder? While the second caravan is completely fictional, I hope you enjoy the flavor of the real caravan and authentic settings. And most of all the spirit of that Greatest Generation.

Many thanks to Susan Downs for approaching me about a historical romantic-suspense story and being every bit as excited about *Stars in the Night* as I was. It has been a thrill to work with Susan. And thanks to Ellen Tarver and Jim Davis for helping me express everything in the way I intended. I am so excited to work with the team at Summerside on this book. Sabrina Butcher, Crystal Miller, and Sue Lyzenga jumped in to help in such an important way by reading the book as I wrote it. They know me and my writing and made sure everything worked. And huge thanks to Robin Miller and Colleen Coble for brainstorming the germ of an idea into a full-fledged plot.

Many thanks to my wonderful agent, Karen Solem, who has always believed in me and never pushed me. On the contrary, this amazing woman constantly urges me to slow down. A message I need to hear even as I struggle to follow it.

Most of all, thanks to my family: Eric for always believing in me and supporting my crazy dreams and the resulting crazy hours; Abigail, Jonathan, and Rebecca for thinking its really cool that their mom is a writer. And to our parents Walt and Jolene and David and Virgene for supporting me in my writing. I couldn't do this without them.

Jesus, may You be honored by the words I write. May they be a sacrifice pleasing and acceptable to You.

PROLOGUE

Friday, June 5, 1942

Just how many changes would she need to make before Artie called with the news he had a contract for her?

Rosemary Schaeffer puckered her lips and studied her image in the mirror she'd perched atop the overflowing vanity crammed in the corner of her studio apartment. The small space had shrunk when her friend moved in a couple of days earlier. Rosemary pulled her focus back to her image. If she didn't hurry, she'd be late. The blond curls swirling around her heart-shaped face in carefully arranged short layers still seemed like they should belong to someone else.

A sigh welled up from deep inside. Nothing had gone as she'd planned when she moved to Hollywood with dreams of landing on the silver screen. Sure, she'd landed an agent quickly, but sometimes she wondered if she should follow all of Artie's advice. Still, she was in too deep now.

If she hurried, her latest "date" would arrive after she finished her preparations for their evening of Hollywood nightlife. A swift dusting of powder across her nose and she could escape her tiny apartment. Not quite the bombshell beauty of Jean Harlow, but more girl-next-door. Directors had parroted Artie's words that she'd never transform into a leading lady looking like this. Even Myrna Loy had an underlying sex appeal. The kind that kept men watching while women viewed Myrna as a friend rather than competition.

"Keep moving, Rosie." It didn't matter how often she studied her image, the results wouldn't change. She was who she was—but she still paused to add a swipe of black kohl around each eye. She kissed the air. "A little enhancement never hurts."

She eyed the leg makeup but shook her head. She didn't have time to mess with the lotion and have it dry. Besides, she had to hurry or this latest so-called date would arrive and see the mess she lived in— the wardrobe exploding with clothes, the desk piled high with stacks of scripts and other papers, and the tiny sink loaded with dishes she needed to wash. The mess didn't bother her. But the tiny space didn't measure up to the image of an up-and-coming movie star. No, it showed the disarray of a life lived on the edge of chaos.

She had learned in about two days that in Hollywood, image meant everything.

She grabbed the blanket she'd tossed on the couch, which doubled as her bed, and folded it. All the while, she tried to ignore the burble of unease that built whenever she spent time with one of Artie's clients.

It might be standard protocol in this town for aspiring actresses to spend time escorting men. But somehow she knew her daddy would not approve and her mother would be horrified—even if she could make them understand she was in over her head. The guilt was compounded by the thought that she'd missed her call home last night. She couldn't force herself to dial the operator. She didn't know how to escape, and talking to her parents only made it worse.

She wanted out but longed to see her name in lights even more.

And so, she continued to do exactly what Artie ordered. What choice did she have?

Still, she couldn't fight the certainty that this simply wasn't right.

The coil of unease that settled in her stomach with each phone visit seemed heavier tonight.

Had Audra noticed it? Somehow Rosemary knew she had, and that realization both comforted and alarmed her. Audra would do something crazy…her protective instincts and self-imposed guilt were too well developed to be ignored. Rosemary glanced at the letter she'd started that tried to explain things to Audra, but for once, the words wouldn't come.

Even if her rule remained that the men didn't come into her apartment, it wasn't enough to justify the night's events.

Someday she'd land a long-term contract with a studio and walk away from this part of her life. Until then, she did what she could. Her appointment book was the only thing here that hinted at her shadow life. It contained careful records of the dates and limited information she had on the men she'd accompanied as well as the purely career-focused events. Rosemary had kept a book like this from her earliest dating days. It didn't matter to her that some of the men wouldn't want anyone to know the beautiful women they took around town were escorts.

Rosemary settled at the vanity and examined her makeup again.

A swift knock rattled the door.

She launched to her feet, the chair spilling behind her. Perfume and cosmetic bottles on her vanity rattled against each other, and she tried to steady herself with a hand on the tabletop.

"Coming." She caught one last glance in the mirror. Her eyes were wider than usual, pupils dilated. This date had her completely unnerved. She'd asked Artie to let someone else handle him, since his reputation for having a short fuse scared her. But he'd insisted she was the one, and she couldn't let her fear show now. "Get ahold of yourself. Play the part." She ran her hands around her glamour bob curls, pursed her lips in a pout, and willed the fear from her eyes.

Rosemary hurried to the wardrobe and shoved the black book under a pair of shoes in the wardrobe drawer, the only place she had to store them in the cramped space. The door shook in its frame as he pounded again.

She glided to the door, straightening the lines of her claret-colored evening gown.

"Are you in there, Rosie?" The words sounded slurred already, the man drunk even earlier than his reputation suggested.

"Hold your horses, buster." She mumbled the words, making sure he didn't hear. She pulled a light wrap from its hook and opened the door just enough to slide through it. "Let's go. You don't want to be late."

Hours later she stumbled from the cab, relieved to be back home. She hurried up the sidewalk to her door. She loved the way her apartment had the privacy of its own entrance. She could almost pretend she lived in a little cottage rather than a tiny apartment.

She fumbled through her bag, hunting for the key. After unlocking the door, she pushed it open and flipped on the light switch. A small groan reached her.

"Rachel?" The word slipped from her lips, barely more than a whisper. Was her roommate ill? Her gaze searched the room, but she didn't see Rachel. Whispers of fear edged up her spine, and she turned to leave. Then thought again.

She couldn't leave Rachel.

The bathroom door creaked open, and Rosie whirled around. She trembled when she saw a man she knew—one whose square build intimidated even before she could take in his blond hair, blue eyes, and the rich tan of someone who spent more time on the beach than working. "What are you doing here?"

He hurried to her side, yanked her arm, and slammed her against the wall. The strong stench of whiskey followed him into the room like a cloud.

"What's the idea?"

He slammed the front door shut then paced the room like a caged lion from davenport to bistro table and back. "You weren't supposed to be back. He promised you'd be kept away."

Rosie huddled against the wall, unable to move in the face of his wrath. The shimmy of fear turned into full-blown panic.

She swallowed and straightened. "I'll give you whatever you want."

He moved over her, his shadow pressing fear deeper into her. "It's too late for that."

CHAPTER ONE

One day earlier
Thursday, June 4, 1942

"Well, well, Audra. I do believe you're ready to take this matter to trial."

Audra Schaeffer soaked in the atypical praise. While Roger Clarion was a good man and fair boss, he did not toss praise around for any and all to hear. Satisfaction pulsed through her. After seven years of school and two years where the only job she could find after law school required her to serve as a legal assistant, Mr. Clarion had given her a chance. If everything went well, in less than a month she'd litigate her first case in superior court. A simple case, but it was hers.

He pulled reading glasses low on his bulbous nose and examined her over the rims. "Don't let me down, or we'll both be the laughing-stock of the Indianapolis legal community."

"Yes, sir." The image of her standing at the podium in front of the counsel table, a legal pad resting on it, filled her mind. She'd finally done it! She'd earned the right to try a case.

He smiled then shook his head. "I never thought I'd see the day when I'd have a woman working for me as an attorney, of all things." After a twist to his bow tie and a tug on his sweater vest, he stood and grabbed the wool jacket hanging on the coat tree in the corner of his office behind the massive cherry desk. "Now get out of here. I understand you have an important call to take back home."

Audra couldn't hide the smile that tugged at her lips. "Fortunately, Rosemary's usually a few minutes late." Since the day she was born a week late, Rosemary couldn't be hurried to join the rest of the world. Audra stood and walked to the doorway. "You can't believe how hard it is to wait for her calls. But it is a blessing her landlady allows Rosie to call us regularly from her phone. I don't think Mother could handle it if we didn't have our weekly report on all things Hollywood."

Mr. Clarion chuckled. "Off with you. Can't stand in the way of that."

"See you in the morning, sir." Audra hurried from the office and scooped her hat and purse from the seat of her desk chair. If she hurried, she'd make the bus that would get her home in time for Rosemary's call. Being a little out of breath would be worth it if she could steal a few moments with Rosemary without her parents listening. Audra pushed through the front door into the bright sunshine of an early summer day. Squinting against the brightness, she merged into step with the other commuters headed to cars or buses. The sidewalks pulsed with energy as people hustled to get home to dinner and their families. The United States had been at war only a few months, but already women outnumbered men on the sidewalks.

Audra glanced at her watch and sped up. Her high heels clicked against the concrete as she all but ran toward the bus stop, one hand squishing her hat securely to her head. Ahead she could see the behemoth belching exhaust as it idled, waiting for passengers. She had to reach it, because she couldn't miss Rosie's call.

The last time Rosie called home, she'd been out of sorts. Short. Distracted. Yet no matter how Audra had tried, she couldn't pull from

Rosie what was bothering her. She imagined her sister doodling non-sense images on a piece of paper as she held close what disturbed her. If Rosie were home, Audra could eventually tease the problem from her and help her deal with the situation. But now, with so many miles separating them, Audra felt powerless to help. How she hated that. She was supposed to smooth out Rosie's problems, as she had all through high school when the boys decided Rosie was the cat's meow—her long legs and sweet face attracting them long before she was aware.

Audra reached the bus and relaxed. She'd made it. She climbed the steps, deposited her coin, and found a seat in the back by one of the lowered windows. Though tinged with the stench of diesel, the trickle of outside air seemed fresher than that in the bus.

"Is this seat taken?"

Audra looked up and smiled at an older woman. "Please."

The woman, burdened with a couple of bags of groceries, collapsed onto the seat next to her. She fanned her face and turned forward. "I didn't think I'd make it in time. My kids would have been mighty disap-pointed if they had to wait for supper while I waited for the next bus."

Audra smiled politely then turned back to the window. She twirled a strand of hair around her finger then tucked it behind her ear.

Tonight, Rosemary would have funny stories to weave about peo-ple she'd observed, stars she'd met, and roles she'd almost landed. The dinner table had been too quiet since she moved to California. She'd set her face toward the West and moved, determined to make her mark on the world.

Memories flowed through Audra's mind of the many times before Rosie had stubbornly set her path. Time after time Audra had stepped in to either help the dream come true or thwart a pending disaster. She hid a chuckle behind her hand at the image of Rosemary's determined attempt to make the costumes for a neighborhood play one summer. She'd written a script, drafted neighbor kids for the various roles, and then decided nothing less than specially made costumes would work for her production. Only problem was, she'd never sewn a stitch in her life and Mother was visiting a sick relative. That had left Audra to fill the gaps, something she'd gladly done. The play had been a neighborhood smash, the parents overlooking the melodrama and applauding the kids' efforts. And Audra stood in the background enjoying Rosie's success.

Similar scenarios had played out through Rosemary's in-between years. And Audra had loved stepping in to smooth the rough spots in Rosemary's big plans. She wondered if Rosie had anyone to do that for her now.

Rosemary would call.

Then Mother would smile, and Daddy would lose the tight lines around his eyes.

Everything would return to normal.

For once, Audra had exciting news of her own to report to Rosemary. Her sister would understand how hard Audra had worked for this opportunity and what it meant to have her own case. Rosemary aspired to appear on the silver screen, but all Audra had ever wanted was to appear in court, weaving arguments that won the day. She had followed her grandpa around his one-man firm for a summer, and the legal bug had bitten hard.

A tremor of excitement coursed through Audra at the thought she would finally get to stand in front of a judge and present a case. Yes, she had news—her dreams were ready to come true.

The bus slowed, and Audra prepared to get off. She walked the several blocks home, darted up the sidewalk to the house, and opened the front door.

"Mother, I'm home."

"In the kitchen." Her mother's alto voice sang from the room down the hallway.

Audra set her purse on the hall table and unpinned her hat. She stuck the pin through it and hung it on the banister. She shimmied out of her suit jacket and walked down the hallway. "How was your day?"

"Usual ladies' luncheon." Mother kissed Audra's cheek, a frilly apron covering her pin-and-tuck dress. "Ready for Rosemary's call?"

"Um-hmm." Lifting the lid on the pot, Audra inhaled deeply. The scent of tomato mixed with tangy spices swirled around her. "Smells wonderful."

"We'll eat after Rosie calls. Don't want it to get cold while we talk to her."

"Are you sure? A few bites sound perfect."

Mother shook her head and pinched Audra's cheek. "No, ma'am. No distractions. Besides, a few minutes' wait never hurt anyone."

Yet an hour later, as Daddy had joined them and they still waited for the call, Audra wondered. Her stomach tightened, but not from hunger. Rosie knew she couldn't stay in Hollywood unless she faithfully called home on the prearranged schedule. Daddy had made that iron-clad stipulation when she begged to try her fortunes out West.

As they waited in the parlor, the lines around Daddy's eyes tightened, even as he knocked tobacco from his pipe and refilled it. Even as he settled in his favorite chair with the sports pages. Even as he tried to show an unconcerned air.

"Daddy, did I tell you the good news?"

He looked up from his paper, a distracted expression covering his face. "Hmm?"

"Mr. Clarion says I'm ready to try my first case." She bit her lower lip, wondering what his response would be.

"Darling, that's wonderful." Mother dropped her knitting long enough to clap. "I'm so proud of you."

"So he's given you a client?"

"Yes, sir. It's a small case, unpaid rent." Audra shrugged. "But it's my case. Have to start somewhere, right?"

"Your grandfather would be very proud."

Heat flushed her cheeks at the praise. She told them a bit about the case. "It goes before the judge in one month, if we don't settle first."

"Does that happen often?" Mother sat in her chair, feet propped on a stool, knitting needles clacking a steady rhythm. Only the dropped stitches showed her harried emotions.

"I'm not sure." She tried to hide a grin. "Is it wrong to hope we actually go to court?"

"That might not be best for your client." Daddy had pulled the paper back in front of his nose. "But I'm sure you'll figure out how to represent them. Imagine that. You have your own case."

"Thanks, Daddy."

"You've worked hard for this, darling." Mother shot a strained look at the phone. "Wait until Rosie hears."

"I'm excited to tell her."

Another few minutes passed, Audra staring at the phone, willing it to ring.

Only the clicking of Mother's needles and the occasional rustle of the newspaper pushed against the phone's silence. Finally, Audra couldn't stand it.

"Do we have the landlady's number?" Audra stood from her perch on the davenport and hurried to Mother's small desk. "We can call her instead of waiting."

Mother shook her head, needles flying. "Rosie's never given us the number. Didn't want us to bother the lady."

"Maybe the lines are tied up. Everyone's calling, and the operator can't connect her."

Her father arched an eyebrow at her over the top of his paper. "Settle down, Audra. There's nothing to be concerned about."

He was wrong. She knew it. Something had happened. Something Rosie couldn't talk about but that disturbed her greatly. This time Audra wouldn't wait too long. She couldn't. Images of her brother Andrew's body as he lay broken on the side of the road collided in her mind. All because she hadn't picked him up on time as promised. Visions of his form still haunted her dreams in the middle of the night.

If Rosie didn't call by tomorrow, Audra would go find her.

She'd do anything to make sure she wasn't too late again.

CHAPTER TWO

Saturday, June 6, 1942

"Are you sure about this?" Audra's father studied her, extra lines filling the spaces around his eyes as he pulled the car to the curb at the airport.

Sure? She doubted she'd ever be certain about this decision. Boarding a plane to Hollywood? All because her sister didn't call? Anyone outside the family would label her crazy. But inside the family, everyone understood communication was the price Rosemary paid for the freedom to live in Hollywood.

"I don't know what else to do."

His gray eyes considered her in silence. Finally, he nodded. "Here's some money to help. I know the ticket wiped out your savings."

"Daddy, you don't need to do that."

"I know, but you're my daughter." He pressed a stack of bills into her hand.

She slowly stuffed them in her purse. She could count them later. For now, she needed to climb from the car and enter the airport before she changed her mind. The Indianapolis skyline beckoned her to stay. If she left, Mr. Clarion had made it clear her position might be filled when she returned. And her chance to try a case on her own, no matter how small, could be permanently lost.

She took a shuddering breath.

It didn't matter right now, in this moment. What did was confirming Rosie was okay. Better to have Rosie laugh at her overboard concern than wait too long.

"Thank you. I need to go or I'll miss the plane."

Daddy reached across the seat and hugged her, strength and warmth flowing from him. "Be safe."

Audra nodded against his chest, not trusting her voice.

"Call me with the details of your return flight. I'll be here when you land." He released her then stepped from the driver's seat. Moments later, he'd pulled her suitcase from the back seat of his Studebaker. "Don't forget to call when you arrive and get settled."

A smile filled her at the thought. Guess she'd get to see how easy it was to find a phone in Hollywood. "I'll hurry back."

"See that you do."

Audra entered the airport, her suitcase heavy in her hand. She worked her way through the ticket line and then waited forty minutes in the lounge for her flight to be called. First a quick hop to Chicago on an American Airlines flight, then the longer journey to Los Angeles on the Longhorn after several hours' delay. If she were lucky, she'd look lively after sleeping on a plane. The ticket agent had assured her passengers slept comfortably on the DC-3, but she couldn't imagine getting good rest, not on a plane.

The thought of climbing on a plane and trusting that thin frame to safely transport her thousands of feet in the air to her destination unnerved her. Only her concern for Rosemary could get her on the contraption. The first flight passed quickly. She had a lone seat against a window separated from two seats in her row by the narrow walkway. Set up for day travel, a maximum of twenty-one passengers could board. They'd barely climbed through the clouds before the plane nosed down. She held her breath, white knuckles clutching the armrests, as the plane fell from the sky and bounced on the tarmac.

Then, before she'd found her courage after waiting in Chicago, the stewardess announced her next flight. Fourteen hours and she'd land in California after several stops en route to let passengers on and off. Fewer passengers boarded the plane in Chicago. Since it was an overnight flight, at some point the stewardess would make up narrow beds for them. With a few hours until the turndown, Audra settled in with a paperback she'd purchased in Chicago. Several passengers gathered around a table to play cards while others read the newspapers and magazines the stewardess handed out. Once her bed was made, Audra tried to relax, letting the steady hum of the plane's engines lull her to sleep, but her mind resisted. Thoughts of what she might find in Hollywood collided with her need for rest.

She shifted on her side, tucking her hands under her cheek. *Father, will You walk with me through whatever I find? Prepare the way? Keep Rosie safe until I find her?* She recited her favorite Scriptures until her thoughts calmed and her body sank into sleep.

Hours later, with the sun barely cresting over the clouds, the stewardess walked through and woke everyone. Audra tried to freshen up in the small lavatory then returned to her assigned seat. She stilled and stared then snapped her jaw shut. Robert Garfield? *The* Robert Garfield? Seated next to her? Her heart stuttered and jumped inside her chest. When had he joined the flight?

"Would you look at that?" The man whistled, seemingly oblivious to her stare.

"What?" The word stuttered from her lips as she sank into her seat.

"Ever flown over the Grand Canyon, miss?" His voice had a soothing baritone richness that mirrored the tones he cultivated in his movie roles.

"I think I've seen a picture or two." Oh my goodness. She sat conversing with Robert Garfield. She couldn't wait to tell Rosie.

"Someday you'll need more than a fly-over. It's breathtaking. An amazing spectacle that God carved for us to enjoy. Here, take a peek. It almost makes the aggravation of flying from Tucson worthwhile." He scooted back against the seat and motioned her to lean forward.

Feeling like she invaded his space, Audra leaned onto the armrest between them. An empty sky dotted with an occasional cloud as fluffy as quilt batting stared at her. "I don't see anything."

"Then you need to look down."

Down?

The thought of looking down when the plane was thousands of feet up—it stole her breath.

"You'll miss an amazing view if you don't take the risk." He pointed out the window then whistled. "Amazing."

Curiosity got the better of her fear. "All right. But I'll have to lean closer to the window."

"Fair enough."

Even though the star did nothing to take advantage of her precarious position, Audra could feel the heat radiating from him. A faint musky aroma tickled her nose.

Suddenly she saw it. A gaping rent in the earth's surface that was layered in rich colors as it tumbled deep into the permanent gash. "Oh my." Words escaped her. "How vast."

"You have no idea. From the rim it is the most incredible sight." He leaned toward the window, his shoulder brushing hers as he pointed at the canyon. "The Colorado River rests in the bottom. At one point, it must have been an amazing river to have carved such a deep and vast canyon." His voice tickled her ear, causing her to turn and meet his gaze, which searched deep into her, leaving her exposed.

Audra collapsed against her seat, feeling the connection break, relieved and disappointed at the same time. "Thank you for showing me."

"Sure thing." He smiled again, a charming grin that quirked at the corner of his mouth. "I'm Robert Garfield."

"I know." He grinned again, and heat climbed her throat. "Audra Schaeffer."

"It's a pleasure."

"Breakfast time. Hope everyone's hungry."

At the stewardess's singsong voice, Robert rubbed his hands together. "Guess we'll have time to talk later."

Audra played with her seatbelt, relieved for the break before she embarrassed herself.

The stewardess placed steaming plates in front of them. "Coffee or orange juice?" Once she'd deposited black coffee, she moved to the next row of passengers.

Audra closed her eyes for a quick blessing over the food. She opened them, surprised to find Robert's head bowed. He opened his eyes and grinned at her. Heat flooded her cheeks at being caught.

He winked at her and raised his fork. "Enjoy."

As soon as she finished eating, she tugged her paperback from her purse, willing the hours to disappear until she finally stood on firm ground. The travails of the heroine swept her away, and Audra lost all sense of time.

The plane descended with a bump that caused Audra to drop her book. She was thrust against one thin arm of the seat, then against the other arm. As she bounced from side to side, her stomach mirrored the plane's ping-pong ball action. Robert folded up his paper—the headline announced Richard Heydrich, the Nazi officer in charge of the Czechoslovakian campaign, had died—and grabbed her book.

He handed it to her with a smile, and Audra could imagine him stepping from the pages of her novel. In fact, as she looked closer, his brown hair waved in all the appropriate spots for someone in pictures. Its length fit the bill for the hero in the novel or a movie. And the clear blue eyes that studied her with a hint of concern matched the placid sky that mocked her through the window. The plane dipped again, and she focused on the broad shoulders that filled the perfectly tailored jacket rather than the growing certainty this plane would topple from the sky.

The stewardess walked the aisle, unaffected by the bumps and dips and seemingly oblivious to the presence of a star. Then she caught Audra's gaze and winked. She stopped in front of her. "Coca-Cola?"

Robert shook his head, picked up a *LIFE* magazine, and flipped to the table of contents.

The plane dropped, taking Audra's stomach and the stewardess with it. Audra reached out to steady the woman.

The stewardess straightened her cap and smiled. "Thank you. Here, have a Coke."

Audra took it, but as the plane dipped, Robert bounced into her shoulder. Drops of Coke sprayed from the bottle and dotted the sleeve of her shirtwaist.

"Excuse me." Horror laced his voice as he pulled the handkerchief from his jacket pocket. He dabbed at the spots then handed it to her, a reddish tinge spreading across the tips of his ears. "I'm not usually this clumsy."

Audra attempted to smile as she pressed a hand against her churning stomach and held the Coke as far away from her as possible with the other. She'd never been good at things like roller coasters, but she couldn't allow the nausea to win. Not in front of others. She might not ever board another plane. Her father had called it a flying cigar; her mother, a death trap. Her mother appeared correct. Would the Coke settle her stomach? She eyed the bottle and then handed it back to the stewardess. "Thank you, but as much as the plane is bouncing, I'd wear it."

The plane sagged to one side and Audra gulped. This plane was going down. Just like Carole Lombard's. When she died in a plane crash in January, Audra promised she'd never risk her life on a plane. Only the certainty that knowing something was wrong with Rosemary could have propelled her onto the silver bird.

"Seatbelts." The stewardess smiled through tight lips as she bumped down the narrow passageway. "We'll land shortly."

God, please don't let this be the end.

This couldn't kill her. Not before she found Rosemary and confirmed her sister was fine. Her imagination had shifted to overactive, territory usually reserved for Rosie. Audra closed her eyes and prayed as she waited for the plane to either land or crash.

"A couple more bounces and we'll get over the mountains. Smooth flying from there." Did he really believe his talking relieved her anxiety?

Audra nodded and turned to look out the window. A mistake, as her stomach rebelled at the jagged mountains.

"Look at me. We'll talk about anything. If your mind isn't focused out there, you'll be fine." His quiet voice pulled her attention.

She latched on to the first thought that crossed her mind. "Are you in a movie right now?"

A pained smile stretched his lips. "Will be again soon. At least that's what my agent tells me." He pointed to the *LOOK* magazine peeking out of her bag. "I even appeared in that a time or two."

"I know. I think I've seen a few issues with you on the cover." While it had always been Rosemary's dream to live in Hollywood and appear in pictures, Audra read each issue of *LOOK* from cover to cover and attended the weekend matinees. She'd pursued a dream every bit as elusive and foolhardy as Rosemary's. She also knew that after investing three years in law school and two years as an over-trained legal assistant, she'd walked away from her chance to appear in court as an attorney. She was a fool. The legal world might change someday, but not fast enough to make a difference for her.

The plane bumped again, and Audra shrieked.

"Take my hand."

She grappled for his hand and felt his large fingers squeeze around hers.

"You'll be fine. I promise." He let go of her hand long enough to pull a piece of paper out of his jacket pocket and scribble something on it. "Here. This is my number. Call me if you need anything while you're in town."

"Thank you." Audra could barely mumble the words, until he retook her hand. How could he be so calm?

"Tell me about yourself." His rich voice held a promise that everything would be okay.

"Audra Schaeffer." Wait, she'd already told him. He must think her a ninny. "Indianapolis."

"What brings you to California?"

"Looking for…" The plane tipped and Audra glanced out the window. The ground rushed toward them at a dizzying rate. She sucked in a breath to stifle a scream. Robert squeezed her hand, and she pulled her gaze back to his steady one.

"Looking for a role?"

"No, my sister." How did he endure the flight in that unflappable manner? None of the turbulence affected him. Maybe she could match that. The plane bounced once, twice, and then slowed to a stop. Audra released his hand. "Did we make it? Are we on the ground?"

Robert cocked an eyebrow. "Yes, Audra, the plane has touched the terra firma of California." He shook his head, a slight grin tweaking his lips, and played with his seatbelt. "Maybe if you're free tonight you could come to a fundraiser. I know that's not a typical welcome-to-Southern California experience, but I'm emceeing the event." He took a breath, a hint of shyness creeping into his voice. "I'd like to see you again."

The plane taxied toward the terminal, and Audra froze. A movie star had just invited her to an event? "I don't know what to say. Or what Rosie's planned. She doesn't know I'm coming, you see."

"Oh." He hesitated. "Enjoy your time in California."

As soon as the plane stopped, he stood and ambled toward the door. Audra watched him, shocked that she'd turned down the opportunity to spend time with the star. He'd already proven himself kind, with a self-deprecating viewpoint. Not at all what she'd imagined. Maybe she'd call him and say she changed her mind about joining him once she found Rosie.

Her mind raced with the realization she'd landed in a strange city and foreign state with no idea how to proceed. She'd wasted time panicking instead of forming a plan. She straightened her box jacket and reached for her hat underneath the seat in front of her.

This endeavor had the earmarks of a half-baked gut reaction. She had no facts to reinforce her need to find Rosemary fast. Daddy had been right. She should have stayed home and made the most of her case.

Her fellow travelers streamed from their seats and off the DC-3. The stewardess walked up the aisle, empty Coca-Cola bucket in hand. "Can I get anything for you?"

"No." Audra plucked her purse from the floor in front of her. "Thank you." The stewardess nodded, and Audra descended the plane's steps. Heat settled around her body like a coat. Palm trees like those in *LOOK* magazine photos dotted the arid landscape. The scenery couldn't be more different if Rosemary had chosen the other side of the world. Where Indiana was dotted with rolling hills and cornfields that melted into Indianapolis, the view from the tarmac contained a diversity of distant mountains, dry landscape, and exotic plants.

She grabbed her suitcase and straightened. Time to find Rosemary and her efficiency apartment somewhere in the sea of buildings spread before her.

CHAPTER THREE

Where now?

The question hit Audra like a blow as she left the airport.

She didn't know.

A line of taxis idled in front of the airport. A man hopped from the front cab and reached for Audra's bag. She pulled it away from him. "I'll keep it. Thank you."

He stepped back and opened the door. "Yes, ma'am. Where you headed?"

She didn't know.

The thought almost made her turn around, flee the cab, and race into the airport. Instead, she slipped in the backseat, pulling her bag after her. What if Rosemary was out of town? Busy for the week? Completely and totally unhappy to see her?

She didn't know.

It didn't matter if Rosemary stomped around or acted miffed. Audra could endure any scorn and charges of being overly protective as long as she was satisfied all was right in Rosemary's world. Part of her even felt excited at the chance to see that world for herself. Rosemary had bubbled about her apartment, the location, the neighborhood, everything Hollywood. Now she could give Audra the grand tour.

She tried to reassure herself that Rosemary's silence meant she was swept up in the excitement of life in Hollywood. Yet a premonition nagged Audra.

"Miss?" The cab driver turned in the front seat to stare at her. "You want to sit in the car all day or actually go somewhere?"

"Sorry." Audra pulled her thoughts from their downward spiral and dug in her purse for the scribbled note with Rosemary's address. The taxi pulled from the curb into traffic, and she leaned against the seat and closed her eyes. In a matter of minutes, the taxi would deposit her at her sister's apartment. Then, if Audra's fears were overwrought, Rosemary would open her door, a look of shock coloring her face that her big sister would make a frivolous and expensive trip across the country based on a missed phone call. Audra prayed that happened. If Rosemary wasn't home, Audra would use the extra key Rosemary had mentioned she kept hidden under a stone. Audra would let herself in and wait until Rosemary came home.

With her role in Andrew's death, she couldn't simply wait and see what happened.

The car slid in and out of traffic, the driver never pushing quite far enough to make Audra concerned for her life. Yet she caught her breath as he came dangerously close to another car's bumper.

As the cab continued down a wide boulevard, Audra couldn't see the appeal of the town. The landscape was dry, almost barren, and couldn't appear more unlike Indianapolis. How could Rosemary like it? Yet she did—at least that's how things had sounded the first few months, as she received callbacks after auditions that led to a couple of walk-on roles. Then Rosemary called, voice vibrating with excitement, because her agent thought a contract for a speaking role was on its way.

The car drove past a red brick building with a sign that read MASTERS STUDIO. Had that studio seen something they liked in a film test? Had someone there landed Rosemary one step closer to her dream?

Rosemary moved closer to her dream, while Audra had fled the opportunity to breathe life into hers. Had she wasted that opportunity? It shouldn't matter. Family was more important than any job. Yet her heart pained at the golden goose she'd killed when she left Indianapolis.

A few more turns, and Audra couldn't tell anymore which direction the cab headed.

Her thoughts returned to Rosemary and the sudden decline in her excitement. She'd turned unusually quiet when she talked to Audra. And then, during their last conversation, there was a panicked edge to her words. She wouldn't tell Audra exactly what bothered her, but Audra had surmised that Rosie had some kind of man trouble.

The taxi jolted to a stop in front of a nondescript stucco building. The front entrance faced the road, but Rosemary's small apartment had an outside entrance separate from the one the other residents used.

Audra handed a dollar to the driver.

"Thank you." He flashed her a smile that revealed a mouthful of crooked teeth. "You like me to wait?"

"No. That's all right." Audra opened the door and slid out of the cab, pulling her bag behind her. She studied the building as the taxi raced into traffic. "Time to confirm how foolish I am."

She hefted the bag's strap over her shoulder. Her steps dragged as she looked for the sidewalk that led to Rosemary's entrance. As Audra edged around the side, she had to step around trash blown along the overgrown hedges. She didn't share Rosemary's enthusiasm for the location. A bus lumbered up a side street. Audra covered her nose against the odor.

Almost at the backyard, Audra found the door. She knocked on it and waited a minute. No one came to the door, so she knocked again then searched for the rock that hid the apartment key. Rosemary hadn't mentioned she had a rock garden next to the door. Audra broke a nail as she culled through the rocks, finding the silver key under the sixth rock. "About time." Audra knocked one last time, but when no one came, she inserted the key and opened the door. The curtains were drawn, and a dusky light coated the room.

Audra stepped into the room but hesitated to go farther as she dropped her bag.

All was silent and chaos reigned, typical of Rosemary's lack of housekeeping. A pillow and blanket were tossed on the floor next to a floral davenport. Bottles were strewn in a haphazard fashion on the vanity that was pushed into a corner of the room. The wardrobe overflowed with a riot of gowns and clothes pushing out of the gap between the unclosed doors. A few shoes had tumbled to the floor in front of the wardrobe.

A clammy sensation coated Audra's skin, and the hair at the back of her neck stood on end. She whirled around, purse pulled tight against her body.

"Oh." She gasped at her silliness. No one waited behind her, ready to pounce. She tried to laugh, but it sounded like a kitten's weak squeak. "Get ahold of yourself."

She swallowed.

Enough. She marched farther into the room, toying with a charm on her bracelet as she absorbed the scene. A davenport. Stacks of paper. A hot plate on a tiny table. Audra wrinkled her nose at an underlying odor that pervaded the room.

The blanket indicated Rosemary slept on the davenport or the floor. Audra moved toward the desk. Paper covered its surface, a hodge-podge of debris, yet somehow Rosemary would be able to find anything she needed.

Some fancy foiled invitations sat on top of the mess. Audra selected one. A fundraiser for the Hollywood USO at the Roosevelt Hotel. Looked like her sister had snagged an invite to appear at the event that evening. Audra noted the address. If Rosemary didn't show up beforehand, she'd borrow one of Rosie's dresses and meet her there.

The next stack caught Audra's attention. They were articles written about the Hollywood Victory Caravan. Rosemary had circled items about the stars who'd boarded the benefit train. Bing Crosby. Desi Arnaz. Abbott and Costello. So many had made that trip, raising money for war bonds at each stop. Underneath the articles was a letter inviting Rosie to participate in a second caravan that was scheduled to leave in a week. Rosie? On a trip like that?

Audra turned to the wardrobe, running a hand along the dresses until she found a navy number she'd wear tonight if she attended the fundraiser. As she studied the overstuffed wardrobe, she wondered how Rosemary could afford the abundance of outfits. And what did she wear when she wasn't at an event? Nothing seemed serviceable for every day. Audra shook her head. Rosemary had not turned into a practical person while out here. If anything, it appeared her flighty, fun-loving personality had lost what little restraint it had.

The wardrobe's bottom drawer puckered out, and Audra tried to push it into place. The drawer resisted and she reached in, expecting to move clothing or a handbag. She tugged out the obstruction and found a little black appointment book shoved among a mishmash of heels and other shoes. The book looked like one Rosemary had kept since high school, when the football team noticed her blooming beauty.

She'd made notes about every boy who asked her out and kept track of what happened on their dates.

Flipping through the pages, Audra whistled as she ran down the list of stars Rosemary had penciled on its pages. As she turned another page, Audra realized her sister rarely had a night at home. No wonder she had an invitation to join the caravan. Everyone in Hollywood had to know her. Had that contributed to her nearing a movie role?

According to the book, Rosemary would attend the USO event with Robert Garfield, the star from the plane. Audra's fingers trembled as she remembered their closeness. His film charisma certainly carried over to the living, breathing version.

She turned back to the book. The calendar cleared after tonight's appearance. Had Rosemary planned a break, or did it indicate a change in her status? Audra would have to ask when she found her. Already Hollywood seemed like a totally different world from Indianapolis. The magazines seemed to have it right—every night revolved around a party or gala. When did the stars work?

Audra turned another page and found a list of names and telephone numbers. Many of the names matched those found on the calendar. Closing the book, Audra tapped it on the table then placed it back in the drawer. Next, she rifled through a few piles on the desk. A note filled with Rosemary's curly doodles stopped her. Names swirled around the edges, mixed with flowers and crossed-out hearts. Rosie only doodled when something bothered her, but the contents of the note made no sense to Audra. She placed it with the black book for easy access when she found Rosemary. She'd ask her about it—and insist Rosie tell what bothered her. Audra stepped away since nothing else there held her interest.

Everything looked all right. Controlled chaos as only Rosemary could enjoy.

Yet the longer she stood there, the more it felt like spiders skittered up her back. There was little left to explore, other than whatever waited behind the lone closed door.

She nudged open the door to the bathroom.

Was that…?

She gulped and leaned against the door, opening it against a weight that pressed back.

A pale pink glob was visible. Audra swallowed and crouched down.

A hand?

"Rosemary?" She shrieked, unable to stop the terror. "Honey? Let me in."

She pushed hard against the door, felt the weight give, and the door eased open.

Audra leaned around the door. She screamed. Then the world opened up as its axis shifted.

CHAPTER FOUR

Robert Garfield bounced his legs as he waited in the lavish anteroom for his agent, Artie Schmaltz, to see him. The other three leather lobby chairs sat miraculously empty at the moment. A cluster of palm trees filled a corner, and one of the leaves tickled his neck when he moved just so. He should slide over to avoid it but couldn't find the energy after rising early to catch the plane out of Tucson.

The trip home had drained him from the moment he heard his mother lay in a hospital. His father hadn't expected her to live long enough for Robert to get there, but she'd rallied. Then she'd ordered him back to Hollywood with the flush of health convincing him she'd be all right. The woman had an iron will. When he'd protested, saying nothing waited there for him, she'd snorted.

"With an attitude like that, I can see why." She'd patted his hand and told him to get on the next plane. "You can't do anything here. I'll be right as rain in no time. But you go back to Hollywood and prove to that group of snobs that the Garfields are worthy of appearing in their silly films." She'd coughed, the deep, chest-rattling sound that robbed her breath. "You go for those of us they snubbed." She smiled then pointed a finger at him. "And do not let that woman steal your career."

Robert had agreed, even as it pained him that his parents still didn't see him as a success. His name had reached second and third billing in a dozen films, but it wasn't enough. All they could focus on was his current, uncontracted status.

So he'd returned to Hollywood, back in Artie's office after two long days, hoping a screen test had turned into work. He fought the urge to let fatigue pull him into a slump. Instead, he pushed his shoulder blades together, straightened the knot in his tie, then kept his hands loosely clasped, stilling his knees in the process. Appearances meant everything here, everyone trained to watch for the slightest sign of weakness. But the façade that every day was sunny with nary a cloud in sight grew harder to maintain. If Artie didn't have good news that a contract was on the way, Robert's wallet might as well shrivel up and blow away in the next Santa Ana wind.

At the very least he needed a few decent roles to keep the rent and other bills paid.

Goldie Simmons, Artie's curvaceous but bubble-brained secretary, looked up from filing a nail. "Don't worry, Bobby. He's about ready to see you."

Robert worked to keep his face blank at Goldie's substitution of that horrid nickname. Robert was a strong name, one worthy of an A-list star. Bobby indicated a kid who hadn't quite gotten his act together. "Thanks."

"You going to the USO event tonight?" She smacked her gum and examined a nail. After the way she'd sawed it, the nail must be honed to a point.

"Artie got me invited, then ordered me to emcee." It seemed a simple enough thing to do to be seen and move his career forward. One well-placed notice would lead to the next role, and then he'd clear the last hurdle to the A-list.

"Oh, great exposure for you. That's what it's about, ya know."

"I know. Making sure the right people see you in the right settings."

"You learn quick, Bobby."

Robert nodded and studied his hands. It didn't matter. Until he achieved Cary Grant's status, Artie would consider him second tier.

"Your chance will return. It always does for the ones who want it most."

"I'm counting on that." Robert rested his head against the wall. He forced his eyes to stay open. Somehow, he'd find the energy to appear peppy and interested as he kept the partygoers entertained. "Any idea who's attending tonight's shindig?"

"Artie said the biggest and best from Hollywood." She waved her file in the air. "That's why it's good for you to participate. He's paired you with his new young thing, Rosemary Schaeffer."

Another aspiring starlet. Robert would never forget the first time he met her. Intelligence had shone from her eyes as she took him in. A flirtatious air surrounded her, but she held it in check. Rosemary Schaeffer had the potential to make it—he could see that special something shimmering underneath the surface. Was this the gal that Audra, the nervous but beautiful woman on the plane, was looking for? What were the odds that her sister was Rosemary? The last name wasn't that common around Hollywood, and Robert wished he hadn't left the plane without a way to reach her. "Have any drinkable coffee back there?"

"I wouldn't touch it, but it's over there." She pointed the file toward a small table perched against the wall.

Robert stood and ambled to the pot. The coffee had a thin film over the top. He lifted the pot, sniffed, and then shuddered. "You're right. That's not fit for my worst enemy." He walked the room, studying the photos lining Artie's vanity wall. Photos of him with the biggest stars crowded the space. Clark Gable. Jean Harlow. Jimmy Stewart. Carole Lombard. William Powell. Bette Davis. Artie never shared which were actually his clients, but the agent made sure people saw him with all the right people. Someday, Robert's photo would move from a corner shadowed by a plant into a more visible spot.

Someday. He hated that word. His life seemed filled with the maybes someday suggested. He was ready for something more permanent.

The speaker on Goldie's desk sparked to life. "Goldie? Goldie?"

She hit a button and leaned in. "Yep, boss?"

"Send that kid in. Right away. I've only got a minute."

"Yes, sir." She yelled the words into the contraption loud enough Robert doubted she needed it for Artie to hear her. "Go on in, Bobby. He's ready for ya."

"Thanks." Robert clenched his jaw and set his back. *God, You know how much I need good news.* If only he could whisper a prayer and know he'd get exactly what he requested. It never worked that way. No matter how he fired them off, his prayers remained largely ineffective.

"You want a shove?"

Robert shook his head. After a quick rap on the door, he opened it, his confident smile firmly affixed. "Artie, my man."

"Robert Garfield. How are you?" Artie stood and moved from behind his desk to meet Robert. The small, rotund man bypassed Robert's hand for a full body hug that Robert endured.

"Back in town."

"So I see, so I see. What can I do for you today?" The agent's words raced around his cigar and tumbled over each other as he settled one hip against his mahogany desk.

Robert shrugged. "Wanted to get an update, see if anything's broken loose."

"Still pushing hard for you. Have a couple more screen tests lined up. Good parts, my boy, good parts. You'll be back to work in no time, I assure you. Check with Goldie before you leave. I'm glad you're here, though." Artie maneuvered to his executive chair and sank into its plush leather. "I've got a proposition to make."

Robert sat on the edge of a chair. "I'm listening."

"The Hollywood Victory Committee wants to send out a second Victory Caravan. The first was a rousing success, and they want to build on that, only through the South this time."

"And this affects me…"

"I want you on that train. You'll be introduced to audiences across America, in the flesh. It'll remind the ladies why they swoon at your handsome mug in the pictures, the gents can see you're an 'every guy' like them. What do you say?"

"Is any pay involved?"

"Nope, just good citizenship, though expenses will be covered."

"I'm not a song-and-dance man or stand-up. What would I do?"

"Whatever they want. Think about the exposure." Artie frowned and tossed his cigar in the trash can next to his desk.

Robert paused, but only for show. What held him here until he got that contract? "All right. I suppose it's my patriotic duty."

"Could be your big break." Artie looked at his watch and launched from his chair. "I'll get it set up. Find Mark Feldstein at the fundraiser tonight. Make tonight a smash, and you're a shoo-in to the caravan and contracts. Come back in a couple days to get the details. And knock those screen tests out of the park."

"Yes, sir." Robert stood and then shook hands with Artie. "Thanks."

Artie waved him off. "Not a problem. Just do a great job tonight. It's all coming together." He pulled a fresh cigar from his pocket and shoved it in his mouth. "I can see it now. Your name in lights." Artie rubbed his hands together. "Now get. You've got an event."

After getting the screen test information from Goldie, Robert wandered the streets toward his apartment. The auditions and screen tests started the following day. Today's only duty was to arrive at the USO fundraiser in plenty of time for his emcee duties. His thoughts traveled back to his companion on the plane. Maybe Audra would be there with Rosemary. He liked that thought. A lot.

The exercise felt good, but the heat left sweat pooling in the small of his back. He covered another block then loosened his tie, pulled off his jacket, and rolled up his sleeves. That felt marginally better, but sweat still dripped down his face. He yanked off his fedora. He reached into his back pocket for his handkerchief, but it wasn't there. He hadn't gotten it back from Miss Schaeffer. After wiping his forehead with his hand, he slapped the hat in place. The sun pounded down and drained his energy. Maybe he should have hailed a cab.

He passed a hacienda with orange and other fruit trees hanging over the stucco wall and slowed to stretch out his time in the shade.

Would participating in the second Victory Caravan work like Artie thought? Traveling the country trapped on a train with the egos of twenty or more stars sounded exhausting. He'd heard the stories of the drinking, carousing, and barricaded doors from those who traveled with the first caravan.

That wasn't him. He might wonder if prayer worked, but he

remained convinced God did not condone certain activities. And the rumors indicated those had occurred on the first caravan.

He reached his building and used the key to access the lobby. Stars on their way up, a few on their way down, along with a few non-cinema types, filled the building. When he'd rented the place, Robert had hoped he'd meet the right people. Hard to do when everyone raced directly to their flats and closed their doors.

Dead fronds littered the floor around the palm trees filling a corner of the lobby. His shoes tapped lightly on the marble floor. It had been easy to afford this place during his marriage, but after Lana left, he wasn't so sure he liked living here anymore. Too many memories. But he hadn't exactly raced to find another place.

He pushed thoughts of glamorous, hard-hearted Lana Kincaid from his mind. Excuse me, Lana *Garfield*. How could she still use his name?

As long as their paths didn't cross, he ignored the pain of her betrayal. The sting of her rising success after their divorce while his career stalled.

If he didn't pull his head together, he'd be in no frame of mind to emcee the fundraiser. Despite Goldie's assurances, it must be a small event if Artie had snagged it for him. Robert hiked the stairs, deciding the extra exercise wouldn't kill him and might help him maintain his Jimmy Stewart build. It worked so well for Jimmy, keeping him in boy-next-door roles.

His phone rang as he unlocked his apartment. In a couple of steps, he stood at the side table, the door still open. "Garfield."

"What do you think you're doing?"

Robert fumbled with the phone at the piercing voice. "Lana?"

"Of course." She took a trembling breath, and he pictured her fingers tapping her elbow as she stared daggers through the wall. "You have to bow out."

"Of what? The USO fundraiser?" What had her blabbering this time?

"No." She snorted. "I couldn't care less that you're participating in some small effort for the boys. Artie's a fool to think that matters."

Robert sank into a chair set against the wall and waited. Eventually, she'd tell him the purpose of her call. If he was lucky, his silence would frustrate her enough to talk faster.

"Still playing games? You are pathetic, Robert." She paused. "Have you heard I have the lead in *Enemy from Within*?"

Calling to gloat? Robert forced his annoyance down. "Congratulations."

"Thank you."

"Can we reach the point?"

"Pull out of the Victory Caravan. I won't go if you come."

Robert rubbed the pulsing pain that erupted in his forehead. Lana was on the caravan? Artie had left out that important detail. Maybe he didn't want to go after all. But he also didn't want to allow Lana to push him around anymore. He had succumbed to her pressure too many times. Probably one reason she'd left.

"Are you there, Robert?"

"Yes, and I'm sorry it makes you uncomfortable, but I will be with the caravan. Artie said it's a done deal, and I agreed to participate."

Her breathing turned fast and heavy. "You can't do this, Robert."

"If they want me, it's my duty to help the war effort in this small way."

"Since when have you cared about anything bigger than you?"

He braced against the pain the words brought. Lana had never understood him. The studio had told them to marry, and he'd lacked the strength and will to say no, a decision he'd paid for ever since. Even with the arranged marriage, he'd tried to make it work and learn to love her. His parents had given him a great example to follow, but everything he'd tried fell short. He'd actually allowed himself to love her, his first mistake. The second came from caring what she thought of him.

The marriage had been doomed from the start, but he'd fought hard for it.

Not that Lana acknowledged that. Instead, she delighted in belittling him every chance she got. If Artie had told him she'd be on the train, he'd have killed the idea of joining at that moment. But now that she wanted him to quit, he'd be there. Forget about making an impression on some studio exec. He had to prove her hold on him had expired.

"I have to get ready for tonight's event."

"You know we'll be uncomfortable."

Robert glanced at his watch then pushed from the table. "I have to go."

"Robert, please. Don't come."

Lana begging? He paused but then stiffened his resolve. Her cajoling had no power over him anymore. "If I do, I'll do something for a cause a lot bigger than you and me. Good-bye, Lana. See you on the train." He hung up as she screeched in his ear.

CHAPTER FIVE

Audra pressed a hand over her mouth. Stared at the body. Heaved in a tremulous breath.

Everything was wrong. Everything.

She forced herself to creep closer to the body. Examine it. She brushed aside the blond hair, sobbing at the realization it wasn't brunette, Rosemary's color the last time she'd seen her. This woman looked a few pounds heavier than Rosemary's slender form, too. Audra knelt down and felt the neck for a pulse, her knee slipping on a towel. Nausea pounded Audra as a putrid smell permeated the tiny room. Nothing pulsed under her fingers.

She hurried from the room and to the front door. Burst through it, gulped deep breaths of beautiful, clean, orange-infused air.

"Help me. Somebody please help." Audra looked around but couldn't see anyone. All the windows on the side of the building were shut. She wouldn't get help this way.

She rushed to the sidewalk at the front of the stucco building and yelled again. Pounded on the front door. "Help. There's a body."

Relief underscored the horror. It wasn't Rosemary. Tears coursed down Audra's cheeks at the thought. It wasn't Rosemary. Thank God it wasn't. But who lay there? Where was Rosemary?

And why wouldn't someone help her?

Audra felt adrift in an alien land. If this had happened at home, she'd know what steps to take. Here, her mind froze and nothing came. She didn't even know where to find a phone if a resident wouldn't help her.

A window opened, and a lady hung out, curlers dotting her head above her floral housecoat. "Young lady, what is all the noise about?"

"Please, call the police. There's a body in Rosemary's apartment." Audra's words rushed out in a high-pitched, reedy tone. Not the voice she'd cultivated during law school. But the image of that body lying in her sister's bathroom... The vivid picture wouldn't leave her. The kaleidoscope of pale skin against blue tile mixed with rich red tones in the evening dress. Audra didn't know who lay there, and that scared her.

"A body?" The woman stared at her, glasses perched firmly on her nose, seemingly taking in Audra's appearance. Why did she stand there staring?

"There's—a body—in my sister's apartment." Audra's knees weakened as the words stumbled from her mouth. "Can you call the police? Or tell me where to find a phone?"

"I'll call." The woman appraised her one more moment then turned away from the window, disappearing behind a billowing lace curtain.

Audra walked up and down the sidewalk, rubbing her arms through her jacket sleeves, trying to create warmth when she felt ice cold. The sun blazed down, yet at the core, she felt nothing but frigid emptiness. Questions. Fear.

Audra shivered uncontrollably. The woman looked like she'd been dead for a while. Audra's breathing raced until she feared she'd hyperventilate. The longer the body had been there, the longer Rosemary hadn't.

Please don't let me have waited too long. She prayed for peace, but felt none. She'd known something wasn't right from Rosemary's last couple of phone calls.

Why didn't I do something? If she'd learned anything in law school, it was to follow her instincts. Why hadn't she? Audra sank onto the front step of the building, the heat from the cement seeping into her.

A police car pulled in front of the building, lights pulsing, siren silent. A man wearing a navy blue uniform stepped out while another stayed in the car, arms crossed.

"You the one who called in?" The thin man stood in front of her, feet apart, arms hanging at his sides. He appeared relaxed, but Audra sensed he would respond quickly to danger. The question and his stance gave no indication he knew why he'd been called.

Audra stumbled to her feet. "I found a body. In my sister's apartment. But it's not my sister." A mix of relief and horror pulsed through her. Tremors shook her. She had to find Rosemary. Before she had to identify her.

"I'm Officer Josh Trainor and the lug in the car is Officer Matt Jones. Take a slow breath." He studied her, concern lacing his eyes. "We'll take care of this if you can show me where you found the body."

Audra squared her shoulders, willing strength to flow through her. Do whatever they requested, and then she could find Rosemary. The officer gestured toward the building and started toward the front stairs behind her.

"Not that way." Audra moved up the sidewalk to the side of the building without waiting to see if he followed. She stalled when she reached the door.

"Would you like to wait here, Miss...?" Officer Trainor's hands rested on his hips as he watched her, eyes soft even as his stance remained firm.

"Miss Schaeffer." Audra licked her lips. "Can I have a moment?"

"Yes, ma'am." He eased her against the wall then pulled his gun and edged around the door. He turned and looked back at the car. "You coming, Jones?"

"Yep." The officer opened the car door and slid from the seat. While the first officer was tall and fit, Officer Jones's paunch spilled over his belt. The car groaned then rocked side-to-side as he stepped out. He ambled toward them, pulling his gun at the last moment. Audra tried to disappear against the building's side, stomach churning as the officers swept into the front room.

"Where's the body, Miss Schaeffer?" Trainor, the thin one, poked back out to look at her.

"Behind the door. In the bathroom." Audra stood rooted to the spot and waited. A few rustling movements reached her. She looked around her but didn't see anything. The noise must have come from the apartment. She frowned. Wouldn't the officers check the body before rifling through papers?

Officer Jones strode out the door toward her, his face set in grim lines. "Did you move the body or do anything in there?"

Audra searched his face, praying for strength. "I looked around the main room before I found the body. I—I didn't expect that. That poor woman may have moved when I opened the door. I had to see if she was alive. But that's all before I ran for help."

The policeman studied her, eyes piercing her in a way that made her want to squirm just like when her professors drilled her during law school. It was as if he tested her words against what he saw, checking for truth. When she thought she couldn't take another moment of scrutiny, he strode to the car without a word. He leaned in and did something with the radio before returning to her.

Audra longed for a place where she could retreat. Her mind spun with horrid images, but worry knotted her shoulders. Rosemary was in trouble. Audra had to find her—even if she had no idea where to start in this strange city where she knew nobody. And Rosie hadn't dropped names of friends or men. Other than the black book, she'd have to get creative about where to start looking.

She should find a hotel room with a bed she could collapse on. Maybe if she took a nap, she'd wake up to find the whole afternoon had been nothing more than a terrible nightmare. Officer Trainor stepped outside and approached her, a sad dip to his mouth. She swayed on her feet, and he steadied her.

"Jones, location called in?"

The other officer nodded. "Of course. Detective's on the way. Should arrive soon."

"Good." Trainor looked around. "Know who?"

"Franklin." Officer Jones rolled his eyes and crossed his arms.

"Great. We've broken his unwritten rules. I'll wait out here with her. You guard the apartment."

Officer Jones saluted with a frown. "I'm the senior member of this partnership, you know."

"And I'm the brains."

Audra's mind wandered as the officers bantered. Jones stalked back to the apartment, muttering as he passed.

She swayed again, and Officer Trainor tightened his grip on her arm and held her up. "None of that, please." He led her to his car, where he offered her the passenger seat.

Audra hesitated then eased onto the seat, the smell of cigarette smoke overpowering. Her limbs felt heavy as she sank against the back and answered the first few questions, almost without thinking. Name. Occupation. Hometown.

"Finding your sister brought you to Hollywoodland?"

"Yes."

"Any reason to think she's in danger?"

"Other than finding a body in her apartment?"

"Good point." The corners of his eyes crinkled before he looked down at his notepad. "All right…" A car roared to a stop at the curb. The black vehicle didn't match the car she sat in, but as soon as she saw the man driving, she knew Detective Franklin had arrived.

He stepped from his car, hat clamped down around his eyes, thin face, lanky form, and stiff posture. His gaze darted around the apartment building. She imagined he already took mental notes, not missing much.

"Everything looks quiet. Where are the neighbors?" Franklin's gruff voice grated.

"It's still hush-hush. Jones is guarding the apartment, and I'm here with the witness."

For the first time, Franklin turned to Audra, his gaze marching up and down her. She fought the desire to melt against the seat and attempt a disappearing act. The detective tightened his tie and strode toward her. When he reached the car, he squatted in front of her. "You witness the murder or find the body?"

"Found the body." She tipped her chin to match his gaze.

"Trainor, why don't you interview the neighbors? Chubby there can guard the door. What's your name?"

She told him. He nodded and she got the impression he never forgot a detail.

"Well, Miss Schaeffer. You're going to wait here while I check the scene. You look like the kind I can trust for a few minutes."

What else was she going to do? Steal the police car? Time slowed to a crawl as she waited for him to return. If she hadn't checked her watch, she would have believed hours had passed rather than minutes.

A solemn expression pulled his face down as he strode toward her. "All right, come here. I want to hear your story in there."

Audra hesitated then followed the detective into the apartment and toward the bathroom.

Officer Jones marched up to Detective Franklin. "You sure about this?"

Detective Franklin stared him down. "She's already seen the body." He turned his back on the officer and pivoted toward her, a guarded expression on his face. "I need you to step in here."

Goosebumps erupted all over her skin. She couldn't go in that tiny space again. Not with the body.

"Come on." Detective Franklin extended his hand and waited. Audra exhaled then took a deep breath. She placed her hand in his and took a step forward.

She peered around the door. The woman lay against the side of the claw-foot tub, her red gown bunched under her. Her shoulder and arm had wedged between the tub and the floor.

"Tell me what happened when you came in." Detective Franklin listened intently, grooves appearing on his nose. After she finished, he studied her a minute. "Let's go back outside. Make sure you don't touch anything on your way out."

A moment later she blinked in the sunlight, wishing the rays would reach to the depths of her. Once she was settled back in the car, Franklin crouched in front of her again.

"Do you know the name of the victim?"

"No. I arrived this afternoon. I don't know much about my sister's friends and acquaintances or Hollywood." Audra bit the inside of her cheek. An unsettled feeling engulfed her as he studied her.

"Really? You come all the way out here and find a body you know nothing about?"

"Of course. How could I know anything?" She wanted to stomp her foot and force him to believe her. He wasted time talking to her when he should be looking for a killer and her sister. Her heart raced at the thought her sister could be held by some killer. It pounded at the thought that that was the best scenario if Rosemary had been home when the killer struck.

The thought rolled around her mind.

Churned her stomach.

She stood and hurried past the detective to the shrubs. Lost what little she'd eaten that morning on the plane.

She bent over, hands on her thighs, trying to ignore the cycling fears and questions.

"You all right, Miss Schaeffer?"

Audra wiped her mouth. Tears traced down her face. She staggered back to the car, pulling a handkerchief from her handbag. She wiped her cheeks then rubbed her thumb along the monogrammed initials. RG.

"Who did your sister talk about?"

"She didn't. That's the problem. She was excited then disappointed. But she didn't tell us many details."

"You've got to give me a name. Something."

Audra leaned forward and put her head in her hands. "Occasionally, she mentioned another gal. I think her name was Rachel."

"A last name?"

"I'm sorry, I don't remember." She shook her head, wishing she could force the knowledge to appear.

"She ever mention anyone who made her nervous or concerned for her safety?" He rattled off the question as if it was one he knew all too well.

Again Audra had to shake her head. "I had a gut sense things were worse than she said. But the lack of details and concrete examples is why I'm here alone. My parents think I'm overly concerned." She had to get away. Find Rosemary. Before it was too late. "I found a body in my sister's apartment. The only good thing is it's not my sister. However, my sister isn't home, and I have no idea if she's safe or where she is." She should call her parents, but couldn't. Not until she knew something. A plan formed in her mind. "Can I call a cab?"

"In a minute. First, I want to try a theory. See what you think." He studied her. "Your sister a lot like you, Miss Schaeffer?"

"No. She wants the big stage, and I'm just an attorney hoping for a courtroom."

"Then think about this: Your sister and this woman get in an argument for some reason. Don't know why, mind you, but we'll learn that. They're arguing, and your sister accidentally kills the other woman. In a panic, she runs from the apartment, leaving the body here."

Indignation stiffened Audra. "You cannot think my sister did this!"

He shrugged. "It's a plausible theory. Things like that happen in real life and on the screen."

"My sister could never kill anyone."

"You'd be amazed how many families are convinced their precious son or daughter didn't kill, but we prove they did. Sometimes life works that way. My guess is you won't find your sister, because she's running."

Audra stiffened her spine. "I'm leaving." She'd find a cab somewhere.

"We can be done for now, but I need to know where you are. Where will you stay?"

Roosevelt Hotel. Wasn't that where Rosemary's event was that night? "I'll be at the Roosevelt Hotel."

He whistled. "You've got rich taste, sister. Here's my information." He slipped a card from his coat pocket and handed it to her. "I'll radio for a cab for you. Don't leave the area without letting me know where you're going. I'll have more questions for you."

She needed to get away and think without the detective watching. "I'll find my way, thanks."

"I have to insist." The hard look in his eyes signaled she needed to tread carefully. "You might not be involved. In fact I doubt you were, but if your sister somehow learns you're here and contacts you or you stumble onto her, you must tell me. Anything else will be obstruction of justice or aiding and abetting. If you're an attorney, you know what that means."

Audra swallowed. She needed to let reason win over passion. She might not like this man at the moment. But he could be an ally later if she didn't find Rosemary tonight at the USO event. She needed to get to the Roosevelt, follow the only information she had. "Thank you." What else could she do? "Can I get my things?"

He nodded. "Point them out and I'll release them."

After he nosed through her bags, she grabbed them and the dress, then he walked her to the curb where a cab waited.

"Be careful. Whoever did this hates your sister. Or might be your sister."

CHAPTER SIX

Robert tugged the sleeves of his shirt, pulling them from under his tuxedo jacket.

Twilight fell outside his window. Time to get a move on or he'd miss his emcee gig. He needed the practice for whatever job he'd have on the caravan. He wasn't a wit like Abbott and Costello. And he certainly didn't have the pipes of Bing Crosby. He couldn't direct a band or make the crowds laugh like Desi Arnaz. Guess he'd have to be Robert Garfield, plain and simple. Lead the crowds from moment to moment with smoothness and a touch of humor.

That ought to bring the fans in droves.

Selecting a top hat and walking stick, Robert pulled on his gloves and headed out. A 1940 Buick followed a '42 Studebaker down the boulevard. Someday he'd own his own vehicle, only his would be something sporty with quick pick-up. A short walk down palm-lined streets led to the Roosevelt Hotel. The Spanish architecture-influenced building towered against the night sky at least eleven or twelve stories high. Red marquee lights spelled out the name of the restaurant sitting in front of the hotel. Robert marched past it and toward the main door off Hollywood Boulevard. A bellboy dressed in rich livery opened the door with a grin.

"Sir."

"Thank you." Robert tipped his hat, removed it, and started across the lobby then turned back to the bellboy. "Can you direct me to the Blossom Ballroom?"

"Certainly." He led Robert across the lobby and directed him up a set of stairs. "From there you can follow the women in ball dresses." He winked at Robert.

"An interesting technique, but looks like it will work."

"Yes, sir. Hone in on a beautiful woman and follow her. Works even better if she's alone for the evening."

Robert laughed. "I'll remember that. Thank you."

No sense telling the man the last thing he imagined doing tonight was finding a woman to twirl around the floor when he wasn't at the microphone. The full rainbow shimmered in the hall as couples made their way to the ballroom. Robert slipped to the edge so he could bypass the crush.

"Robert Garfield." A sweet soprano voice called him.

Robert turned on his heel, pasting a grin on his face. "Who's calling?"

A brunette adorned in a silver gown that clung to her body until it fell away from her hips in waves held out her hand. "I heard rumors you'd make an appearance."

"Elizabeth McAllister. You are breathtaking tonight." Robert leaned over her hand and brushed his lips across it.

She tittered. "You are kind. Escort me inside?"

"You're unescorted?" Robert glanced around. "I never thought that day would come."

"Me either." She shrugged. "Willing to help?"

"I don't know that being seen on my arm will make a difference, but let's make like it will." Robert offered her his arm, and the two moved across the ballroom.

When they reached a table with an empty seat, Robert bowed toward her and slipped from her grasp. "Here you go, mademoiselle."

"Thank you. Good luck tonight." She kissed his cheek. "You'll do a great job."

Robert pulled out her chair, cheek hot where her lips had brushed. He glanced around the expansive ballroom. Artie's instructions echoed in his mind. Find Mr. Feldstein. If he didn't, the caravan gig might not happen.

He had to hit a homerun tonight.

"There you are." Goldie smacked her gum, her platinum curls in a crazy wave around her face. "Artie sent me to watch for you hours ago."

"Not that long."

She rolled her eyes and blew a bubble. "Maybe, but I've turned down too many dances while cooling my heels. This way." Her skirts swished around her calves as she turned without waiting to see if he followed.

Robert smiled at a woman he passed. They'd both worked a crowd scene in a movie. Looked like someone had worked with her since then. She'd dropped a few pounds, glammed up a bit, as she now wore the latest form-fitting style. She looked ready to become the next Marlene Dietrich. Exactly what the world needed at a time like this—another pin-up girl for the troops to dream about.

He brushed his gloves down his jacket sleeves and bumped into Goldie when she halted.

"Watch it." Goldie pushed Robert away. "Here's Artie."

"Thanks, Goldie." Robert turned to the table where Artie Schmaltz held court. Instead of the typical two- or four-topper that filled the glittering ballroom, this table had a sea of chairs shoved against it and chairs two or three deep behind it. The starlets that filled each chair added to the illusion Artie had landed in the middle of a rhinestone-bejeweled collage.

"Keeps your paws off, Garfield." Artie's eyes glittered like black coals.

Robert held his hands up, palms out. "No interest, I assure you."

No, if he ever developed a serious interest in a woman again, it would be someone far removed from the superficiality of Hollywood. Yet another strike against him if the studio heads knew. He didn't fit easily into their system of dictating every action and relationship of the stars. They did that once and it had been a disaster with a world of heartache at the end.

Artie snorted and stuck a smoldering cigar in his mouth. "Come here, Babycakes."

A dolled-up blonde in a skintight blue gown that left little to the imagination slid onto Artie's lap and snuggled close. Robert shifted to the side, grateful his kid sister, Louise, had never shown a desire to move into the family's business. With her angelic looks and naivety, the vultures would circle and tear her to pieces before she knew what happened.

Even if this kid snapped out of it before she was used up, there were a dozen more eager and ready to take her place. And that was limited to the women he could see here. Disgust coiled in his gut. He jammed his hands in his pockets. "So where's this Feldstein I check in with?"

Artie gestured toward the head table. "See the gorilla up there? He's with the big studio. He'll get you set up, not only for tonight but— if he likes you—for the caravan. Break a leg."

No pressure. He always auditioned in front of a few hundred

strangers who all wanted him to fail. Maybe he should have taken more opportunities with the vaudeville act to test his chops in front of a live audience. Tonight he'd aim to exude a debonair aura, far removed from the sticks of middle country vaudeville.

Robert strode across the distance with a nod here and a handshake there before reaching Mark Feldstein, who turned to him with an impatient air. As Robert studied him, he decided gorilla was a bad descriptor. He was larger than most in Hollywood but wore a well-tailored suit and flashy tie that made him fit in with the style-conscious.

"Robert Garfield."

The man eyed him up and down before brushing a strand of hair away from his eyes and sticking out a hand. "Mark Feldstein. I'm glad you're here. Your hostess is late." The big man eyed his watch. "Artie promised she was the next Kate Hepburn."

Robert shrugged. "I suppose. I would think you could get the real Kate."

"True. She didn't want to drive back into town for the night, and the bosses said it was okay. You won't pull things like that on the road?"

Robert shook his head, feeling a slow grin spread on his face. "I'm a team player."

"That will get you only so far. The rest requires something extra." Feldstein looked Robert up and down. "You'll do fine. Show me you can string some thoughts together, maybe get the audience to relax, and you're on the caravan. No pay, but all expenses."

"Understood."

"Good. I get the honor of babysitting the lot of you B-listers for the tour."

"I'll keep your job easy."

"They all say that. In fact, that's probably what your co-host thought until she decided to run an hour late. You go on in five minutes with or without her. Welcome to showbiz and the art of going with the mood." A few minutes later, Robert had the agenda as well as instructions on who to introduce. Then Feldstein strode off, muttering under his breath.

Robert took a deep breath and placed his hat, walking stick, and gloves at the head table. He set the agenda next to them. Time to figure out the audience.

While it was a Uniform Services Organization fundraiser, it wasn't overwhelmed with military uniforms. Which made sense in a way, since it wasn't the USO itself. But there were a few dress uniforms mixed with tuxedos and the colorful dresses. Small square tables were set around the ballroom. Only a few people like Artie held court in the corners of the room. Waiters circulated with plates of hors d'oeuvres. The aroma of the food mixed with the cloying scent of a dozen perfumes. If he stayed near the front, the mix didn't overpower him.

Several couples waltzed in the center of the room on the dance floor. In a minute, the bandleader would raise his wand, the music would stop, and Robert would step to the podium. Or maybe he should step to the podium and wait for the band to stop.

He shook his head. If he wanted to make it, he needed to do this in a big way. And he'd never run from a challenge before. It was time to break Lana's hold on him. All the things she'd said about his lack of acting skills weren't true. Time to get his head back in the game and focus on what mattered—doing a phenomenal turn as emcee.

The violins and trumpets reached a crescendo and fell silent.

"The dancing will continue after the program. Thank you again for joining us. Take it away, Bobby." The bandleader swiveled on his heels and pointed his baton at Robert.

Robert stumbled to the microphone, bumping into it and sending a screech through the ballroom. "Sorry about that, ladies and gents. Didn't mean to give you such a loud wake-up call. Welcome to tonight's festivities in honor of the Uniform Services Organization. Let's give a round of applause to thank the representatives of the USO who are with us tonight. What great work they do."

A smattering of applause met Robert.

"Now, folks, let's give them the applause they deserve for the great work they do raising and maintaining the morale of our troops. We're here tonight to do more than applaud their efforts. We'll all be digging deep—" He made a show of searching through his pockets, pulling out one and then another until his monkey suit had lost its stiff formality. "—Some of us deeper than others, to help them with a few dollars to continue their good work. So let's start with the easy part. If you have served at one of the local USOs, please stand so we can thank you."

Men and women stood, a few reluctantly, and others bounding to their feet to receive their recognition. Robert led the crowd in applauding them then took a moment to stuff his pockets back inside.

"Before we get to the part where we eat and then separate you from your hard-earned moolah, please welcome Miss Janice Lucille to sing 'The Star Spangled Banner.'"

A lovely redhead joined him at the podium. With a quick peck on her cheek, Robert backed from the podium as the United States flag with its field of forty-eight stars was marched into the middle of the ballroom. Miss Lucille's tremulous voice soared impressively over the gathering. As soon as she finished, Robert strode back to the podium, trying to portray the image of an urbane gentleman.

"Many thanks to Miss Lucille for that stirring performance. In a moment, the waiters will come with our meals. Before they do, let's take a moment to thank God for His many blessings and ask His protection on our men fighting around the globe. If you'll bow your heads... Heavenly Father, we ask that Your sheltering hand would be on our troops as they train and fight around the world. Give our leaders wisdom. And guide us tonight. Bless this food and be honored. Amen.

"You may enjoy your meal."

Robert eased to his seat. It could be a long evening if he had to sit at the front alone.

"Excuse me, is this seat taken?"

He looked up into the beautiful face of his traveling companion from the plane. Her hair tumbled in loose waves around her face, a face that looked even whiter than it had when they landed. The rich color of her navy gown did nothing to heighten her color. A slight tremor coursed through her body.

What was she doing here without Rosemary?

CHAPTER SEVEN

Her room in the Roosevelt Hotel struck an opulent note compared to Rosemary's flat. Audra stood in the middle of the room dressed in only her foundation items, feeling torn. Should she go downstairs and pray Rosemary had shown up at the fundraiser? Or should she call the detective and see if the apartment had been cleared? See if he'd learned who that poor woman was and who had killed her?

Her stomach tightened and a rush of panic coursed through her.

Never one to wait for others to tell her what to do, Audra marched over to the closet and pulled out Rosemary's gown. She might not belong in Hollywood, but she had to do everything she could to locate Rosie—before it was too late. A wave of nausea burned up her throat. She rushed to the bathroom and leaned over the toilet.

A moment later her stomach was emptied again.

Lord, I can't do this. But I can't sit here either.

Her pale image stared back at her from the ornate mirror. She felt like a phony, spending a chunk of her precious reserves on this room. It had made sense when she needed to go somewhere. She didn't know the hotels in Hollywood, but figured if the fundraiser was here then it should be a nice hotel. She'd been right. Almost too right.

The hint of the sapphire gown behind her shimmered in the mirror. She could sit here, or she could go downstairs and do something.

She splashed cold water on her face and braced. Time to act. She applied her cosmetics as if she preparing for an audience with the president himself. First, the pancake layer, then the rouge, followed by a hint of color on her eyes and a swipe of lipstick. Then she shimmied into the dress. She twisted her hair into a knot but decided that looked too formal. Letting her hair fall around her shoulders, she felt like she'd slipped into a role. Almost as if she played Rosemary. If she found Rosie, it would be worth it. She glanced at her watch and jumped. The fundraiser had started forty minutes earlier. How could she slip in now without being noticed?

As she studied the mirror, she imagined everything she'd seen in Rosemary's bathroom. A shiver coursed through her. That poor woman!

Audra felt the tears gather in her eyes at the thought of what the dead woman's family would experience when they learned she'd been killed. So brutally. So callously. So cruelly.

How could she pretend to have a good time with that image locked in her mind?

Rosemary.

Audra grabbed her handbag, tossed her room key and a tube of lipstick in it, and hurried from the room before her courage fled.

Minutes later, she stood at the entrance to the ballroom, the invitation in hand.

"Do you need assistance, ma'am?" One of the hotel staff standing in front of the door eyed her curiously.

She pulled from her reverie. "No, I'm fine." She would be fine. She had no choice.

The strains of the swing band pulled her into the crowded room. All she saw was a sea of unfamiliar faces. She slowly gazed around the room but in the half-darkness couldn't see features and distinctions well enough to determine whether Rosie was there. Her gaze reached the front of the room and the other person in town she knew. Robert Garfield sat at the head table, looking debonair in a tuxedo, the picture of the next Cary Grant.

Her feet carried her toward him, his kindness from the morning drawing her. Maybe he could help find Rosemary. And if she were here, the invitation had indicated she should be with him. "Excuse me, is this seat taken?"

Robert hurried to his feet. "Well, hello again." He gestured to the table. "There's plenty of room if you'd like to join me." He pulled back a chair, and Audra eased onto its edge. A smile stretched his face as he sat down next to her. "Is Rosemary with you? She's running late."

Audra felt her face slacken. "I'd hoped you would tell me she was here."

Robert frowned. "She didn't show for the event. I'm emceeing alone, but we can wander around the room later. See if she's hiding."

"I suppose, though I doubt she'd do that when she had the option to sit up here."

"True, but other than calling for her from the podium, I'm not sure how else to search." Robert eyed her. "Anything you want to tell me that might help?"

Audra bit her lower lip and considered the situation. Rosemary would be furious if she learned her own sister had gossiped about what happened. Audra should talk to her first and then, together, decide what to say about the body. She shook her head. "I can't say anything now. Maybe after we find Rosie." She squared her shoulders and glanced around the ballroom. "What an impressive place."

"Yes, I suppose it is. You go to enough of these, it's easy to miss the grandeur."

"I guess it's a nice side benefit of making the trip." She fanned her face as if on the edge of swooning. "I'm just sorry I made such a fool of myself this morning."

"You didn't." His warm smile settled on her. "So where is Rosemary? Artie's annoyed by her tardiness."

"Artie?" Audra wrinkled her nose and rubbed her forehead. "I don't know who he is or where Rosemary is. She wasn't at her apartment." A waiter placed a plate of food in front of each of them. Audra pushed the plate away and covered it with a napkin, her appetite abandoning her.

Robert picked up his knife and fork and cut into his steak. "After the meal, we'll walk around. It's a long shot, but we might find her."

"Thank you for offering. It can't hurt." Audra tried to smile, but the aroma of the fish and steak on the plate wound around her. She swallowed hard against the urge to gag. She should eat. She hadn't had anything since the plane. But the thought of eating when she didn't know where Rosemary was—or what had happened to her—or who the body in her apartment was. She couldn't do it.

Robert must think she'd gone crazy. Between her strange behavior on the plane and now, she certainly hadn't put her best foot forward.

She played with her bracelet then stood. "I'm sorry. I should leave you alone."

Robert shot to his feet, steadying his chair behind him where it rocked. "Please stay." He shrugged, a strangely endearing gesture. "It's kind of quiet and lonely up here." He leaned closer. "Shh, don't tell anyone. The life of a second-tier star isn't everything it's billed."

"All right." He really had looked lonely up here by himself. "I guess we'll give the columnists something to write about in the papers."

"Who was that mystery woman seen with the darkly handsome Robert Garfield?"

"Precisely." Audra eased back onto her chair. She peeked at the food under the napkin then pushed a hand against her stomach. She had to get her mind on something else. "Tell me why Hollywood."

Robert repositioned his napkin on his lap and settled in. He sliced a piece of meat and popped it in his mouth. After swallowing, he pointed at hers. "You really should try it. Hollywood? What can I say? It was in the blood. Mom and Pop had a vaudeville act. Grew up in it. Saw pictures and knew I had to try. Starve or not, see if I could make it." He shrugged. "There's nothing like breathing life into a role. Then watching the crowd interact with the characters." He leaned closer. "I like to go to the theatre and watch the crowds. When they get the performance, it's wonderful. But let's keep that our little secret." Though he whispered the words, Robert smiled at her in a way that made it seem they were alone in the room rather than surrounded by several hundred people.

Audra felt heat travel up her neck. What must this man be like when he really wanted to impress someone?

Robert scanned the ballroom. "People have worked their way through the course. Time for me to get back to work. Would you like to fill in for Rosemary?"

"No, thank you." Audra waved him off. "The only audience I'd like is a judge."

He winked at her, and her heart stopped. *Get ahold of yourself, Audra. He is a movie star. He flirts with all the women. Comes with the job.*

While he entertained the crowd and got them relaxed, Audra nibbled at her food. Once she slathered a roll with rich butter, she could force it down. She poked at the baby potatoes but left the meat. She could imagine any number of her friends who would envy her this moment. Dinner with a movie star in Hollywood. Being seen by those who mattered in the business. But she couldn't think of that. Not when Rosemary hadn't shown. All that was left was for Audra to wander among the tables until she'd checked each one for her sister. Where was she?

Audra shivered in the gown she'd borrowed from her sister's wardrobe. She felt exposed. As if everyone could look at her and see at a glance that she was a pretender.

She knew she didn't belong here.

She didn't want to.

But that didn't mean she wanted everyone to identify her feelings with a glance.

"Feel free to make your way to the dance floor as the Johnny Richards Band takes to the bandstand again." Polite applause followed Robert as he made his way back to his seat. "There. Duty is done for a while."

Audra tried to relax. Smile. But the image of that body—she couldn't make the switch.

"Hey, how'd you like to skirt the room with me? See and be seen?"

"Don't you have a date?" She chewed her lower lip, wondering how he'd respond.

"I am free as the proverbial bird. Someone else is handling the money talk." He smiled at her in a way that probably made most women melt. "Besides, we can look for Rosemary without raising suspicion."

She nodded and stood. Even if Rosemary had decided to shirk her emcee duties, Audra would at least know she'd shown up. Though it was a remote possibility, finding her here would be better than the fear.

And the body…

A shudder overcame her. Robert studied her, concern etched on his brow.

"You okay?"

"Yes." Audra licked her lips and tried to smile. "Let's wander. It's not every day a girl like me gets an opportunity like this."

Robert shook his head and laughed. "I know you don't really mean that, but let's promenade anyway. You're different from the other women here. I like that." He extended his hand to her and waited while she slipped her hand into his. The strains of Harry James's "Music Makers" flowed from the band as she and Robert stepped around the table and down onto the floor. "Besides, it's my job to make sure you head home with plenty of stories to turn your friends' heads."

"You have no idea." Audra followed Robert as he whisked her between tables, stopping here and there to introduce her to someone. Nowhere did Rosemary make an appearance. Audra strained her eyes, trying to search the corners of the large room. And once people began circulating among the tables and dance floor as the band switched from Tommy Dorsey to Glenn Miller, the task of locating her sister became impossible. Eventually, Robert swung her by a beverage table and obtained glasses of punch for them. Audra sipped hers, enjoying the coolness as it slid down her throat.

"Any idea how long you'll be in town?"

"No. It all depends on Rosemary. As soon as I know she's safe, I can go home."

"You've no interest in trying the city?" Robert looked at her, a question clear in his eyes.

"I'm not much of a West Coast or desert girl."

"It's not so bad. And Hollywood itself is pretty small. There might be some good opportunities here for a woman with a legal background."

Audra let the idea roll around a minute. "No, I need to focus on finding Rosemary and then head home."

The music started again, this time with a swinging waltz. Robert took her cup and handed it to a passing waiter. "Then enjoy tonight." He swept her toward the floor, and soon they danced cheek to cheek. He hummed along with the band, his voice a smooth baritone that tickled her ear. "Are you sure you can't stay?"

Audra sighed and tried to push a bit of space between them. "You say that to all the women."

"No. I assure you my ex-wife has spoiled me to all women save you." He pulled her next to him again and swept her back into the fray with a smooth hum.

Audra stepped back and eyed him. Even if she were looking for a man, she wasn't sure how she felt about one who'd been divorced. That didn't bode well for future relationships. He must have seen something in her face.

"Next time I marry, I'll decide who my spouse is rather than letting the studio dictate that decision to me. Hollywood isn't Middle America. The rules are different in ways you might not understand."

A couple bumped into them, and Audra realized she and Robert had halted in the middle of the floor. Robert must have realized it, too, because he lightly eased her back into the dancing couples.

Audra closed her eyes, longing for one instant to get lost in the moment. To pretend she was young and carefree and could enjoy the undivided attention of the star holding her. To pretend that she didn't need to find her sister. She blocked the thought and focused on the moment. One moment. That's all she asked.

CHAPTER EIGHT

Robert enjoyed the sensation of the woman in his arms. Somehow he doubted she'd believe him if he told her how rarely he let himself enjoy the company of a woman like he enjoyed being with her tonight—that words of wooing didn't naturally trip off his tongue.

His status as a star left most women acting strange around him. They swooned and made fools of themselves because of his job. Add in Lana and any trust he had in the fairer sex had disappeared. Living with her had left him undercut. The thought of spending more than a passing moment with a woman didn't hold much appeal.

But this one—the one in his arms—she already seemed different. While at first flustered, Audra had quickly recovered and seemed to ignore the fact he acted for a living. A welcome change.

He tucked her closer to his side, enjoying the moment as long as it lasted.

Audra sighed, and some of the tension evaporated from her shoulders. Whatever had happened since she'd arrived in Hollywood, it hadn't meant finding her sister.

Should he be concerned? Press Audra for details? A woman alone in a strange city. Why would she let him close? He would share the burden if she'd let him, but he didn't really know Rosemary—just her reputation as a woman who did whatever it took to make it. She'd taken all of Artie's instructions. One dinner with her before tonight didn't give him much insight. Even then Artie had insisted they be seen together.

Robert tucked Audra closer. He'd shield her as long as possible from the truth he knew about Rosemary. She likely didn't know the sordid underside of Hollywood or understand that it had affected her sister. That would be unwelcome news. The kind that added to the worry that had driven Audra here.

The saxophone wailed a last, piercing note. He dipped Audra then spun her.

When she opened her eyes, a dreamy look had cloaked her face.

"Hello, doll."

"Oh." Her mouth formed the perfect rosebud, and he must have stared because she jerked back a step. "Thank you for a delightful distraction."

Distraction? Did all women know instinctively how to hit a guy's ego where it hurt? "The night doesn't have to be over."

"Yes, I think it does. It's late, and I'm ready to get back to my hotel room. Maybe Rosemary's left word there." The flash of a shadow hid her face, as if she really didn't expect to hear from Rosemary.

Robert hoped he kept his face schooled from the disappointment. "Rosemary's a grown woman. Surely she can take care of herself while you stay for another dance." He grinned, the smile that made his fans swoon. "Please."

She shook her head, and tears filled her eyes. "I can't. I'm sorry."

He hesitated then reached up to brush a tear from her soft cheek. "I didn't mean to make you cry."

"I'm just worried." She blinked hard and transformed before his eyes into a woman with a strong grip on her emotions. "My brother died in an accident a few years ago. I guess that turned me into a nervous big sister. I couldn't stand it if anything happened to Rosemary too." A tremulous smile graced her lips. "I'm sorry to leave, but I assure you, it has nothing to do with you and everything to do with my imagination. Spending this time with you has been beyond anything I've dreamed." She clapped a hand over her mouth, as if horrified at what she'd said.

Robert tried to muffle his laughter. This woman certainly had no artifice, something he liked very much after all his time surrounded by women aiming for their next role.

She stared at him, eyes large, and he realized how his joy could be misinterpreted. "I'm so sorry. Losing your brother must have been terrible." He shook his head, worried his words only worsened his faux pas. "See? I need scripts to keep from stumbling all over my words." He took a breath and studied her. "I can't imagine what it would do to me if my sister died." The thought was terrible. "I hope you find Rosemary and everything is fine. She seems like a great kid and has potential to make it here." Robert offered her his arm. "Are you sure you can't wait until I can escort you?"

"That's kind of you, but I'll be fine." She patted her hair as if suddenly self-conscious. "It's already been too much to spend the evening with you. You don't know how the girls back home will squeal when they learn I danced with you—*the* Robert Garfield."

"I'm no Cary Grant or Clark Gable."

"That may be. But we all loved your role in *Before Tomorrow Breaks*." She grinned at him, her grief of moments earlier swept aside. "There are many reasons I read *LOOK* and magazines like it."

"At least let me know where you are staying."

"Tonight I'm here. Then I'll likely be at my sister's until I return home." She sighed and frowned, then shook her head slightly, as if to clear it. "Well. Thank you for a welcome change of pace. I needed it. More than you'll ever know."

"Then you're welcome."

Audra headed to the dais at the front of the ballroom. She grabbed her purse, and he followed like a boat wallowing in her wake on a lazy lake.

"Wait."

She stopped and turned toward him. "Yes?"

"If you need anything, call. Hollywood can be a lonely town." He stepped away from her and rubbed his hands together, fighting the surge of fire that had shot through him when they touched. "Anyway. Thanks for a great evening."

A bulb exploded near their heads. He looked up to find several photographers poised to shoot their photo. "Ready to be a star?"

She looked at him with a dazed look in her eyes. "They don't do this in Indiana."

"Come with me."

He tucked her arm under his and swept her out a side door. By the time they reached the front sidewalk and he'd hailed a taxi, she'd joined him in laughing. "Take the taxi around the block a few times, and the photographers will find other targets."

"All right." Audra leaned against him, her body light and small. "Do you ever get used to it? The photographers, I mean."

Robert opened the cab door for her and considered his words.

"There they are!"

"Oops. They found us." He scooted her into the cab and then slid in next to her.

"What about your duties?" She looked at him, her eyes round in her narrow face.

"Looks like I'm done for tonight. I'll explain to Feldstein later. Either I passed his test or not."

"Where to, kids?" The cab driver watched them in the rearview mirror.

Audra shrugged. "Actually, I have a room back at that hotel."

"Jokes on you, huh." The cabbie chuckled.

"Guess so."

Robert laughed, threw his arm along the back of the car seat, and snuggled Audra next to him. "Guess you can drive us around the block a couple times. Then drop us at the other entrance."

"Yes, sir." The cabbie saluted him in the mirror. "Young love…"

"That's right, mister. That's right." With Audra next to him, Robert considered the idea love might be in his future.

But one good night couldn't wipe out a hundred nights of bad memories. Or the bitter taste they left in his mouth. No, he wouldn't rush headlong into another terrible mistake. He'd protect himself before he'd risk the word *love* with anyone again.

CHAPTER NINE

Sunday, June 7, 1942

Warmth flooded Audra as sunlight tickled her nose. She stretched lazily in the magnificent bed, feeling like a princess in the beautifully appointed room. It had been foolish to spend so much money on a hotel room, but she'd enjoyed every moment.

Now as the sun cascaded through the open windows, she decided to enjoy the extravagance. It had been after midnight by the time she returned to the room.

Sneaking back into the hotel with Robert Garfield had been a fun cap to the evening. He had certainly made the evening more enjoyable and helped her forget the horrible day—if only for a while. How many times had she daydreamed of spending time with a real movie star? Meeting him and seeing a glimpse of the real man had been amazing. She could understand a little better now why Rosie loved Hollywood.

Last night Audra had closed her eyes a time or two during the evening's events and allowed herself to imagine it was real. That he cared for her and flirted with her for no other reason than she was beautiful and desirable.

Last night had been hers.

And she'd treasure every moment.

Now that her Cinderella adventure was over, she needed to face reality and call home. Let her parents know she'd arrived, but also break the news that she hadn't found Rosemary. Audra didn't know how to begin to tell them about the body she had found. She closed her eyes and prayed for wisdom. She wished she had a church to slip into, a place to quiet her heart before God and soak in His presence. As she prayed for peace, she felt His sweet presence meet her. Somehow, He would guide her.

Audra opened her eyes, slipped out of bed, and pulled on the fleecy robe that waited in the closet.

After she got ready, she'd slip downstairs and place the call. Since her parents wouldn't be home from church yet, she'd wait a bit longer. Maybe she could buckle down to the task of finding Rosemary in the interim. The thought chilled her, and she burrowed deeper into the robe. How should she start?

She'd never felt more alone and unsure than she did at that moment.

A heavy pounding shook the door. She jumped and clutched the fabric at the throat of the robe. "Yes?"

"Miss Schaeffer? Officer Trainor with the Hollywood Police Department."

A quiver skittered up Audra's neck at the name. Maybe he knew something about Rosemary.

"May I come in?"

Audra swallowed and opened the door as far as the security latch allowed. Just because he used that name didn't mean it was the same man. "Can I see your badge, please?"

The officer slid his badge toward her. She studied it then unlocked the door and returned it to him. "Where's Detective Franklin?"

"He asked me to bring you to him. Can I come in out of the hallway?"

"No, I need a moment to dress." She closed the door and leaned against it. The detective was waiting for her somewhere. That couldn't be good. No, all she could see is how that meant she needed to see or do something. She slid down the door, hand pressed against her mouth. *God, help me face whatever is coming.*

Audra dragged in one breath, then another. She could do this. She had to. Squaring her shoulders, she rose to her feet. She swayed a moment then hurried to the small sink in the bathroom and splashed cold water in her face. The fairytale dream of minutes before had evaporated, replaced by the harsh reality that Officer Trainor would take her to Detective Franklin, who would tell her something about her sister. Audra rubbed her arms, trying to find warmth while she longed for Daddy to stand next to her through whatever awaited. *Father, I can't do this alone.*

She couldn't imagine a scenario where the detective's words would be hope-filled.

The thought of planning how to transport a body weakened her knees. *Father?*

She sucked in a shaky breath as a modicum of peace settled on her. Not enough to wipe away the reality of what she had to do, but enough to do what the day required.

Audra pulled a basic boxy gabardine suit from the wardrobe. Most of the wrinkles had fallen out of the garment overnight. The solemn navy seemed appropriate for whatever task awaited her. And the severe lines fit her mood. Rosemary's lacy navy evening gown lay where she'd tossed it over a chair the night before, the gown a stark contrast to the day's agenda. If she hadn't seen it there, she'd wonder if it had all been a beautiful, romance-laden dream.

She slipped on the suit then tugged on navy Mary Janes. She brushed her hair, pulled it into a French twist, and checked her image in the mirror. Circles darkened her eyes, and she almost wished for time to swipe cosmetics on.

A knock sounded at the door. "Are you ready, miss?"

No time. She took a deep breath, pressed a hand into her stomach, and moved to the door. Her navy hat sat on the hall table, and she perched it on top of her up-do. She picked up her handbag and opened the door. "Let's go."

"Right this way." The officer strode down the hallway toward the elevator.

"Wait. Should I check out before we leave? Will we be back in time?"

"I'll handle it at the front desk. Detective Franklin isn't fond of waiting."

"No, I suppose not." She followed Officer Trainor into the elevator and then waited as he spoke to a man at the check-in counter.

"We're all set. If you'll come with me." He gestured toward a dark, nondescript car that sat at the curb.

"This is a police vehicle?"

"Unmarked. I'm not supposed to tip all the bad guys off that we're coming today. Besides, Officer Jones has my usual car."

"Where are we going?"

"The hospital."

Audra's pulse started to race. The hospital? Maybe Rosemary was still alive. Injured she could deal with. She just wanted her baby sister in one beautiful piece. Then she could take Rosemary home and help her parents nurse her back to health.

The officer opened the vehicle's door and closed it behind her. She shifted in an attempt to get comfortable on the cloth seat. Her fingers twisted her purse straps as he drove through the unfamiliar streets. The radio screeched in the background, making a grating noise that was hard to understand. Audra tuned it out and watched the dry landscape dotted with flowering cactus and unfamiliar bushes pass in a blur. Tall, nondescript apartment buildings transformed into a dry park with a slide and handful of palm trees followed by a city block with a stretch of mom-and-pop type establishments.

The car turned into a long driveway. A sign at the entrance read HOLLYWOOD PRESBYTERIAN HOSPITAL. Audra sucked in a couple deep breaths. *God, help me.*

"Detective Franklin should be in the lobby." Officer Trainor pulled the vehicle to a stop underneath an awning. The radio squawked to life, and he cocked his head toward the noise. "I've got to provide back-up, but Franklin will meet you and make sure you get back to the Roosevelt."

"Thank you." Audra slipped from the vehicle and then watched as it zipped back toward the road. It disappeared from view, but still she stood. She couldn't make her feet move. The news could be good, very good, but all she could think about was the terrible feel of the cold, lifeless hand she'd touched the day before.

It might not have been Rosemary, but she was someone's Rosemary. Someone's sister. Someone's daughter. Maybe someone's wife.

Audra pivoted and moved toward the front door. Cool air hit her face as she opened it. A quiet intensity propelled people up and down the corridor. Directing them to their various destinations. Audra watched, not recognizing anyone, and finally moved toward an information station.

"May I help you, miss?" An older woman in nurses' uniform with Windsor-style eyeglasses perched on an aquiline nose smiled at her.

"I'm supposed to meet Detective Franklin here."

She wrinkled her nose as she considered Audra. "Don't know anyone by that name. But you'll often see the police over by the emergency room, down that hallway there." She gestured across the lobby toward a section that buzzed with activity.

Audra glanced around the lobby again. Still no sign of the detective. "I'll see if he's over there. Thank you." She headed down a hallway, but froze when Detective Franklin stepped from a room.

"There you are." He stomped toward her, a scowl darkening his face. "I told Officer Trainor to bring you to me."

"He had to leave. Said he had to provide back-up?"

"I don't usually leave women wandering through strange hospitals by themselves." He guided her toward a chair that sat against a wall. "Have a seat."

Audra sank onto the edge, not sure whether she wanted to run or hide.

Franklin knelt in front of her, his rumpled jacket swinging open. "You're here because officers found a body in a local park this morning."

Her breath came in quick sips as his words sank in.

"We don't have an identity yet. You may be here for no reason at all. But she could be your sister. She wore a red evening gown when found in the park."

"I don't know what Rosemary would be wearing or her life here."

"That's right." He rubbed his hands over his hair, mussing the sides. "I don't like to ask women to view bodies. Don't need you fainting. Is there anyone else you would rather have identify the body?"

Audra stiffened her spine. "If it's Rosemary, I need to do this. I don't know anyone else to suggest."

"All right. We'll hope it isn't. But…"

Something in what he wasn't saying indicated Detective Franklin had reached a determination about who they'd found. Audra stared at the door, recoiling at the thought of walking through it to what lay beyond. If Rosemary is in there… *Let me be strong enough to do whatever I have to, Father.*

She lurched to her feet before she could change her mind. "I'm ready."

He opened a door and ushered her into a small examination room. A sheet covered a body lying on the table, a scrap of red silk trailing below. Audra paused at the door. Everything in her rebelled at the task. *Please don't let it be Rosemary.*

"Are you sure you're able?"

Audra nodded, a hand covering her mouth, stopping the cry that crawled up her throat.

"I will pull back the sheet, enough to show her face. If you start feeling weak, speak up." He studied her, a glint of compassion shining through the hard edges. The detective must do this so often.

"Do you ever get used to it?"

"What?"

"Doing this?" Audra gestured at the room, the table, the body.

"If I do, it's time for me to retire and move on to something simple like acting."

Audra took a breath. Squared her shoulders. Nodded. "All right."

Detective Franklin pulled the sheet down. The first thing Audra noticed was the hair. Blond, bleached from a bottle. Surely Rosemary wouldn't have done that to her beautiful hair. Audra's gaze followed the sheet down the woman's face. It was so pale, pasty. The eyes were closed, but as the sheet slid further down her face, Audra bit back a scream.

"It's her?"

She nodded, hand still covering her mouth. Audra swallowed and then lowered her fingers. "It's Rosemary. What did they do to her?"

She studied her sister's face as the detective sketched the details.

"A man walking his dog found her tucked behind some trees. Hard to see. Probably dead a day."

"How?" It wasn't a question she should have to ask. Rosemary should be alive and on her way to movie stardom.

"Are you sure I can't fill someone else in? I hate breaking it to you."

"I need the answer. Somehow, I have to leave this place and explain to my parents what happened to their baby girl. And telling them the police decided we didn't need to know won't be satisfactory." She crossed her arms, biting the inside of her lip hard. She couldn't let the hardened detective see the emotion building in her. A coppery taste tinged her mouth. She released her lip. As her gaze traveled down her sister's smooth cheeks, Audra felt a tear trickle down her own cheek, followed by another.

"Coroner says she was strangled."

"Like the woman in her apartment?"

"Yes." Detective Franklin pulled the sheet over Rosemary's face, hiding her delicate features. "Anything come to you on who that woman is?"

Audra shook her head. "I'd hoped Rosemary would tell me."

"We all did."

She wiped her cheeks. "What do I do next?"

"Once the coroner releases her body, you can ship it home."

Her mind spun—how did she even do that? She'd think about that later. Right now—right now she could barely form a thought around the bubble of rage that filled her at the sight of Rosemary's unnaturally still form.

"Who did this to her?" Hot flashes of anger coursed through her, pushing the pain to the side. She would survive this. And she would find the person who did this to her sister, just like she'd fixed the wrongs when they were girls. She had to do something. The need to act poured through her with a force that stole her breath.

Detective Franklin studied her, a mix of darkness and intensity in his eyes. "We don't know. Officers are looking for witnesses, but right now we have nothing. This murder is similar to one from last year. A girl with an escort service ends up murdered. We're still investigating that one. We'll work hard to find your sister's murderer, but these cases aren't always solved overnight."

Audra rubbed her forehead, trying to press the pounding headache away. "What does an escort's death have to do with Rosemary?"

"Maybe they're unrelated, but I'm checking everything."

"Can I move into her apartment?" From there she could look for something—an idea of who might have killed her. Maybe she should study Rosemary's black book if the police had left it, see if she missed something.

"Don't get any ideas of becoming a lone ranger. Leave this to us."

Audra nodded. "Someone has to clean out her apartment. And I'm the only one here."

"That's the only idea in your pretty head?" He crossed his arms. "What did you say you do again, Miss Schaeffer?"

"I work in a law office."

"As long as you promise to only clean out her apartment, you can go today. Leave the investigating to us."

"Then find her killer." Audra raised her chin and met the detective's direct gaze.

"I will be watching you, Miss Schaeffer, and I think my efforts could be better spent finding your sister's killer. Remember that if you make me keep you out of trouble." A tight smile twisted his lips. "I already have two dead women and no motive for why they were killed. I'd hate to have to do something like send you out of town to keep you safe."

She gave a slight nod with her chin. And that quickly, the fight left her. She smoothed the sheet, playing with the edges.

"We'll do all we can to find whoever killed her. Last thing I want is a killer roaming Hollywood. And I want whoever did this to go to the gas chamber. But I cannot do that and worry about you being next."

"Yes, sir. I understand. Can you pull the sheet down again? Just a bit?" Detective Franklin did, and she studied her sister's features. Memories flashed through her mind. All the times Rosemary had pretended to star in a new show and Audra had reluctantly agreed to play a part. She squared her shoulders and lifted her chin. Nobody had asked her if she wanted to do this. But she would.

How was she supposed to transport a body or handle any of the other details? The walls of the small room closed in on her. All she saw, anywhere she looked, was Rosemary's sheet-clad body. Her earlier strength abandoned her.

"Excuse me."

She bolted from the room. Dashed down the hallway, blinded by the light that bounced off the white walls, white floor, white ceiling. She bounced off someone and kept moving. She had to get out. Away from the place of healing that had turned into a den of death.

Someone pushed the doors open in front of her, and Audra dashed into the sunlight. The light blinded her, and a car honked shrilly. She stopped, feeling tears course down her cheeks.

A car door opened and a man stepped toward her. "Are you okay, ma'am?"

"No. Do you know where I can find a cab?" She needed to get back to the hotel, check out, and then go to Rosemary's apartment. A trickle of fear tickled her at the thought. What if the killer came back? It didn't seem likely, and she needed some place to stay. She pushed her fear aside. There might not be anything she could do for Rosemary. But she could find the killer and make sure he paid.

CHAPTER TEN

One week until he boarded the train out of Los Angeles. His list of tasks grew the longer he thought about the tour.

Robert had heard stories of the escapades that filled the first Hollywood Victory Caravan, and knew the train he'd live on would have its own unique mix. One week until he'd board the train with about forty other stars and staff.

After the fundraiser last night, he would play the emcee.

Three weeks of playing the host in city after city.

All while living on a train.

It sounded like craziness now, but he was committed. Robert grabbed his hat, shoved it on his head, and left his flat. His wingtips clacked against the floor as he strode toward the elevator. Its wrought iron gate slid open as he approached.

"Just the man I was looking for."

Robert stopped in his tracks. "Artie?"

"In the flesh." Artie thrust his arms wide like he expected a hug. Robert stared at him. "You don't think I make house calls?" He shoved a cigar in his mouth. "We've got a problem."

"O-kay. Do you want to come into my apartment?"

"Walk with me."

Robert nodded. The agent could be a little over the top in his style, but he had made stars out of less deserving men. Robert could humor him until he told the problem.

The elevator grate clanged shut behind them, and they coasted to the lobby in a silent, uncomfortable trip. Artie led the way to the street and waited until they'd walked half a block before speaking. Robert shoved his hands in his pockets, determined to wait Artie out. Artie's games seemed ridiculous. With the sun shining, Robert determined to enjoy the excursion.

Artie kicked at a rock on the sidewalk. "Rosemary Schaeffer has been found."

Robert stopped. Turned to look at Artie. "What?"

"Some Joe Blow found her at a park. Her sister identified the body this morning."

That poor kid. Robert couldn't imagine having that task. It must be horrifying to walk into a room and look at a body, a mere shell of the person you loved. "Is she okay?"

"Who?"

"Audra." Artie gave him a blank look. "Rosemary's sister."

"Don't know. You can bet dollars to donuts she's headed to Rosemary's apartment."

"Sure. Where else would she go?"

"And when she gets there, she might learn information about Rosemary she doesn't like."

Robert was ready to shake Artie. Make him speak plain English and move on. "I don't see how that involves me."

"That's why you have me. I catch everything you miss. Including things that could kill your career."

"Speak plainly or move on, Artie. I don't have patience for games."

Robert followed Artie as he entered a street-side café, walked to a table in the back corner, and then gestured for Robert to sit down. "Have a seat."

Robert dropped onto the chair opposite Artie and crossed his arms.

"Rosemary did anything to get her chance in Hollywood. Anything."

"And you encouraged that, didn't you? I don't want to know anything more." He'd heard rumors Rosemary had accepted the *extra* duties some agents talked their girls into, but had hoped to spare Audra that knowledge. He wouldn't want his little sister in an escort role and couldn't imagine what it would do to Audra if she learned that about Rosemary. "She was a sweet kid the time or two I bumped into her."

"Sweet and willing to do anything. Hollywood's a tough place. Do you know how many people are carried on contract by the big studios? Maybe fifty at Warner Brothers, a hundred over at Metro Goldwyn Mayer. Flip 'em around. It doesn't matter. What matters is that the steady-pay jobs are few and far between. You're making it, but how long can you last without a studio taking you on? Another couple months?"

"I'll find a way."

"Sure you will. That's what everyone says until they're out of dough. Then they crawl to me or someone else, desperate for a leg up. These opportunities form the backbone of this town. Whether you and others get it or not."

Robert looked at the agent, his esteem for him tanking. "You really set the gals up?"

"If they've got the looks or the temperament. Sure. Why wouldn't I? It's lucrative."

"It's immoral."

"You're in Hollywood."

Should he just leave? Or would it make any difference? Artie clearly didn't think there was anything wrong with his side business. With a choice, he'd go somewhere else. His recent treks from office to agent had shown him he wouldn't be an overnight success, especially without the visibility of being Lana's husband.

So why did it feel like he needed a hot shower? Something to wipe the grime away? He'd believed coming to Hollywood was the right thing. Something God could honor and bless. Yet his life hadn't gone as expected since arriving.

"Shouldn't you focus on the fact someone murdered one of your future stars?"

Artie waved a hand at him. "Let me worry about those things."

"Then why find me?"

"Because she may have considered the USO event an escort duty." Artie looked at him with arched brows then pushed out of the chair. "With you." He studied Robert a moment, and then flung his hands out. "Forget about it. You've got your next screen test this afternoon. Knock it out of the park and make us both happy." Artie strode from the café without a backward glance.

Robert watched him a moment, disgusted by the direction of Artie's insinuations.

* * * * *

Audra staggered up the sidewalk to Rosemary's apartment after checking out of the hotel, her bag weighing her down almost as much as the image of Rosemary's still face. So much had changed in the thirty-six hours since she'd arrived. The building looked darker, even though the sun shone through the palm trees. Death had marked it, and cold soaked deep into her. The only thing that brought her back was the determination to find a killer.

I'll find him, Rosemary. I promise.

When she got inside, she had to find the strength to call her parents. Tell them their baby had died.

She pulled the apartment key from her skirt pocket and slipped it into the lock. The door eased open, and Audra stumbled inside.

A shuddering breath shook her as she leaned against the wall. Rosemary was supposed to be here. Supposed to be alive. Supposed to be angry Audra had overstepped her big sister role. Instead, she'd died.

Just like Andrew.

The door closed with a click, and Audra slid to the floor.

"What am I supposed to do, Lord? How do I tell Mama and Daddy?" She tipped her chin as tears coursed down her cheeks.

Time passed as she sobbed. Cold seeped through the wood floor and her skirt, into her legs. The tears trickled to a stop, and she struggled to form how she'd tell them. Part of her wanted to send a telegram. Let someone else tell them. But she couldn't do that. Instead, she'd borrow a phone. Wait while the operator connected lines until enough were patched together.

Maybe the landlady would let her use her phone one last time.

Audra stood then went into the bathroom. The skin under her eyes was puffy and red-rimmed. With a last glance in the mirror, she left the flat and headed around to the front of the building. She climbed the stairs and pressed the button for the landlady's flat.

"Yes?" The woman's voice scratched across a speaker.

"Hello. This is Audra Schaeffer, Rosemary's sister. I wondered if I could use your phone."

The door buzzed, and Audra slipped in. A door at the end of the hallway opened, and the landlady peeked out, her housecoat a bright mix of colors and flowers. At the sight of Audra, she straightened then waved her down the hallway.

"Do you have news?" The landlady clutched the neck of her dress, wrinkles creasing the crown of her nose.

"The police found Rosemary. I need..." Audra swallowed the sudden lump in her throat. "...I need to call home, tell my parents."

"Oh, honey. I'm so sorry." Her face collapsed, mirroring Audra's grief. "She was such a good girl. There was no mistake?"

"No. I identified her."

"You come right in. Use my phone. I'll fix tea while you talk to the operator." The woman ran a hand up and down Audra's arm as if to warm her as Audra walked by. The small sitting room held a davenport adorned with a collage of doilies protecting the fabric. Movie magazines covered the surface of a small oval table. The phone teetered precariously on a stack of *LIFE*s. "I'll be right in the kitchen."

"Thank you, Mrs...."

"Oh my, how rude of me. I can't believe I haven't introduced myself. Mrs. Margeson." She patted her cheeks as if to cover the sudden rush of color.

"The tea sounds nice." Audra stared at the phone as Mrs. Margeson disappeared into the other room. She picked up the receiver. Pulled the unit close and dialed the operator. "I need a line to Indianapolis."

"I'll call as soon as I have it."

"Thank you." Audra leaned back against the davenport. She couldn't believe it had come to this.

First, she had to make this call. Then she would start a list of who could have harmed Rosemary. It wouldn't be easy. But she would learn who Rosemary's friends were, who her enemies were, and how she could get close to them.

"Here you go, dear." Mrs. Margeson handed her a cup filled with hot water and a swimming teabag. Then the plump woman slipped to the edge of a dining chair opposite the couch. She balanced a second teacup on her knee, and a thin smile stretched her lips. "So are the police done in the apartment? I was so horrified when that detective told me about the body. I didn't want to believe him. Then he insisted I stay out while they searched the place." She trembled, the cup shifting precariously on her knee. "When they came back this morning, I couldn't imagine what they'd missed. But if they'd found your sister… What terrible things you've been through."

"It's been awful." Audra studied her cup, braced for the phone to ring. "Detective Franklin said I could return to the apartment now. I'll stay there if it's okay."

"Rent is paid through the end of June." Mrs. Margeson shrugged. "Might as well stay there if you like and he says it's okay. But are you sure you want to, considering what you found?"

Audra nodded, words catching on the lump in her throat.

"Well, I'm truly sorry about Rosemary. She didn't stay home much, but was always pleasant when I saw her." She blew on her tea then took a sip.

"Can you see who comes and goes from that side entrance?"

"Depends on where I am. It's certainly not as easy to watch as the front door. But your sister seemed to like the added privacy. Didn't want anyone to bother her." A shiver shook Mrs. Margeson's rounded shoulders, and a few drops of tea spilled from the rim of the cup. "Maybe she'd still be here if she'd chosen a different apartment."

Was it that simple? A change of room could have changed her fate?

"Whose apartment is over hers?" Maybe they had seen something. Audra could start there.

Mrs. Margeson wrinkled her nose and tapped a finger against her chin. "Well, I guess that would be Shelia Sloan. Yes, she's been in that flat for a couple months. I don't think she's around right now though. Seems like she went somewhere a couple days ago."

The shrill ring of the phone startled Audra. She placed the cup on the table and rubbed her damp hands along her skirt.

"Let me get it." Mrs. Margeson grabbed the phone and licked her lips. "Hello?" She nodded then thrust the phone at Audra. "It's the operator. She's got your connection."

Audra accepted the phone and took a deep breath. "Hello?"

"I have your connection with Indianapolis." The operator's voice was calm, professional, and utterly unaware of the terrible news those lines would carry.

"Thank you." Audra told the Indianapolis operator her parents' exchange then waited for them to get on the line. How many neighbors would eavesdrop? She only hoped it would be those like Mrs. Butterman, who would rally around and comfort them.

"Hello?"

"Mama and Daddy?" A hollow sound echoed across the line. She tried to be patient until she heard them speak.

"Audra?"

"Hi, Mama. Is Daddy with you?"

"Pressed next to her at the phone." The sound of his deep voice comforted her.

Audra heaved a sigh. She hadn't wanted to tell Mama about Rosemary without Daddy there.

"What do you have for us, girl? It's about time you called." Her daddy's voice had an edge, whether from her not calling the moment she landed or him having a sense about the call, Audra couldn't tell.

She tried to block out the image that rose up in her mind. Being too late to get her younger brother at a high school event. Andrew catching a ride with a friend. Both killed when a delivery truck hit their car head-on. Now, she'd been too late—again.

"Yes, sir. It's about Rosemary."

Mama's sharp intake of breath made its way to Audra. "She's fine, isn't she?"

There was no easy way to say it, and a solid lump filled Audra's throat. She opened her mouth but couldn't force anything around the mass. She closed her eyes, and tears slipped down her cheeks. She startled when a soft hand rubbed up and down her arm. Mrs. Margeson settled next to her, a comforting arm around her shoulders. Strength filled her. She wasn't completely alone.

"The police asked me to identify a body this morning. It was Rosemary. Somebody killed her." Audra covered her mouth with trembling fingers. "I didn't find her in time. I'm so sorry."

"There must be a mistake." Daddy's gruff voice cracked. "It couldn't be our Rosie."

"I wish I were wrong. How I wish."

Silence stretched longer than needed for the voices to travel to Indianapolis and back. "When will you bring her home?"

"I don't know yet, Daddy."

Soft sobs hiccupped on the line. Audra imagined her mother plastered to Daddy's side, a handkerchief shoved against her mouth to muffle the sounds of her grief. The ladies from church would descend within the hour with a mix of food and comfort. Who would comfort Audra in Hollywood? Is this how Rosemary had felt? Isolated and alone?

Her father's voice in her ear. "I need to take care of your mother."

"Yes, sir."

"Where can we reach you?"

The question stumped Audra. Without a phone in Rosemary's apartment, she'd have to rely on Mrs. Margeson. She glanced at Mrs. Margeson, who nodded. "I don't know the number."

Mrs. Margeson took a pen and paper from the corner of the table and scribbled her exchange on it. Audra repeated it to her parents.

"Audra." Her daddy's voice sounded weaker than she'd ever heard before. "I want you on the next plane home."

"Daddy, I can't."

"Then catch the next train. I won't have you alone in the city that killed Rosie."

Audra sucked in a breath. "Sir, I have to stay. Figure out what happened. I promise I'll be careful, but I have to find some answers."

"How will you stay safe?" Her mother's words whispered across the line.

"All I can promise is I won't do anything foolish. I'll be careful and if I think things aren't safe, I'll leave."

Her daddy sighed. "Then I insist you call home as often as you can. At least every couple days. Your mother and I won't be able to sleep otherwise."

She could do that. "Yes, sir. I love you, Mama and Daddy."

"We love you too. Stay careful."

Audra hung up and then stood. "Thank you for the use of your phone."

"Are you sure you're okay by yourself down there?"

Audra nodded and fled from the apartment and the landlady's concern.

CHAPTER ELEVEN

Dusk settled on the apartment, the sunlight thinning as darkness approached, but Audra couldn't rouse herself from the couch. It might be only eight o'clock, but she'd pulled a blanket from the stack on the floor and spread it over her, tucking it under her chin. Her stomach grumbled. Had she eaten today? She tried to remember, but probably hadn't. The police had arrived before she had breakfast, and the thought of food turned her stomach after identifying Rosemary.

Another rumble shook her stomach. Whether or not she thought she could eat, her stomach demanded sustenance. Last night's dinner seemed so long ago. The memory of dancing in the circle of Robert's arms and then running from the press warmed her for a moment. But memories wouldn't fill her stomach. Did Rosemary even have anything?

She needed to think—develop a plan—but couldn't do that if her brain felt fogged.

After throwing off the blanket and struggling to her feet, she stumbled to the small kitchen area, opened the cupboard doors, and found nothing to eat other than a lone can of tuna. Too tired to try to locate a grocer in the strange area, she found a cracked glass in the cupboard and filled it with water from the faucet. Maybe that would be enough to satisfy her stomach until morning when she could ask Mrs. Margeson for suggestions.

Audra turned to Rosemary's desk. Time to shuffle through its piles. The desk showed all the signs of Rosemary's chaos coupled with the police search as they investigated both deaths. Audra found a blank pad of paper in the mess and, after digging, found a fountain pen. She froze when she realized it was a Parker 51. Where on earth had Rosemary gotten the money for a pen like that? Only the attorneys used the elegant and expensive pens at the firm where she worked.

Audra shook her head then put the pen to paper. Time to start the list of things to do the next morning. First, she needed to ask Detective Franklin if they'd identified that poor woman yet.

Then her mind blanked.

She was trained in legal matters. Surely something she'd learned in her studies or witnessed in the last couple years could help her now.

What would Mr. Clarion do if she walked into his office as a client, demanding justice for her sister? He was well respected in the Indianapolis legal community and had earned his reputation as a skilled attorney and gifted investigator. Maybe she'd call him tomorrow.

Maybe somewhere in this mess Rosemary had left a clue about who would want to kill her. Surely Audra could find something, even if the police missed it. She knew her sister in a way no one in Hollywood could.

The stacks of papers and books overwhelmed Audra. She preferred to keep her desk ordered so she could quickly locate everything she needed. There was only one way to tackle the mess. Simply start. Audra selected a small stack of papers. As she flipped through it, all she saw was a random assortment of bills. She set them to the side on the floor and grabbed the next stack.

Methodically, she tackled the mess until small piles of paper surrounded her on the floor. The scripts might make interesting reading, but for now she had stacked them in teetering piles. Even so, the left-hand side of the desk remained untouched. She'd almost decided to quit for the night when she remembered the black volume she'd tucked in the wardrobe drawer. She tugged the drawer open and pulled it out.

Why hadn't the police taken it? She stroked the cool, leather cover then took it, some notepaper, and the pen to the couch. She sank on the cushions and opened the book First, she examined the note she'd stuck inside. Now she'd never have the opportunity to ask Rosie what it meant, if anything. As Audra studied the doodles and swirls, they made no sense to her. She almost crumpled the paper. Instead, she placed it on top of the pile and flipped through the first few pages of the notebook. She scanned them, not sure what to look for. It wasn't like the murderer would have written his name and phone number on the right date. That didn't even happen in the movies.

Since so many of the names didn't mean anything to her, she decided to go back a few months and compile a list of the people Rosemary had recorded in the book. Then Audra could try to determine why they were listed.

Soon two sheets of paper were covered with columns of names and dates.

Royce Reynolds. Quincy Cambridge. Jim Collins. Winston Portland. All actors Audra had seen in *LOOK* or movies. The list continued with an impressive assortment of men. Why had Rosie spent time with them?

One name jumped out. Robert Garfield. What was the connection between Rosemary and Robert? There were so many men listed that Audra couldn't imagine he meant anything to her sister.

She stared at Robert's name. At least she'd met him. She could call him and ask more questions about Rosemary.

The quiet in the flat overwhelmed Audra. She glanced at her watch. Nine thirty on a Sunday evening. What would she find on the radio? It didn't matter, she needed some noise to distract her from the silence. She flipped the power on the radio and waited as it crackled to life.

Heavy knocking flowed from the machine, hard enough that Audra almost jumped to her feet to check the front door.

"What's the matter? What is it?" a woman's voice asked with a worried tone.

"Another case for Nick Carter, Master Detective," a man's voice said.

Audra didn't know this show but settled back on the couch with the black book and paper. She tucked the blanket back around her as the organ music played and the announcer introduced the show. Before long she was engrossed in the efforts the detective went through to solve the mystery.

Maybe she should go undercover too. The only problem was, she didn't have any idea where to do it. It had to be somewhere she'd gain access to the people who knew Rosemary. Ideally, people from the list she'd formed. Many were in movies, but was everyone? And would they be in one place?

Her mind swam with the odds of locating anyone who knew anything.

Audra inched the blanket closer to her chin. Closing her eyes, she succumbed to the tug of darkness and her exhaustion.

Scratch. Scritch. The noise poked through the dark images that had filled Audra's dreams. Images of women in red evening gowns. Each with bruises lacing their necks rather than pearls. She trembled and shifted on the narrow couch. A thunk sounded as something fell to the floor next to her.

Screetch.

Audra struggled to untangle her legs from the hold of the blanket. What was that sound?

The awful noise made her want to cover her ears. It sounded as if someone were running their fingernails across a chalkboard.

Her heart pounded and she couldn't see anything. She jumped up, clutching the blanket.

The doorknob jangled, and a sliver of silver light crept across the room toward her as the door eased open.

Audra hunted for something she could use as a weapon but couldn't see anything in the dimness. A gloved hand slipped around the door to the inside as if groping for a light switch before a large blob entered the tiny entry area. Audra screamed as loudly as she could and slipped behind the couch.

"What the…" A deep voice spoke as the hand hesitated.

Audra screamed again. The small window behind the couch wouldn't give her an escape. *Oh, God. Please help me. Hide me from him or get him away from the apartment.*

"What's going on in there?" an unfamiliar voice sounded outside the door.

Audra screamed again. "Help!"

The shadow swore then took off running.

"Hey, stop." Echoing footsteps chased the first set.

Tremors shook her body. Why would someone break into the apartment? Did they know she was there, or were they looking for something?

Light flooded the room, and Audra looked up. Mrs. Margeson and a strange man hurried into the apartment.

"Are you all right?" Worry tightened the lines around Mrs. Margeson's eyes as she studied Audra.

"Someone broke in." Her voice trembled in a way that embarrassed her.

The man nodded. "My brother is chasing him, and Mrs. Margeson called the police." He squatted in front of her and eyed her carefully as if examining her for harm.

"He didn't get in all the way." Audra blew out a breath.

"Bryce, can you check the lock for me? Make sure it still works?" Mrs Margeson turned to Audra. "Miss Schaeffer, you can't stay here tonight."

"I don't have anywhere else to go." Her pocketbook couldn't afford too many nights in a hotel. The plane ticket had almost wiped out her small savings, and Daddy's money would evaporate if she didn't use it judiciously. She hated the thought of wiring home for more money. That would only add to her parents' suffering.

"Don't worry. I've got a spot in my apartment."

Audra wanted to protest, but the thought of sleeping here after the break-in seemed impossible. "For one night."

Mrs. Margeson patted her hand. A siren pulsed in the distance. "Help is on the way." She shook her head. "What is the world coming to?"

Bryce came back with a bag of tools and knelt in front of the door.

"Don't touch that." Audra cringed at the tight voice. Detective Franklin strode into the room. "Miss Schaeffer. Getting into trouble already?"

CHAPTER TWELVE

Silence fell as Detective Franklin stood over Audra. Mrs. Margeson wrung her hands and looked from one to the other. Bryce stood and stepped barely inside the door.

"I'll have someone dust for prints. Did either of you touch the door?" He directed the question at Mrs. Margeson and Bryce.

Both nodded.

"If I didn't tonight, I know I have in the last week or so." Mrs. Margeson rubbed her hands together faster.

"Then we'll fingerprint you both. Don't want to get your prints confused with whoever was at the door." Detective Franklin pulled out a thin notebook from his inside jacket pocket. Audra had never seen him in anything but a jacket and rumpled pants. With the temperature spiking past the eighties each day, he couldn't be comfortable.

The bass of a car pulling up outside reached through the open door. A minute later, two uniformed officers appeared in the doorway. Audra looked around the room and wondered where they'd fit. The apartment felt cramped with the extra people. She leaned against the davenport, taking up as little space as possible.

Detective Franklin pointed at one of the officers. "Go ahead and print the door. We've got a unit patrolling the neighborhood for someone on foot."

"Yes, sir." The officers rummaged through the bag of equipment they'd brought.

Detective Franklin returned his focus to Audra. "All right, Miss Schaeffer. Tell me what happened." While his words were brief, concern tinged his eyes as he took notes. She told him the little that she could. "Okay. Anything you two have to add?"

Mrs. Margeson shook her head. "I heard screams. After everything that's occurred, I hurried down the stairs and ran into Bryce. He sent me to call the police while he checked on Miss Schaeffer. By the time I talked to the police, whoever it was had disappeared."

"That sounds right." Bryce shrugged. "A man ran from the doorway when I got here. I came here to check on the lady. Maybe I should have chased him."

"Leave that to us." Detective Franklin flipped back through the pages he'd filled with scribbles. "Miss Schaeffer, did you see the man?"

"Only a gloved hand and the impression of a blob. He must be large."

"You still want us to fingerprint?" One of the officers looked up from the doorknob.

"Yes." The detective nodded his head. "We have to be thorough."

"Sure." The man shrugged. "But we can't collect fingerprints from someone wearing gloves."

The other officer strode over with an inkpad and paper. "I'll take your prints now."

Mrs. Margeson grimaced as he ran her fingers across the pad and then pressed them against the paper.

Detective Franklin turned his back on the officers. "Mrs. Margeson, you can leave."

"All right. Don't forget to come upstairs when you're done, dear."

Audra nodded. Something told her she'd already gotten all the sleep possible for tonight. Her already dark dreams might turn to nightmares after this.

"So you'll stay with her?" Detective Franklin asked.

"Tonight. Then I'll be back here if you say it's all right."

"What do you think this person was after?"

"I don't know. But I can tell you it was a man. He had a distinctly male voice."

"That's something to go on."

"Cuts out a whole fifty percent of the population." Judging from the dark glare the officer received at that comment, he wasn't gaining any credit with Detective Franklin.

Detective Franklin glanced around the room. He snatched the black book. "What's this?"

"Rosemary's calendar and address book. I found it yesterday, but looked through it tonight."

He flipped the pages then tucked it in his pocket.

"What are you doing?" Audra sat up straight and reached for it. "It's not yours."

"It is until I confirm whether it contains anything that assists the investigation."

"When will I get it back?"

"When I'm finished. Is there anything else you found that might be helpful?"

"Not yet." She gestured toward the desk. "I only got through half of it."

Bryce cleared his throat and held up inked fingers. "Can I leave now? It looks like you're well protected, ma'am."

Audra tried to smile, but feared it fell short. "Thank you for your help."

"My pleasure."

Detective Franklin collected Bryce's contact information then allowed him to leave. The detective watched her in silence, then pulled out the book and perused the pages. "Quite the list of individuals. Reads like a who's who of Hollywood up-and-comers. Even a few real stars. I thought your sister hadn't landed a big role yet."

"That's right. She thought she was close, but her break hadn't arrived yet." Audra shrugged. "She seemed so excited a few weeks ago, and then a week ago that changed. But she wouldn't tell me why." Audra tugged the blanket around her shoulders and pulled it tight.

"She's made notes next to some of the names. Any idea what they mean?"

"I didn't notice them."

He handed the book to her. "See here at the end in the address book section. The notations might indicate a way she tracked activities with the men."

"I doubt it." The way he said *activities* made Audra's skin crawl. It didn't sound like he meant something innocent. She studied the symbols. They looked like more of Rosie's doodles, but nothing that meant anything. She closed the book and held it a moment.

"Make anything out?" Detective Franklin reached for the book.

"No, I'm sorry. Maybe if you let me look at it awhile…"

"No can do. If the marks are more than doodles, we'll figure it out." Audra released the book when he tugged. "May I leave?"

"You'll be at Mrs. Margeson's?"

Audra nodded.

"I think you'll be safe there. Keep someone with you and don't come back until I clear it. I'll have an officer escort you to her apartment."

The words had the same edge as all his others, but Audra sensed a shift. Maybe he really had a heart under all that gruffness.

"Mike, please escort Miss Schaeffer to Mrs. Margeson's apartment."

"Yes, sir." The officer moved to her side.

Audra collected her toothbrush and cosmetics from the bathroom and her bag from beside the couch.

"I'll be in touch in the next day or two. Stay where I can find you."

"Yes, Detective." Audra followed the officer out of the apartment. The fresh air had a hint of something sweet. Orange blossoms? She took a deep breath and exhaled it slowly, trying to release the stress that had built since she arrived in this terrible town.

"Where to, ma'am?" The officer stood next to her, a solid mass of muscle that towered a good foot over her head. Maybe she should find someone like him to act as a bodyguard and keep her safe.

"I'm staying in an apartment on the first floor. Main entrance."

"All right." He led her to the sidewalk then paused, looking both ways as if looking for some kind of trouble. Then he hurried her around to the front door. "Which apartment?"

"Two-A."

He pushed the button, and Mrs. Margeson granted access.

"Thank you."

He followed her inside. "I'll make sure it's safe in here before I leave." He stuck his head in each room, hand on his gun. Audra would have laughed if Rosie had been with her. Instead, his movements seemed serious and necessary, if a bit overdone.

"All clear. You're safe."

Maybe he was right. But she'd thought that several times since arriving. Yet each hour seemed to hold something more unsettling than the last.

"I'll take care of her." Mrs. Margeson settled an arm around Audra's shoulders. "You'll be fine here. I've already got the couch set up for you. It was that or sleeping on my twin. I didn't think you'd mind since the couch was what you're using downstairs."

Audra accepted the comfort of the landlady's embrace, closing her eyes and imagining her mother held her. Her muscles turned to jelly as if weighted down by bags of sand. She sagged against Mrs. Margeson.

"I need to stop talking and let you get some rest. The stress you have been under." She tsked, a comforting sound. "I've got the tea brewing. A nice cup of tea to help you relax after everything."

"I don't know that tea will help."

The landlady's chins jutted. "It can't hurt anything."

"Thank you." Audra collapsed on the couch. A blanket and sheet were pulled across it with a pillow resting on one end. The cushions were wider than the davenport at Rosie's. Maybe she'd sleep after all. Though, as she settled down, Audra thought she could sleep on a boulder if it allowed her to escape.

Mrs. Margeson walked back from the galley kitchen with two steaming china cups. "I've been thinking."

"Oh?" Audra tried to smile her thanks when she accepted the cup.

"I think you should find a job with a studio." She settled on the chair and stared over the top of her cup at Audra. "It could be a good way to get to know people who knew Rosemary."

"I don't know." Audra considered the idea. "I've never had an interest in the movies. That was always Rosemary's area."

"If you want answers, that's where you start."

"Why?"

Mrs. Margeson shrugged. "My nephew works for a studio and he's told me some about how they work. I think it could give you quick insight."

"But Rosie hadn't broken in yet."

"As far as you know. I guarantee she was at the studios. That's where all the hopefuls spend their time. Her agent had her out and about. Screenings. Film tests. It didn't matter if she had a part or not. Sometimes you have to be in the right place at the right time to be noticed."

Audra tried to follow but got stuck on something Mrs. Margeson had said. "Her agent? Do you know who that was?"

"I'm pretty sure it was Artie. You know, that Schmaltz guy."

"Of course." Audra sipped the weak brew. What she wouldn't give for a heaping spoonful of sugar. Her brain must be fogged to have forgotten a name like that. "I guess I should go see him."

"Sure, but get to the studios." Mrs. Margeson tucked a gray piece of hair behind her ear. "Well, it's been another long day, filled with too much sorrow. I think we'd better get to bed. Are you done with that?" She grabbed Audra's half-full cup. "I'll see you in the morning. Make yourself at home and knock on my bedroom door if you need anything."

Audra quickly slipped into her nightgown and brushed her teeth. She settled on the couch, hugged the pillow to her chest, and rocked. A deep emptiness settled over her. What had happened to her faith that God was good all the time?

She should pray, but the words wouldn't form. And the emptiness seemed to sink deeper into her soul. Today she'd had to do unimaginable things, and God had seemed distant after her morning prayers.

Where did You go?

The words cycled over and over in her mind like a broken record. She'd always thought her faith was so strong, so solid. Unshakeable even. Yet in two short days, it felt like waves of grief and anger had crashed over it, revealing how very weak the foundation was.

Pulling her Bible from her bag, Audra flipped to the Psalms. She'd slowly been reading through them, and the book opened to Psalm 126 where her bookmark rested. She reread verses 5 and 6. *They that sow in tears shall reap in joy. He that goeth forth and weepeth, bearing precious seed, shall doubtless come again with rejoicing, bringing his sheaves with him.*

Rejoicing? That seemed so impossibly far away. A mirage that she could not imagine.

Audra closed the Bible and tucked the pillow behind her head. She curled on her side and pulled the blanket over her shoulders. The promise felt hollow and empty. For right now, she'd have to rely on herself and hide her tears.

CHAPTER THIRTEEN

Monday, June 8, 1942

Artie had called a meeting in his office for first thing Monday morning. Robert wondered if he really wanted to update everyone on the status of the second victory caravan. Or did he want to keep an eye on his clients?

The agent had acted nothing but strange since Rosemary Schaeffer's murder. It didn't make any sense to Robert, but there was little he could do other than ignore Artie. He'd do that to make the climb to the top of the marquee. He'd eventually prove to everyone that he was as good an entertainer as his father. Maybe even better, if he got the chance to work hard. The klutzy kid had transformed into an urbane man.

So Artie would get the benefit of the doubt since he'd taken a risk on Robert. Only believe the best about everyone. Words his mother had drilled into him. And she'd raised him in show business. If she could do it, he'd train himself to do the same.

Artie's office was standing room only when Robert arrived. He nodded at Victoria Hyde and Quincy Cambridge and found an empty spot against the wall. Several other rising stars had filled the seats. The caravan would provide the exposure he needed to land a role in his own strength and not because he was Mr. Lana Garfield. He'd always been surprised she hadn't taken her last name back, but her first big roles had come during their short marriage.

"Robert, how are things?" Victoria's soft voice pulled him from his thoughts.

He shook off the bad memories and studied the beautiful brunette. Her green eyes sparkled with intelligence and caring. "Just waiting for that next role."

"It'll come. Don't worry." When she said the words, he almost believed her.

"At least the caravan should be an experience."

"I'm glad the studio released me." She rolled her expressive eyes. "I wasn't sure they wouldn't create a reason to keep me here. I'm ready to get out and do my part."

Robert felt small in light of her words. Here he was focused on exposure and launching into roles. Victoria truly seemed to have a sense of why they were going. "You deserve each piece of success you're finding."

Soft color tinged her cheeks. "You're kind." She shrugged. "I'm going to enjoy it while I have it. But face it, most of us don't have Katherine Hepburn and Bette Davis's staying power. I'll be glad to entertain on celluloid as long as I can."

The door bounced open and Artie breezed into the room, making his way to the desk. Before the door closed behind him, Lana blew in wrapped in a silver fox stole. Her electric beauty pulled all attention to her. She posed a moment with hand on her hip as she studied the room with casual indifference before moving to Artie's desk.

"Here you go, doll." He pulled his chair around for her, and she settled into it like a queen accepting her throne. Artie paused a moment as if waiting for thanks. He should know by now Lana's vocabulary rarely used the word. Especially when it came to people she believed lived to serve her. Robert swallowed back the threatening bitterness. *Keep my thoughts, Lord.*

Artie pulled a different chair behind his desk, sank into it, and crossed his hands over his belly. He glanced around the room, seeming to take roll. "Everyone's here. Good news—the plans for the caravan are well under way for you to leave Sunday." He pulled a cigar from his desk drawer and clamped down without lighting it. "Bad news. The studios think they need more staff to shepherd you around the country. I tried to tell them you're big kids, but they aren't biting."

Quincy cleared his throat. "What's that mean for us?"

"If we're lucky, and they find someone fast, you'll leave as scheduled. For some of you in this room"—he looked at Victoria—"that's key. Any delay means you won't be on the train. Each of you can benefit from going."

"I don't know why this is so important." Lana rolled her eyes at Artie and examined her nails. "It won't save your contract with me."

Victoria shifted uncomfortably, while others focused away from Lana and Artie. Leave it to Lana to air her contract issues in front of everyone. Robert had heard she'd threatened to move to a different agency. Seemed now that her star was on the rise, she'd decided to trade up. Maybe it was a good career move, but Robert had to wonder what Artie thought. His personality was forceful enough to not like being played like that.

"Patriotism, baby. It's all about doing your part." Artie twirled the cigar through his fingers.

The Lester twins conferred in whispers. The two looked like peas in a pod—just like the Tarleton twins in *Gone with the Wind,* down to the curly red hair—except one had put on more weight than the other.

Their comedy routine had been added to the line-up of one radio network, and they should bring some laughs to the audiences around the country. But would they be as good as Laurel and Hardy on the first caravan?

Well, it would be his job to make them seem as good.

"I've got the caravan contracts for you to sign. Goldie will give them to you before you leave." Artie chomped on his cigar, seeming to have forgotten the thing wasn't lit. "Make sure you stay where we can get a hold of you quickly in case things change on the fly."

The door flew open, bouncing off Victoria's chair.

"Sorry, boss, I tried to stop this woman." Goldie smacked her gum and tried to snag a lady's arm with her sharpened fingernails.

Robert stared at the gal when he realized who it was. Audra Schaeffer? What was she doing here? She stopped short when she looked around the room.

"Oh." Her voice sounded small and uncertain.

"Who are you?" Artie's lips curled down as he stared at her.

"Audra Schaeffer."

"All right, everyone. Meeting's over. Go see Goldie. Move it, move it."

Lana stood first, staring at Audra before speaking over her shoulder to Artie. "Don't think we're through."

The men scuttled from the room with sidelong glances at Audra. She stood as they streamed past her, her hair pulled back in a severe bun, no makeup on her face save a swipe of color on her lips. Her suit had a severe cut that did nothing to soften her look. He wished he could erase the events that had led to the purple shadows darkening the skin under her eyes.

Victoria eased to her feet, every inch a graceful star in the making. "I am so sorry to hear about Rosemary. I didn't know her well, but she seemed like a swell gal."

"Thank you." Audra's eyes teared, but she blinked quickly.

Robert stayed rooted in his spot. Maybe Artie would forget he was there, and Robert could make sure the older man didn't bite off the poor gal's head.

Artie studied her from behind his throne. "So you're her sister. You weren't much alike."

"No."

"What can I do for you?"

"Can you tell me more about my sister's time here?"

"Nothing I didn't tell the police."

"Please. Somehow I have to explain this to my parents. And right now nothing makes sense." Her chin trembled, and she took a deep breath. She glanced over and caught Robert's gaze. Her back stiffened as if her body had been shocked. "Hello."

"Audra, I'm sorry about Rosemary." Robert tried to smile but felt it die at the thought of all she'd endured since landing in Hollywood. "I wish I could have helped you this weekend."

"It must be fate she's here now." Artie rolled his eyes. He schooled his features and turned back to Audra. "Look, Miss Schaeffer, your sister did what a thousand aspiring actresses do. Anything they can to get an agent and then a role. It worked, too, because I had a contract offer to show Rosemary this week."

"That's all she's ever wanted. I wish she'd known before she died."

Artie crossed his arms and leaned back in his chair. "It is unfortunate."

Audra collapsed into one of the vacant chairs shoved in front of the desk. Not sure what she was thinking, Robert slipped onto the chair next to her. At least he could let her know she wasn't entirely alone in this terrible situation.

"So when are you headed back to Iowa or wherever you're from?"

"Indiana. And I'm not leaving until I know what happened to Rosie." A determined glint shone through the tears shimmering in her eyes. Robert had the odd desire to reach out and shelter her from the terrible turn of events.

"How do you think you're going to do that, young lady? The police are on the job. I'm sure they'll find the killer."

"You really should listen to him, Audra." Robert couldn't stay silent. "What if something happens to you?"

"It won't. I'm a nobody from Indiana who couldn't harm anyone here."

"Unless you get them sent to jail."

"Well, I'm a long distance from that goal." Her shoulders slumped and her voice got quieter. "But I will do this. I've always taken care of Rosie. And this time I failed. I won't fail in finding who did this to her. If the police find him first, great. Then I can go home sooner."

Artie studied her a moment, a thoughtful look on his face. He steepled his fingers in front of his chest. "So do you have a plan?"

"Beyond talking to you and others? I hope to spend time with people she knew."

"That I can help you with."

Robert stared at Artie. "You can?"

"Sure. You, young lady, may be exactly who we've waited for. How'd you like to spend three weeks on a train with many of Rosemary's peers? Her rivals and friends will all be on that little ride."

"Doing what?"

Robert shook his head and stood to his feet. What did Artie have up his sleeve? "This is a bad idea."

"Why would you say that?" Audra turned to him, her face closed.

Artie smiled his Cheshire cat grin, the one that made him look like he'd eaten a prized canary. "What do you know about the Hollywood Victory Caravan?"

"I didn't see it if that's what you mean." Audra worried a piece of lint on her skirt. "The closest it got to Indianapolis was Chicago."

"They're planning a second one." Robert stilled her fingers and held her hand as he tried to stroke the cold from her fingers. "An entirely new group is going. The other night at the fundraiser was my audition to join the caravan."

"That's what your emceeing was about? A practice run?"

"Yes."

"And the second caravan might be postponed if they don't find the right woman to go along as chaperone and gopher for Mark." Artie continued to stare at Audra in a way that left Robert disturbed. Something hid behind Artie's decision that Audra should join the caravan. "It won't be an easy job. The participants got a little crazy on the first one. You should hear some of the stories that came out of it."

Robert studied Artie, uncomfortable with Artie's quick decision that Audra should join the caravan. She didn't understand the studio system or Hollywood. She didn't know the actors and performers. His agent had to have an ulterior motive, but Robert had no idea what. Maybe it would be better to have Audra on the train with him where he could keep an eye on her rather than joining the caravan uncertain what would happen to her in the next three weeks. The idea she needed protection bothered him, but after what had happened to Rosemary, he couldn't walk away without trying to keep an eye on her until she left.

"Then why would I go?"

"Maybe it would be a good idea for you after all." Robert sucked in a breath and leaned toward her. "In addition to spending time with yours truly, you'd get to investigate those your sister associated with to your heart's content." In a place that shouldn't pose much of a threat to her either. And if she were on the train, he'd make sure nothing happened to her. Her parents had lost one daughter; he didn't want them to lose the second from being headstrong and stubborn.

A shadow crossed over her face, weighing down her muscles. What would cause that? Robert jolted. Rosemary's funeral. By asking her to join the caravan, they'd asked her to miss the funeral. "You can't come."

She looked at him, the slight movement seeming to take immense effort. She must think him crazy to keep changing his mind. "Why?"

"Rosemary's funeral."

The simple words clouded her eyes. "I should be there. But every time I imagine it, I see my brother's funeral." She closed her eyes and shuddered. "I can't—I just can't do it." A tear slipped down her cheek before she swiped it away.

She bowed her head as if praying. Artie tapped his fingers on his desktop, only stopping when Robert frowned at him. After a moment she looked up. "All right. I'll do it. When do we leave?"

"In six days." Artie grabbed his phone and bellowed into it. "Goldie, connect me with Mark Feldstein. Tell him I have the solution to his problems." He slammed the phone down and considered Audra. "There you go, young lady. Hang around a bit, and we'll get you squared away. If Mark says you're in, you're in." He grinned at her in a predatory way.

"And Mark always does what I tell him. So count on three weeks swaying across the country on a train."

"Thank you."

"Now go wait in the lobby. I've got work to do." Artie selected a fresh cigar and jabbed it at Robert. "And you, get over to the studio pronto. We've got to get your screen test finished so we can get your contract signed before you leave. I want that signed yesterday."

"Yes, sir." The leap from screen test to contract was a big one, but Robert liked the sound of it. He was ready to move to marquee status and this role might do it. Add the exposure of the caravan, and his luck could be changing.

He offered Audra a hand and helped her to her feet. A tremor of connection shot up his arm. If she got on the caravan, they'd spend lots of time together. The thought stopped him as he opened the door. She looked at him quizzically, and he shook himself. He couldn't believe his thoughts had headed in that direction.

CHAPTER FOURTEEN

A couple of hours later, Audra hailed a cab to take her to the Masters Studio. Throughout the ride, she couldn't shake the question of whether she should travel home for the funeral. Of course Rosemary's sister should attend, but her stomach churned so at the thought that she'd feared she'd get sick in the cab. She imagined looking in the casket and seeing Rosemary, feeling the waves of accusation and guilt that she hadn't done enough, just like when she'd walked past her brother. Surely it was more important to find Rosemary's killer than attend her funeral. Even as the thought entered, the anger and grief competed.

This had to be the right thing. If only someone else would tell Mother and Daddy. They would never understand.

The red brick warehouse-style building wasn't what she expected. Newsreels showed complexes—multiple buildings with every square inch covered with sets, people, and chaos. Instead, this felt more like a school after all the students had gone home.

"Want me to wait for ya?" The cabbie turned around in his seat to glance at her.

"I don't know how long I'll be."

"Just call the company and someone can come get you when you're ready."

Audra paid the cabbie and slid from the vehicle. Working for the studio on a victory caravan? She felt singularly unprepared for the task.

What did she know about babysitting movie stars? Surely they all had oversized egos—except Robert, who seemed to have avoided that. She shook her head. Everybody had an angle. His would come to the fore soon enough.

Until then, she'd guard her heart. Love was the last thing she needed to add to the mess of her life. The one time she'd opened her heart to a man, he'd made it clear after a month of wooing that he was only interested in her as a way to get her close to him. Her cheeks flushed red at the memory of what he'd tried to talk her into. After that experience, she didn't trust herself to read men correctly. And in her field, she needed to hide her femininity as much as possible to be taken seriously. While romance bloomed on the pages of the novels she read, it never graced her life until she met Robert. But romance, especially with someone who lived here, and a star at that, just didn't seem right. Not now. She'd lived a fine, if lonely, life in recent years. She'd make out all right for another couple months until she rebuilt her life in Indianapolis.

Audra entered the building through a set of doors on the left-hand side. All the peace showcased on the outside of the building disappeared in the lobby. People ran every which direction, some bouncing off each other in their haste to get wherever they were going. Audra stood inside the door and stared. It didn't seem safe to venture into the fray. Especially when a woman who sat at the desk on the far side of the room scowled as she yelled into her phone.

"You see here! Those costumes were supposed to be delivered yesterday. Do you want us to send you a bill for the cost of every hour delay in filming? I can have it on your desk first thing in the morning." She listened a moment and a satisfied smile curved her lips. "I thought so.

We'll expect them here within the hour." She hung up without even a thank you.

Before Audra could attempt to get her attention, a second phone on the desk blared to life. Maybe this had been a terrible idea. Even worse than she initially thought.

She should catch the next flight headed east toward Chicago and begin the process of returning to Indianapolis. She could tell the police where to ship Rosemary. Prepay for the delivery and get out of this crazed town. Yes, that was the thing to do.

The door blew open behind her and Audra stumbled. A firm grip on her arm steadied her. She disengaged herself and turned to look.

"Jumping Jehosaphat!" Audra staggered backward, away from the star she easily recognized from Saturday matinees.

Royce Reynolds laughed, revealing perfectly even teeth. "I get that reaction all the time."

"I guess you do." Audra closed her eyes and ordered her pulse to return to normal. Wait until the girls heard about this. As if telling them about her magical night with Robert Garfield wasn't enough, now she'd bumped into Royce Reynolds. His blond good looks were even more eye-catching in living color than in black and white on the big screen. His hair looked rumpled and stood on end as if the wind had blown him in. He towered a good head above her and wore casual clothes that made it look like he'd breezed in from a golf course.

"So what brings a fair lady like you to this madhouse?" He cocked his head and studied her a moment. "I don't know you, do I?"

"No, I'm quite certain we've never met."

"Hmmm, your eyes are familiar. And I make it a practice to never forget a beautiful woman."

Audra suppressed a sigh as she jolted out of the star-struck moment. Slightly curved, cornflower blue eyes were the only feature that Rosemary and she had shared. "That sounds like a tried and true piece of dialogue. And I assure you, you're thinking of my sister, Rosemary Schaeffer."

The star snapped his fingers. "That's it. But that still doesn't explain why you're here." He swept his arms across the expanse of lobby. "You look a tad shell-shocked."

"I'm here to meet with Mark Feldstein."

Royce frowned, the light fading from his eyes in an instant. No wonder he was so good on film. "I can think of a dozen ways you could have more fun. Mark likes to spend all his time with a movie, book, or escort. Really you'd enjoy lunch with moi more."

"Oh, no. I mean—I'm sure I'd like that, but I have an appointment." She remembered seeing Royce's name in Rosemary's book and wondered if she should abandon the meeting for lunch with him. But maybe he'd join the caravan and she could talk to him then. She needed this job to finance her extra time in Hollywood.

"Well, if you insist on being a spoilsport." He paused, as if giving her time to change her mind. "Let's get you taken care of. Betty, this gal needs Feldstein." He yelled the words across the room to the receptionist.

She waved at him then gestured to the phone she held to her ear. Audra grimaced as Royce grabbed her arm and led her through the maze of people to the desk. The guy would leave a mark in his eagerness to help.

The circular desk looked like a piece of sculpture. The surface curved in front of Audra with inlaid wood, forming a mosaic that featured a camera and some other film equipment. In contrast to many of the people running around, the receptionist was fairly plain with her dark hair held back severely in an ear-pulling bun. Intensity emanated from her in a way that seemed to fit the pace of her job.

Betty hung up the phone and looked at Royce. "Yes?"

"Not me, her. Miss Audra Schaeffer here to see Feldstein."

A soft look swept across the woman's face. She reached for Audra's hand. "I am so sorry to hear about your sister."

Audra swallowed hard, undone by the sympathy. "Thank you. Is Mr. Feldstein available?"

"Let me check for you. Are you expected?"

"I think so. Mr. Schmaltz arranged everything."

Betty nodded and hopped on the phone.

Royce looked at Audra from under hooded eyes. "Artie, huh? That man is always arranging something, though you don't seem his type."

"Yes. I mean I'm not trying to be his type."

"Be careful around him." Royce shook his head. "You don't seem the sort to fall in with him."

Heat flared up Audra's neck. "It's nothing like that."

"That's what they all say. Well, I'll be seeing you, kid."

"Mr. Feldstein will be out in a moment." The phone rang again, and Betty picked up another receiver. "Masters Studio."

A moment later a large man in a finely tailored suit bustled into the lobby, his blue gaze fixed on Audra. "You must be Miss Schaeffer."

"Yes, sir." He took her hand and thrust it up and down twice in a vigorous motion.

"Mark Feldstein. Come with me." His blond hair flopped over his forehead in long waves, leaving Audra to wonder how he could see. He strode through the crowds, not waiting for people to get out of his way. Audra followed in his wake. "So why do you want to do this? Babysit a bunch of stars for three weeks?" He turned and studied her a moment. "You don't seem the star-watching type."

Should she be offended? Audra looked down at her evergreen suit. She might not have Rosemary's flair, but maybe in this town she needed to develop another style to be taken seriously.

"Honestly, I need a job."

He took off again. "My office is in here." He gestured toward a door then opened it.

Audra paused in the doorway. Papers, books, and paraphernalia covered every available surface and were piled at least a foot high on the lone visitor's chair. "Are you sure there's room for me?"

He arched an eyebrow then moved to the chair and swept the papers to the floor. "Better?"

"Thank you." Audra kept her chin high and eased onto the chair.

Mark moved around the desk and sat. "All right. This caravan will mirror the earlier one. This studio is in charge of providing the support staff, but the stars will come from across Hollywood. If you're hoping to meet Bing Crosby or Cary Grant, you've selected the wrong train. They won't make this trip. Instead, we'll have Victoria Hyde, Royce Reynolds, and folks like that. Think you can handle that?"

Audra nodded. Based on what she'd seen of Victoria earlier, she'd be fine.

Mark studied her, beating his hands against the edge of the desk in some kind of rhythm. "Okay. You're on to help babysit twenty or so stars and performers. Should be a laugh a minute. Come back tomorrow, and we'll get organized. We've got less than a week to get those stars on the train, finalize venues, and work with the papers and radio stations to get the word out."

"Yes, sir." She played with her purse a moment. This whole job seemed too easy. "Don't you need references or more information from me?"

"While that might be nice, I don't have time. You're willing and available and Artie vouched for you. That's good enough." He pulled a stack of paper in front of him and flipped through it. "Don't forget. First thing in the morning, here with me. And do something about that hair. You have to look the part, even if you aren't a star."

"Nobody will care if I'm on the train or not." In fact, she hoped she could blend into the background and learn what she needed. It would be easier to watch others if they forgot she existed.

"You've got a lot to learn about this city. It's all about appearances." He flicked a hand at her. "Now get out of here, and check in with Betty in the morning."

Before she could stand, Mark signed a paper then picked up his phone and started barking orders. Audra clutched her handbag and slipped into the hall. If she was going to live on a train for three weeks, she'd better raid Rosie's closet and do some shopping. Her suitcase and its contents weren't prepared for the extension to her trip. With her small caravan salary she could purchase a few supplements to what she'd brought with her.

Maybe she'd stop by the police station first. Try to learn new information about Rosie's murder or whether police had identified the other woman. Surely the police knew something by now. Detective Franklin wasn't the type to let grass grow under his feet.

Betty looked up when Audra entered the lobby. "Everything okay?"

"Yes. I'll be back tomorrow. Do you know where I can hail a cab?"

"One minute." Betty picked up her silent phone. A minute later she smiled and hung up. "You're set. You can wait here or outside."

"I'll wait out there." Audra headed to the door then remembered something Betty had said earlier. "Did you know my sister?"

Betty chewed on her lower lip and nodded. "I can't believe somebody would kill her. She seemed to fit right in with people around here. I'd heard one of the producers was ready to try her in a film."

"Really?"

"That's what I heard."

"She would have been thrilled to know she was close. All Rosemary wanted to do was be in pictures. It's what she dreamed about since her first trip to a theatre." A splinter of sadness punctured Audra at how close Rosie had been to her dream.

"The picture was slated for production immediately after the caravan. I've heard the studio's already contracted another actress."

"Who?"

"Lana Garfield."

CHAPTER FIFTEEN

Rabbit trails. That's what life had become.

Audra waited in the police department's lobby, shopping bags filled with toiletries and clothing scattered at her feet. She should leave. Detective Franklin either wasn't coming back or wanted to avoid her. In the fifty-five minutes she'd sat in the uncomfortable, hard-backed wooden chair, all she could do was stare at the peeling paint and steady parade of characters that uniformed officers led through the lobby. The occasional attorney rushed in, briefcase clutched in hand, no doubt on a mission to save a client.

Much as she wanted to know the mystery woman's identity, Audra also needed to know if she could return to Rosemary's apartment. She'd never felt so uprooted in her life.

The outer doors clanged against the cinderblock walls.

"Come on, Angelina." An officer dragged a beautiful woman in a party dress into the lobby. Audra stared at the handcuffs that clashed with her diamond bracelets. "You can tell your sob story to the judge later."

"I only joined him for dinner. That's all." She spoke in low, cultured tones.

"That's what they all say. You might try a creative angle."

The woman's high heels clicked across the tile until the officer took her through a door and into a hallway. Audra could only imagine what lay beyond.

She glanced at her watch. More than an hour had passed while she'd sat in that uncomfortable chair. She should return to Mrs. Margeson's and place the call home she'd put off. Explain her decision to her parents. She stood and walked to the information counter. If she didn't leave soon, she'd be in the same position she'd been the night before. In an empty apartment with no food. "Can I leave a message for Detective Franklin?"

The officer behind the desk slid her a pen and paper. "Jot a note there. I'll see he gets it."

Audra scribbled Mrs. Margeson's number down and left the message. "Tell him I'll be at that number until I hear from him."

The officer nodded and focused on the next person demanding his attention. Audra returned to her seat and collected her bags. She stood to leave, only to be pushed into her chair as Detective Franklin brushed past her. He startled and turned toward her.

"Miss Schaeffer, what are you doing here?"

"Waiting for you." She rubbed her shoulder where it had connected with the seat back. "Can I have a moment?"

He rubbed his hands through his hair, which already stuck out in a dozen directions, as if the Santa Ana wind had brushed its fingers through the strands. The hat he usually wore had disappeared and his suit looked even more rumpled than usual. He sighed and his shoulders slumped. "Five minutes. That's all I can give you."

"Thank you."

He opened the door that separated the public areas of the station from the rest. "Come on. Follow me to the part of this fine establishment where the real work gets done."

She grabbed her bags then followed him past a couple of rooms with closed doors. He escorted her into the first one with an open door.

"Sorry for the appearance. We don't have much in the way of conference rooms. We like to keep the suspects uncomfortable."

The gray walls closed in on Audra. She couldn't imagine sitting in that small space under a bright light for interrogation. He gestured to a chair on one side of the table.

"Have a seat."

The hard wooden chair bit into the back of her legs. Detective Franklin perched on the table opposite her. Silence fell and she shifted, trying to find a comfortable position.

"This is your show. What can I do for you?"

"Can I return to the apartment?"

"Yep. Left a message with the landlady to that effect. You didn't come all the way down here for that."

Audra took a breath. He was right, and she couldn't predict how he would react to her next statement. "I'll be leaving Hollywood in a few days."

He studied her, and she resisted the urge to shift in her seat like a guilty two-year-old. "Headed where?"

"I'll be working on the second victory caravan, since you don't have anything to report."

"That's like letting the hen loose in a den of foxes." She stared at him until he slouched and spread his hands in front of him. "Look, today's been a mess. Wrong path after false turn. None of which led to any concrete leads. The victim in your sister's apartment was Rachel Gibson. Sounds like she was on her way to early stardom. A few walk-on roles, with a second or third billing role coming opposite Lana Garfield and Royce Reynolds. Shared their agent, too. Had a few questionable brushes with the law about serving as an escort."

"Why was she at Rosemary's?"

"I'm not sure, but best guess at the moment is she'd moved in with your sister since she closed her apartment a week before her death. Rumor has it she was leaving town with no plans to return. Odd, since people talk about her being close to success. Like I said, no concrete leads. It's not clear why anyone would want to kill her. But at least we have a name to chase down. Maybe the agent can connect some dots for us. Could be as simple as she stayed with Rosemary to save cash until she left. Wouldn't be the first time for an arrangement like that. She could have been there when someone came looking for Rosemary. We'll keep digging."

A name. It was something. "Thank you."

Detective Franklin studied her a moment. "Why are you really going on the caravan?"

Audra opened her mouth then shut it. What could she tell him? That she had to do something to track down the killer? That she wanted to understand Rosemary's world? None of those answers would satisfy him. Instead, they'd bring his scrutiny. But she couldn't lie either. So she kept her mouth shut.

As she met his gaze, she knew she hadn't fooled him. He shook his head then stood. "Miss Schaeffer, leave the investigating to us. I can't stop you from going on the trip, but I hope you know how foolish it is to try to discover something about your sister's death. That's work for the police and certainly not for a woman."

She squared her shoulders and met his stare. "My parents have lost one daughter. I won't do anything to compound that pain. After all, what can happen on a train? Everyone will be too busy to do anything nefarious."

"Sure. Bad things only happen on terra firma." He rolled his eyes then crossed his arms as a serious look cloaked his face. "Look. I understand the need to find answers. Really, I do. But leave that to me. We will find them. Maybe not as fast as you like."

The mystery woman he'd mentioned earlier flashed in her mind. She couldn't just leave it to the police. "Then the caravan will give you time to arrest her killer without me to interfere or get in your way."

"You're a funny one."

"I'd call it determined."

"When do you leave?"

"Sunday. It sounds like we'll go to Washington, D.C. Start there like the first caravan, but head south rather than follow the northerly course back to Hollywood."

"All right." He rubbed a hand through his hair. "Be careful in that apartment. I'm not convinced it's a good idea for you to stay there, but I can't stop you. Remember we don't know what whoever was breaking in wanted."

Detective Franklin escorted her from the building. "Take care of yourself." He disappeared back inside the building.

Audra stared after him then squared her shoulders and hailed a cab. When she reached the apartment building, she knocked on Mrs. Margeson's door.

"Come in, come in." Mrs. Margeson hugged Audra and pulled her into the front room.

"Can I use your phone?"

"Of course. Make yourself at home. I'll make some tea." She bustled into the kitchen while Audra worked with the operator.

Finally her mother's voice came on the line. "Audra?"

"Hi, Mama. Is Daddy home?"

"No. It's his Lions Club night. Do you have details about when we should get you? We're scheduling Rosie's funeral."

Audra took a deep breath. It might be easier telling Mama and let her update Daddy. "I won't be coming home yet."

"Why not?" The shock in her mother's voice wasn't hidden by the distance.

"I've taken a temporary job that will let me get close to many of the people Rosemary knew. Maybe I can learn something that will help us find her killer."

Mama's inhalation sucked any hope that her parents would understand. "You would miss your sister's funeral for that?"

"I just can't do that…not again."

"You listen to me. This was not your fault and neither was your brother's death. You have to let go of that false guilt. And you need to come home. You'll regret it if you don't."

"Mama, I can't." The words whispered around the lump in her throat. "I just can't. I'm so sorry, Mama. I already have nightmares of when I had to identify her body. I want to remember her like she was, not the shell she is now."

Silence settled between them, Audra too close to losing control to say anything.

"What if you wish you'd come?"

"I can't do anything for her there, but I can do this. I need to try."

Audra could almost hear her mama's prayers. "All right. If you think you must, but promise you'll be careful. You hear me?"

"Yes, ma'am. I promise I won't do anything foolish."

"Okay." Mama blew out hard. "I'll find some way to explain this to your father. Do not make me regret that. I love you, girl."

"I love you too." Audra hung up then refused a cup of tea from Mrs. Margeson before running to Rosemary's apartment.

The rest of the week passed in a rush. Audra met herself coming and going as she spent long hours at the studio and then even more time running around the unfamiliar city trying to get revised contracts couriered to the caravan's participants. Mark must have decided she was cheaper than a service even though she had to use a taxi to find anything. The number of people who looked at her and saw Rosemary surprised her. Audra had never thought they'd looked alike. And their friends and family never spent much time identifying similarities. Instead, it was always, "Rosemary's the looker." Lose a few pounds and she could turn heads like Carole Lombard. While Audra had pretty eyes and intelligence. Not that Audra wanted to be known for her looks, but the comments had stung. In ways that didn't even make sense to her.

She stared out another taxi window, watching the buildings zip past. She should make an effort to understand the city, but instead she let the drivers deliver her without paying much attention to her surroundings.

The envelope in her lap felt heavy. This time she carried it to a bona fide star. Lana Kincaid Garfield. The thought of meeting the vixen who'd broken Robert's heart bothered her.

And that disturbed her.

It shouldn't matter who the woman was or what she had done.

It certainly shouldn't matter what she had done to a man Audra barely knew.

It shouldn't— But it did.

The only time Audra worried about the caravan was when she considered she'd be in such close proximity to the star and his former spouse.

Then her chest tightened in a way she didn't like.

"Here you go, miss." The cab driver pulled to the curb.

"Can you wait for me?" Everything would go faster if she could tell Miss Garfield her cab waited.

"Sure, but only for twenty minutes. And if you pay me in advance. Otherwise, I have to go find my next fare. Company rules."

"All right. Here's what I owe you for getting here and here's a dollar to wait for me." Audra closed her handbag, making a mental note to ask Mark for reimbursement. Her cash had reached dangerously low levels with all the cab fares.

The cab driver pulled his cap low over his eyes and slouched in his seat. "I'll be here."

Audra slipped from the cab and hurried up the sidewalk. Lana hadn't been around the studio all week. That would have made delivering her contract too easy. Instead, she'd insisted on taking the week off. A time to "center" before spending all her time with the others on the train.

The apartment building was impressive, with a façade that dripped importance. The stone front had inlaid marble and some other stone Audra didn't know. A doorman watched her from under the shade of a crimson canopy as she strode up the stone walk.

"May I help you?" His high voice didn't match what she'd expected.

"I have a delivery for Miss Garfield." She showed him the envelope.

"Is she expecting you?"

"I'm not sure. The studio might have called ahead."

"You'll have to wait while I check." He turned and entered the building, holding the door for her. She followed him to a desk in the corner of the lobby. He picked up the phone, and she looked around.

Persian rugs lay scattered across the highly polished marble floor. Towering palm trees clustered in groups around the edges of the narrow room. And paintings that looked to be authentic Impressionist masters' works lined the walls.

Miss Garfield must be doing well.

"She'll see you." The doorman pointed across the lobby. "Take the elevator to the fifth floor. Hers is the third apartment on the left."

Audra nodded and walked to the elevator. The doors slid open and a man sat on a stool inside.

"Floor?"

"Five, please."

The grate doors slid shut and the machine jolted to life. It jerked past floors in a manner that didn't quite fit with the lobby's ambiance. It bumped to a stop.

"Here you go."

"Thank you." Audra stepped from the box and stopped as the doors slid shut behind her. The hallway stood in stark contrast to the lobby. The cream paint looked fresh and the woodwork cleanly varnished, but none of the visible signs of affluence filled the halls. A nice carpet lined the floor, but there was no marble. No paintings or prints lined the walls. Maybe the show in the lobby was enough to set the stage. Appearances mattered even in the buildings? Further confirmation this was not the place for her. Audra needed to get on the caravan, learn what she could, and then return to Indianapolis.

She followed the hallway to the left and found the third door. She knocked and waited. A minute later she knocked again. Lana had to know she was on her way up.

"Coming." The word sounded imperious and unbothered.

A moment later the lock turned and the door opened. Lana leaned against the doorframe with a bored air. "Yes?"

Audra cleared her throat and held out the envelope. "The studio sent me with your contract. We need your signature on it today."

The star's blue eyes held an icy quality as she studied Audra. "Wait here while I read it." She turned and headed down an entryway, leaving Audra in the doorway.

Audra felt the brush-off. A spike of heat filled her, and she knew chances were good Lana wouldn't read a word of the document. Audra might not be a star, but she had value. She stalked down the hallway after the star, her heels clicking on the wood-paneled floor.

"So Mark's got you set to babysit us?" Lana didn't raise her gaze from the paper in front of her.

"I'll help with logistics, yes."

"Honey, there is no way you are prepared for what you'll see and experience." The star shook her head, perfectly coiled curls bouncing. "Let me take you out. I'll make you my pet. Get you all set to turn some heads. Maybe even land a movie star to take care of you the rest of your life or until he loses interest."

Audra longed for olive skin as she felt the color race to her cheeks. "I'm not here to find a man. I don't need one for security."

"That's what we'd all like to think." Lana's lips curled. "You won't last long here without someone to take care of you. I can guarantee that."

"Is that what happened to Rosemary? She needed someone to take care of her?"

Lana looked up from her pretend perusal of the document. "Who?"

Audra stiffened. She hadn't meant to say that out loud. "Rosemary Schaeffer."

"Her problem was too many men, and none looking after her."

CHAPTER SIXTEEN

Sunday, June 14, 1942

Time to leave. The taxi would be here in a minute. Robert shoved another roll of socks in a pair of wingtips and stuffed both in the side of his suitcase. He pulled out a sports coat and shoved it in. He closed the lid and tried to get the latch to snap on the case.

The phone buzzed, and he plucked the receiver. "Yes."

"Mr. Garfield, your cab is here."

"I'll be right down." Robert hung up and turned back to the stubborn case. He didn't have time to waste. The train left in one hour from Union Station down in Los Angeles. The first small step in what could become a long journey. Finally, the last latch caught, and he nabbed the bag and his keys. He hustled out of the apartment and locked the door behind him.

He kept glancing at his watch as the taxi puttered along. A strange tightness in his gut left him slightly nauseous. He hadn't been this flustered since his first audition. Did it have more to do with the tour or the fact he'd share the trip with his former wife? Add in Audra and his new role as emcee and stand-up comic, and it was no wonder he tensed every time he thought about the caravan.

Last week's screen tests had gone well. While the promised contract hadn't materialized yet, Artie remained convinced he'd have at least one contract for a good role waiting for Robert to sign when he returned. If it was good enough, he'd threatened to meet Robert wherever the caravan stopped and have him sign it before the ink dried. Robert's job was to make the most of the exposure he'd get on this trip. Sell a record-breaking number of bonds. No pressure.

Who was he kidding?

This business was tough, and he'd never had a clear shot to success. He'd crawled his way into roles like most did. But could he do it without sinking to the levels so often required?

The cab pulled to the curb at Union Station with a bump. "Here you go, mister."

"How much do I owe you?"

"Nothing. The studio covered it."

Robert pulled some coins from his pocket. "Well, here's a tip for getting me here in one piece."

"Say. Thanks!" The driver tipped his hat. "Have a safe trip."

"Will do." Robert hopped out of the cab and strode toward the main doors.

"There he is."

"That's got to be Robert Garfield."

"You bet it is."

Several men rushed toward him as cameras flashed around his head.

"You anticipating this trip?" A man with a pencil stuck behind his ear fired the question.

"Sure am. It will be a great opportunity to see America and sell war bonds." Robert shut his mouth before he said anything fractured and unintelligent.

The lone woman in the group pushed her way to the front. "Do you have a quota of bonds to sell?"

"I'm sure we do, but whatever the quota, I know the American public is generous and will buy even more."

The bulbs continued to flash, and Robert waved to the reporters. "Excuse me, but I've got a train to catch."

He hurried through the towering curved arch of the station's Moorish exterior and into the cool interior. The marble floors were inlaid with an elaborate red, gold, and black zigzag pattern. If he watched it too carefully, he'd stagger down the hall like someone who'd been drinking.

His steps slowed when he caught sight of someone who looked like Audra. Only this woman's hair was cut in a soft bob that looked like it would tickle her neck, rather than pulled back in the harsh, professional way Audra wore hers.

"No, you dolt, I said to stack them there."

Robert sighed. That screeching voice could belong to none other than Lana. He pivoted on his heel and there she stood. Her navy tea gown was topped with a fox stole, her curls with a plumed hat. A gold cigarette holder dangled from her perfectly manicured fingers. Lana in all her glory.

"If it isn't Robert Garfield. You were a star once, weren't you?"

"Hello, Lana." This trip already felt like an eternity and hadn't even started.

"Maybe you can explain to the porter how I like things."

Robert pointed to his bag. "I've got to find the train. See you there." He quickened his pace. *Note to self: don't stop at Lana's voice.* He needed to act like her hold had died. Eventually reality would catch up with his actions.

Uniforms filled the halls as he hurried toward the track. Many of the servicemen raced past him while others lingered for a last kiss with the gal on their arm. Still others slept on the floor, a bench, anywhere they could find a spot to rest, hats pulled low over their eyes.

A photographer snapped some shots, the flash popping. Robert wondered which publication he was with but didn't have time to ask. The big clock dominating the wall in front of him urged him to hustle if he didn't want to get a reputation for holding the train up on the first day. He'd leave that distinct honor to Lana or another star.

He entered the terminal lined with trains. Scanning the board, he identified the platform where the Hollywood Victory Caravan was stationed. As he read the number of the platform in front of him, he realized it was at the far end of the terminal. Increasing his pace, Robert hustled toward the train, trying to avoid breaking into a sweat.

Mark Feldstein stood in front of the train, a clipboard clutched in his hand. "Mr. Garfield. Nice of you to join us."

Robert grinned at him. "Thank you."

"You're in the first car behind the coal car, berth four."

"Sure." He could imagine the soot coming in through the windows.

"Here's today's itinerary. The dining car will be open most of the trip. But there are certain hours it will close each day. Orientation is at five, or as soon as the train clears the city. Miss Schaeffer or I will come through to announce the start."

Robert accepted the sheet of paper. So far everything sounded like he'd expected.

"I think that's all for now. Go get settled, and we'll see you at the meeting."

"Yes, sir." Robert saluted Mark and then headed down the train until he reached the first sleeper car. He hauled his bag up the narrow steps and shuffled into the hall. He laughed when he saw the stars someone had pinned to each berth's door. He didn't need a number. All he had to do was locate his name on a star.

He opened the door to his berth and threw his bag in, loosening his shirt collar and pulling off his tie. The room wasn't large. It'd feel downright cozy by the end of three weeks, but Robert was pleased he wouldn't have to share with anyone.

He settled in on the narrow bed. Might as well catch some shut-eye while he waited for things to start.

Sometime later, he was startled awake when someone knocked on the door. "Time for the meeting. Everyone to the dining car."

Robert sat up and rubbed his eyes. He stumbled to his feet, surprised to feel the rhythmic motion of the train rumbling down the track. He pulled a tie out of his bag and laced it around his collar. After knotting it, he grabbed a brush and smoothed his hair. The sounds of banging faded. Time to join the others.

* * * * *

Audra leaned against the wall in a corner of the dining car. Booths lined the outside walls, the backs providing a tiny bit of privacy. Linen tablecloths covered the tables, each with a small vase containing a single daisy sitting on top.

Mr. Feldstein told her he'd insisted the dining and lounge cars be between the men's and women's sleeping cars. Hopefully they would build a natural separation and avoid some of the mishaps from the first caravan. As Audra watched the open flirting as the stars gathered with air kisses and hugs, she doubted that would be enough to keep the amorous apart.

As the dining car filled, Mark rapped a hand on the bar. "Ladies and gents, we are under way."

Muted applause broke out.

"It'll take us several days to reach D.C. That's good since we'll need the time to plan who does what in the show and rehearse. I've got some great scripts, but you'll have the freedom to create your own material starting tonight." Mark ran through the details and general rules. "Remember, first and foremost we are on this train to sell war bonds. The government has assigned a quota to this trip, and personally, I'd like to see us beat it—and the amount raised by the first caravan. Let's show them we can work even harder."

The stars shifted in their seats, and Audra wondered if Mark would notice the signal. Time to move things along.

"Audra Schaeffer is on the tour to help with logistics. If she tells you something, assume it comes from me." Audra waved from her spot on the wall then faded back against it. "Dalia Carver will be in charge of costumes and set pieces. We've got a good many in the baggage car, but will collect more as we need them."

A large woman with coffee-colored skin curtsied from the other side of the car.

"All right. Grab some supper. Finish unpacking. Then, be back here by eight for rehearsals. You're dismissed."

The stars dispersed one by one, with a few collecting in the corners of the car. Mark approached Audra. "Tonight take notes and get a sense of the personalities. We've got more than a few egos on board. We won't be able to accommodate all of them when it comes to building a program. But we'll try to minimize the bruising as much as possible."

"Yes, sir."

"Go relax until eight. You won't get much opportunity for that on this trip."

He had no idea. It might sound like a fun trip, but Detective Franklin had given her no indication he knew who had killed Rosemary. She had as good a chance as he did of learning something important. And that was her true priority. She could grab a sandwich after the performers.

She jostled down the swaying aisle, across the car's walkway, and into the lounge car. Behind the lounge car, she'd reach the sleepers that housed the women making this trip. There were twelve sleeping berths to a car, and Mark had placed her in the first one of the first women's sleeping car. He said she should keep the men away. She'd wanted to laugh at that suggestion but had nodded instead. How did he think she could stop a determined man? Especially if she hoped to get any sleep while on board.

A few people gathered in the lounge car. She swayed as the train rounded a bend on the tracks and found herself falling against a bolted-down chair. Robert reached up and steadied her.

"I'm so sorry." She pulled from the contact, embarrassed as several of the men laughed.

Robert made a show of looking up and down the car. "You don't have anything to be sorry about. Ignore those lugs. They've forgotten any manners their mothers taught them. Here, have a seat if you've got a minute."

She eyed the vacant chair then decided she might as well. "For a moment." She looked at the book he held. "What's that?"

He flipped it over. "My Bible. I thought I'd take a few minutes to read. I have a feeling our berths are going to feel mighty small by the end of this trip."

"Oh."

"You seem surprised."

"It's not the book I expected you to read."

"Don't believe everything you read in the magazines, Audra. My faith is very important to me."

"I'm glad to hear that." She stood and straightened her skirt. "I won't keep you from your reading."

He studied her with a knowing look in his eye. "You are up to something, Miss Audra Schaeffer. Promise me it won't get you in trouble."

Audra met the questioning interest in his gaze and almost shared the burden. She sank onto the vacant chair next to his.

He reached out and touched a curl where it had slipped into her face. "I like what you've done with your hair. The bob looks very nice."

Her heart raced as he stroked her cheek. Could she trust a star, especially one listed in Rosemary's book? Especially one who affected her with a mere touch? No, she wouldn't make any promises to Robert. Not when any trouble she found would be worth it if she could identify her sister's killer.

CHAPTER SEVENTEEN

The dining car overflowed with performers again. Audra stood against the back corner behind the bar, watching as men and women greeted each other and found seats on the covered benches. The men covered the women as if anchored in orbit by their beauty.

Lana Kincaid Garfield sat at one table, overdressed, as usual. Her satin gown shimmered in the light, topped by yet another ridiculous fox stole that would look more appropriate in a Chicago winter than on a train headed across a desert. Royce Reynolds lounged on the bench next to her, an arm casually draped against the back of the seat. His message couldn't be clearer—he'd staked his claim on Lana. From the way she leaned slightly away from him, it wasn't clear whether she agreed with him or not.

The Lester twins filled a booth by themselves, their size making them look permanently squeezed into the tight space. They waved at everyone who walked by, friendly grins plastered on their faces. Audra looked forward to meeting them, since she'd enjoyed the slapstick variety of their radio spots. Based on the way everyone responded to them, no one saw them as a threat.

Several attractive gals had clustered together, inviting the men with come-hither glances. Though not immediately placing them, Audra could tell she'd need to keep an eye on them to ensure the rules weren't breeched by visitors of the male persuasion.

One auburn beauty puckered her lips in a pout as Robert walked past the empty seat next to her.

"Well, there he is. Mr. Trouble." Lana's voice was coated with a thick dose of sugar. Audra followed her gaze, wondering if she meant anyone other than Robert.

"Robert, my man." Quincy Cambridge jumped to his feet from his booth near the door and pumped Robert's arm. "Glad you made this shindig. Should be an adventure, wouldn't you say?"

Robert smiled and slapped Quincy on the back. "Wouldn't have missed this for the world." He marched passed the clustered beauties, and Audra released her breath, then felt foolish. What did it matter to her whom he sat by? "Miss Victoria Hyde, the loveliest lady in Hollywood, may I have the pleasure?"

A soft color heightened Miss Hyde's perfect cheekbones as she smiled at Robert. "Of course. I'd be delighted for some civilized company in this group." She slid over to make room for Robert.

Audra bit her lip as the Lester twins wolf-whistled.

Of what she'd seen so far, Victoria was a far better person for Robert than the other assembled women. But even as she thought that, Audra's heart betrayed her with a hitch in its beating. She silently scolded herself. She had no business thinking about a man like Robert on any day, let alone when she had a mission.

Robert met her gaze and winked. Did he realize she mooned over him like a silly schoolgirl? A flash of heat climbed her face. If only he wouldn't wear his perfectly tailored suits and shirts. Dressed like that, he was the spitting image of Cary Grant—style with an incredibly handsome face.

The door behind Audra slid open and Mark Feldstein strode into the car. "All right, ladies and gents. We have three days to reach Washington and our first performance. Barely enough time to memorize a skit, let alone plan an entire night's festivities, but that's exactly what we are going to do—starting now."

Conversations slowly ended as he stared from one table to the next.

"Thank you." He straightened his tie then turned to Audra. "You ready to take notes, Miss Schaeffer?"

Audra resisted rolling her eyes. As if taking notes of a conversation was the hardest task he would assign. "Of course." She lowered her clipboard and got her pen ready.

"All right. Robert Garfield here will be our emcee. He'll come on to string all the acts together and be the handsome face America loves. We've got slapstick, singers, a couple dancers…" Gene Costos and Annabelle Kelly tapped their toes in a rapid beat on the floor. "…Thank you for that…. And Constance and Frank will sing for the masses."

On cue the two hummed a measure of "Auld Lang Syne" in an off-key duet.

Good-natured laughter filled the car as Mark pulled his hat low over his face.

Mark turned to Audra and popped his fedora back on his crown. "See? This is exactly why three days isn't enough time. We can shoot an entire movie in two or three weeks, but I can't get these yahoos to be quiet and respectful long enough to plan one night's agenda."

"Maybe if you stopped talking, we'd listen," Jim Collins hollered from the opposite side of the car. Hoots and whistles followed his words until Mark brushed his hands at the performers.

"Whenever you're ready to scheme up the perfect evening of entertainment to get Americans to open their pocketbooks and fork over their hard-earned cash for war bonds, let me know. Until then, Miss Schaeffer and I will do some work over here."

"Why don't you order up a round of drinks for us, Markie boy." Winston Portland, a star of more westerns that Audra could remember, rapped the table in front of him. His cheeks bore the flushed, veined look of someone who didn't let much come between him and his night-caps. "It's mighty thirsty business, listening to you." He caught Audra's eye and winked. "In fact, I think your lovely assistant should be the one to serve."

"The bar's closed until the work's done. Feel free to drink some water, though, if you're parched." Mark banged his fist on the bar. "People, the government and the boys are counting on us. It is our patriotic duty to take this seriously. Don't worry, we'll leave you plenty of time to cut it up, but we have to do the work first."

"I'm sure everyone knows why we're here, Mr. Feldstein." Victoria looked at Mark, a composed expression coating any irritation she might feel.

Lana stifled a yawn and shrugged her fur-wrapped shoulders. "How will you use the actors among us? Only one can emcee."

"That's where you come in, Sweetcakes. You're talented or you wouldn't ride with us. We'll create skits. Find an organ-grinding monkey to stand in front of you. Anything to keep the audience happy. If you want input on your image, I suggest you start working with me."

Lana wrinkled her nose and settled against the bench. Royce squeezed her shoulder and Audra caught Robert watching the interplay, his brows knit together. What must he think as they carried on?

Charlie Lester leaned forward. "I think we should start with a little vaudeville routine. Loosen the crowd up with some grins and giggles."

"Of course you'd say that. That means you'd start the show." Royce rolled his eyes.

"Then what's your idea? And what's wrong with warming the audience up with some laughs? We could at least incorporate one or two of these pretty ladies into our routine. Then we could have the tappers and a singer or two. Followed by whatever talent you can display in front of a live audience. You know there won't be a camera focused on your mug." The intense speech seemed to deflate Charlie. His shoulders slumped, shrinking his silhouette. "I've been 4-F'd. This is the only way I'll make a difference in the war effort. You'd better believe I'll give it everything I've got. Whether I'm first in the line-up or tucked in the middle and never mentioned in a solitary column inch in the papers or one moment over the airways. This is about more than any of us."

Silence settled on the train. Audra wanted to clap at his impassioned words but clutched the clipboard instead.

Mark stepped into the pause. "That sounds like something to start with. What would the focus of your skit be?"

"Something about a G.I. Joe. Maybe coming home and finding his girl with a buddy."

"Oh, that sounds funny." Royce snickered.

"Or dreaming of Mom's good home cooking during basic." Danny Lester patted his stomach. "There're all kinds of ways we can take it once we know what works best for the show."

Robert snapped his fingers. "Hey, maybe we could base the skits on that Rockwell character. What's his name?"

Audra thought a moment. "From the *Saturday Evening Post* covers?"

"Yeah."

"Willie Gillis."

"That's it!"

Mark nodded. "Jot that down. Good ideas. Charlie, grab a couple people and see if you can come up with something by tomorrow afternoon. All right. Keep 'em coming. We need more, folks."

Constance bounced on the seat, one hand raised in the air as her blond curls jiggled around her shoulders. "Oh, we could put together a trio with some swinging tunes that sound like the Andrews Sisters. Even cover a couple of their songs. I bet the crowds would like that."

"Yeah, we should build it like a radio variety show. Coming on and off with the suave emcee to keep us all moving." Quincy nudged Robert, who made a show of massaging his ribs.

Mark rubbed his hands together and looked at Audra. "Catching all this? Now we're getting somewhere."

An hour later, Audra had captured a list of ten or twelve possible acts. The performers had a lot of work to do before the next meeting the following afternoon. As the group broke up, she wondered how she'd have time to learn all the personalities and get some of the performers to even acknowledge her presence, let alone talk to her. While many of those on the train seemed friendly and glad to know anyone, some seemed standoffish.

Lana Garfield gave no indication she'd even noticed Audra, let alone remembered she'd stopped at the star's apartment. Audra could imagine Lana's face twisted into a mask of disdain at the thought of talking to someone of her status.

After all, she was merely an assistant.

Audra tapped the pen against her lips, a smile forming. Maybe she could use that to her advantage. Lana wouldn't be the first or last person to underestimate her. Many attorneys and law professors had treated her as less skilled than her male counterparts. She'd waited until their perceptions trapped them then destroyed the illusion. It worked in legal settings. That strategy should work here, too. Her smile bloomed until she couldn't hide it.

Robert sidled up next to her. "You look pleased with yourself."

"Shouldn't you be with a starlet? Someone who can build your public persona?"

He studied her a moment, serious blue eyes searching through the barriers to her soul. "My mission is to convince you that's not me." He sighed. "You'll see plenty of people playing to the media while we're on this trip."

She crossed her arms. "Admit it. You're here for the exposure."

"Sure, that's part of it. But I'm not looking for a mate." He stopped abruptly as if realizing what he'd said. "Not a Hollywood mate anyway." He shrugged. "This is why I work from a script."

She felt drawn into his gaze. "Are you always so…self-deprecating?"

He straightened his cuff links. "That's a mighty big word from such a small person."

"I guess it is." She should turn away. Find something to do. Something. To. Do. Yes, she should. Instead, she stood mesmerized and liked it. The realization startled her.

His gaze settled on her lips, and she swallowed around a suddenly dry throat.

"Robert Garfield." Lana's voice reached screeching levels. "You cannot be engaged with this woman."

Audra jerked as the words broke the spell. What craziness was Lana spouting?

"I've thought about it." Robert smiled his lazy, star smile.

For just a moment, Audra wondered if she'd somehow fallen into *You Can't Take It with You*, the delightful Jean Arthur/Jimmy Stewart romantic comedy. All the screwball friends and family were missing, but the intensity between Jean and Jimmy's characters had appeared in this moment. The almost proposal... She shook her head. What had gotten into her? He was only tweaking Lana's words, trying to get her goat. Less than two weeks in Hollywood and she'd let her mind run away with her emotions.

CHAPTER EIGHTEEN

Monday, June 15, 1942

Chaos reigned in the lounge car. The actors and actresses couldn't do much about the car's setup. After all, the seats were bolted to the floor. Then a studio head had the brilliant idea to cram a piano next to one wall. Someone had strapped it against the wall so it didn't roll all over the end of the car. But that meant the singers and dancers had to practice and scheme in the same small space as the actors.

Robert watched the mishmash of activity from a safe spot. He'd found a vacant bench in the middle of the car so he could observe everything. As emcee he needed to know everyone's role in the show. So he hovered, not really participating in anything. It would be a challenge to make everything fit together in a seamless procession.

Sacrifice.

Somehow it would all come back to the willingness the boys had to lay their lives down for others. And if they did that willingly, shouldn't those left at home make sacrifices, too?

Yes, that was it. Robert snagged a small notebook from his inside jacket pocket and sketched some notes down. The words of John 15:13 slid through his mind. *Greater love hath no man than this, that a man lay down his life for his friends.*

Jesus had been the truest example.

But each young man fighting in or preparing for a battle right now—whether in Africa or the Pacific—would do the same. Die for others if called to.

The thought settled on Robert.

What he did was of no consequence compared to that. Truly his efforts as emcee looked insignificant and so worthless in light of the sacrifices of life and health.

Maybe he should hop off the train at the next station and find the nearest enlistment office.

"There you are." Lana's voice pulled him from his thoughts with a start.

"Lana."

She looked stunning in a blue dress that matched her icy eyes. Her stylist must have told her to only wear blue gowns that fit her like a glove, advice she seemed determined to follow. The eyes of every man on the car locked on her as if she were the only woman there.

"You mind?" Without waiting she settled onto the bench, squishing so close he could feel the heat from her body. Robert sucked in a breath and waited. "I need a protector."

He looked at her and laughed. "You might start by changing into something less revealing. That would help quite a bit."

She stuck out her lower lip in what he used to find a charming pout. "Robert."

"Look, Lana. I'm not your husband anymore. You made that decision. You are no longer my responsibility."

"You're a horrible man." She started to slide away from him then stopped. Robert followed her gaze as a soft look came over her face and she snuggled close. Royce stared at them, arms crossed and a deep frown etched on his face.

"Oh, no." Robert stood, and Lana lurched forward. "I will not be part of your games. If you want him, go get him. But don't use me as a pawn in your game."

He slid past her into the aisle. Where could he go to get away from her? He was trapped on this train until it arrived in D.C. in two days.

Suddenly that seemed like an eternity rather than a mere forty-eight hours.

"Robert." Lana pulled on his arm. "Please don't go."

He stared at her hand on his sleeve then shook her off. He held his head high as he strode to the dining car, ignoring all the eyes focused on him.

* * * * *

Audra tried to shrink behind the piano as Robert passed. Everyone had witnessed the scene with Lana. What a conniving woman. But even as she thought that, Audra wondered if her thoughts were fair.

Maybe something really bothered her.

Audra couldn't imagine what problems a star had. Decked out as Lana was, Audra could envision all kinds of man troubles. The pawing-hands kind. But those were easily resolved.

Then again, she doubted Lana would agree.

"Miss Schaeffer?" Frank Crosby sang her name in his signature smooth, sweet style.

She laughed. "I don't think I've ever heard my name quite like that."

"Then stick around, kid. I'll do it every day, all day if you like." He waggled his eyebrows.

The Lester twins wolf-whistled. "You tell her, Frank."

"That's quite all right." The whistles continued, and Audra put on the face she imagined she'd use in court someday. "If you don't need me for something serious, I'll move along."

Frank struck a pose, hand clutched over his heart. "You slay me, love."

"Oh, give the girl a break. Seriously, Frank." Constance Smythe shook her head and shrugged. "I'd apologize for him except he's not sorry."

"Not a solitary repentant bone in my body."

"Exactly what I was afraid of." Constance sighed. "Seriously, we need an opinion. We thought Frank could croon 'I'll Never Smile Again.' Get everyone in a melancholy mood, thinking about their love fighting overseas. But we're not sure what to do with me."

This was far outside her training. Audra thought a moment then she snapped her fingers. "I've got the perfect song. How about 'I'll be Seeing You.'"

Constance stared at her, a blank look in her eyes.

"You know. The song from Broadway." Audra hummed a few bars. "I bet you could cover it well with your emotional singing. And we could put you in a beautiful gown. A single spotlight on you. Oh, it will be perfect."

"I need someone to play it for me."

Jim Collins hurried to the piano. "This the song you're thinking of, Audra?" He plinked a few keys then swung into the sweeping lyrical part of the song. Audra hummed along then sang, "*I'll be seeing you, in all the old familiar places…*"

She stopped abruptly. "Surely you remember it now."

Constance nodded. "I'm sure someone can help me if I don't."

"Great. I—I need to go—see the costumer." Audra hurried down the aisle. How could she do something so embarrassing? They must all think she's crazy. Why else would she sing in front of two of the country's most famous crooners?

She'd clearly lost her mind. She needed to find Rosemary's killer and get back home to Indianapolis where she didn't do insane things like that. Audra passed her berth and considered going in and hiding for a while.

No. They needed full sets of costumes for a two-hour program that didn't yet have a rundown. As the program came together, Dalia could work her magic. Mark had assured her the costumer was a miracle worker. Audra hoped he was right since she couldn't do much more than sew on a button anymore. It had been a long time since she crafted costumes for Rosemary's plays. Even that she'd never done to her grandmother's exacting standards. Now Audra was glad to buy her clothes readymade.

Dalia's berth was at the end of the last car before the baggage car and caboose. What a lonely place—cars away from the action, excitement, and good-natured bickering that filled the dining and lounge cars.

Audra rapped on Dalia's door. "Ma'am?"

"Who is it?" The rich lyrical voice wafted through the door.

"It's Audra Schaeffer."

"Of course you is." The door opened. "Come on in, child." Audra found herself clasped against the large bosom of the black woman. "How'd you sense I was a mite lonely back here?"

"I didn't." Audra bit her lip, wishing she'd been more creative with her answer. "Do you have time to look at the clothing?"

"Course I does. What else I gonna do but sit here readin' the Good Book?" Dalia plopped a hat on her head and hurried Audra back into the small hallway. "Right this way. You'll see what we have to work our needle magic on."

"You don't think I'm helping?" Dread filled Audra. She could imagine all the blood she would shed on beautiful gowns in her efforts to improve them. "I'm truly dreadful with a needle."

Dalia studied her. "Ain't nothin' a little time and trainin' can't fix. Too bad we ain't got the time." Dalia led her to the baggage car. "This here's where all the props and costumes are." She pulled a key from her bosom and unlocked the door. "Welcome to Oz."

Audra stepped into the room and understood immediately why Dalia had nicknamed the car Oz. It held a riot of color, with little organization.

"Don't you worry none about the looks of things in here. I'll fix some order tomorrow. What I needs to know now is what we needs for the White House."

How should she know? Audra was an attorney, not a Hollywood director. She must be nuts to think she could do this job. She could imagine her mother's reaction. She had tried to make Audra interested in domestic skills like sewing and event planning, and Audra had successfully resisted. Now she'd have to chase up every piece of advice she'd ignored.

"Honestly? Mark hasn't mentioned we're going to the White House on this trip." Audra bit her lower lip and walked along the first rack of gowns. She could imagine Rosemary looking lovely in any of them. "If we are, you have years more experience than I ever want to have." She pulled an emerald gown out to examine. "This one would be perfect for a number that Constance will sing. Will it fit her?"

Dalia eyed the garment then took it from Audra. Examining the tag and then the seams, she nodded. "Yes, ma'am. We can have it lookin' like it was sewn just for her."

"We'll have a trio of the girls singing popular tunes like the Andrews Sisters." Audra pivoted, taking in everything that was crammed into the space. "Do we have matching outfits?"

"Sure we does. You want gowns or more uniform lookin' get-ups?"

"Uniforms. For variety."

"Sure thing. Missy, you tell me whats you need, and I'll make it happen."

"If only I knew. They're still arguing over who will do what. And we arrive in two days."

"Then we'll have to ask the Good Lord to stretch time. He did it for Joshua. Maybe He'll see fit to do it for us."

Audra giggled. "I don't know if this is as serious as that battle, but I hope He answers your prayer. We'll need every moment."

"At least we don't have to worry about Mizz Garfield's dresses. The studio sent everything she could possibly need." Dalia gestured to a long rack filled with rich blue gowns. "The woman needs some variety in her life. That's all I'm sayin'. Um-hmm."

"I don't know. She's doing fine."

"You is new to Hollywood, ain't you? Don't you be thinkin' money and fame makes for happiness. I seen it destroy more people than it's ever made happy. That Mizz Lana ain't happy. You've noticed that. Cain't be around her more than a couple minutes before you knows. Actress or not, she is one vitally unhappy woman. And she'll bring you down with her. Just look at that poor husband of hers."

"Husband?"

"Robert Garfield."

"They aren't married."

"Maybe not no more. Don't mean he don't still bear scars of bein' with that woman. And she gonna try to keep him tied to her on this here trip. Mark my words." Dalia shook her head. "Fact is, Robert's fightin' her, which that lost little lamb don't like."

CHAPTER NINETEEN

Tuesday, June 16, 1942

The train jerked from side to side as it slowed. Audra rubbed her forehead, feeling a bone-deep weariness. They'd finally reached St. Louis. The train had only rolled across the country for two days, but she already wished the tour had ended. How would she survive another two and a half weeks?

It was like traveling with a bunch of juveniles. And she had to referee all of them. She'd love the option of banging down a gavel and sending them to their rooms. Already she'd stopped Royce Reynolds from barging into Lana's berth. If she'd thought the star would be grateful, she'd been disappointed.

Lana had stormed into her berth without a thank you.

And that was only one incident.

The hardest part was that she couldn't go to bed until the stars did. Leaving the performers without their babysitter seemed a clarion call for disaster. So Audra hadn't let herself sleep longer than a couple hours at a time since boarding. She could sleep when they'd safely returned to Hollywood. Until then she'd drink black coffee by the pot.

Mark wandered about the train, keeping an eye on things, then disappearing for chunks of time. Audra wouldn't venture through the men's cars to find him. No need to invite trouble. Not when a lot of the men seemed to think they were entitled to pinch anyone who came along their path.

Yes, two days down, and she was thoroughly sick of all things Hollywood. She didn't care if she ever saw these people again.

Her heart clenched at the thought. That wasn't a complete truth.

But there was no point thinking about Robert Garfield. He'd been completely friendly and professional. Refreshing, but not fodder for dreams.

She yawned. She needed to get off the train. But that wasn't possible, so she'd settle for leaving her berth. Maybe the coffee in the dining car would be fresh. And she could hop off the train if they actually pulled into the station. Most of the stops so far had been in the middle of train yards as the workers swapped engines. If that happened here, she wouldn't be able to detrain and feel solid ground under her feet.

The dining car held only a few people when she reached it. A touch of solitude.

Walking to the bar where the coffeepot warmed on its coil, she examined the brew. It looked like it'd sat there for an hour or so. She took a mug and filled it. She drizzled sugar across the top. She'd love some rich cream, too, but would settle for sugar.

When she turned around, Victoria Hyde had entered the car. She approached Audra. "How are you holding up?"

Audra plastered on a smile. "Fine. What's not to like?"

Victoria studied her as if seeing through the words. She filled a mug then gestured toward a booth. "Come sit with me. I'd like to get to know you."

Finally, an opportunity to see what someone knew about Rosemary. Victoria was an easy person to start with. She couldn't be involved with the murder. But she might give Audra a better idea of what Rosemary had done.

Audra eased onto the bench opposite Victoria. The rising star's quiet beauty was as breath-taking in person as on the screen. But the glow of inner peace set her apart from so many of the other women on the train.

A friendly smile lit her face. "What do you think of our gathering?"

"It's very different from the circles I'm used to in Indianapolis."

"Don't let them get to you. It's easy to forget that we don't have to perform all the time." Victoria ran a finger along the rim of the mug. When she looked up, her green eyes studied Audra. "Some of them are kids who forgot to grow up. Others have learned their on-screen persona so well, they've forgotten who they really are."

"Has that happened with you?" Audra bit her lower lip before she said anything else intrusive. "You don't have to answer that."

"It's all right. I work hard to remember who I am. A small-town girl from Nebraska who happened to be in the right place at the right time to catch the right person's eye. I can't be too proud, since I had little to do with it." She shrugged, a move that looked elegant and refined. "I'm blessed but hold it lightly. I won't be young forever."

Audra rolled her eyes. "Right. You're over the hill at twenty-three."

"Twenty-one." Victoria's eyes twinkled. "You've read the wrong articles."

"I guess so." Audra took a deep breath. "Did you know my sister? She wasn't much younger than you."

"Rosemary?"

"Yes."

Victoria looked over Audra's shoulder as if hunting through her memory. "I think we first ran into each other at Artie's office. She'd signed with him and was over the moon. She looked so innocent and vulnerable. I wanted to take her under my wing, but if she was going to make it she had to stand on her own."

Audra stiffened when she saw tears in Victoria's eyes.

"How I regret not giving her a few tips. Maybe she'd be in Hollywood right now memorizing lines for a role. It was perfect for her. I'd read for it but knew I didn't have the right look."

"What role was that? I keep hearing she was close to her first real part."

"Artie sent several of us to try out for the next big Andreson production. Rumor had it she was a favorite for the second lead."

Rosemary had been that close? Audra's heart constricted at the thought Rosemary hadn't known. "What movie?"

"The working title is *The Enemy Within*. I was so pleased for Rosemary. Hollywood can be a rough place for someone who wants to break into movies." Victoria lifted her coffee mug and then set it down without taking a drink. "There are many traps for those who haven't lived here awhile and know what to beware of. And Artie can all too easily push the gullible toward dark places."

A chill shook Audra's frame. She looked around the car and noticed that where it had been fairly empty a few minutes ago, it had now filled.

One of the performers she didn't know yet sat uncomfortably close to the booth she and Victoria shared. He sat there with a newspaper on the table in front of him, but she felt certain he focused on them rather than the headlines. Why? He must have sensed her attention, because he stood, tipped his hat, and walked past her with a grim smile.

Audra leaned across the booth. "Do you know who that is?"

"Who?"

"That man who walked by. He sat at the booth behind you."

Victoria twisted to look for the man. "From the back he looks like Dexter Snow."

"Why is he on the train? What does he do?"

"I think he hopped on at our last stop. He's a magician who's played bit parts in a couple of not very good movies. Mark must have decided to add him to the mix."

Maybe. She'd have to ask Mark the next time she ran into him. Until then, she had to get more information about Rosemary. "Did you run into Rosemary at any events? At any screen tests or auditions?"

Victoria shook her head. "Artie likes to send us to different ones. He doesn't believe in his clients competing against each other—at least until they're established. *The Enemy Within* was unique, but a great opportunity so he sent several of us."

"I still don't understand why Rosemary would need a warning."

"Men come to Hollywood longing to spend time with beautiful women."

Why did it feel like she had to pull the information from Victoria? "And?"

Victoria took a deep breath and met Audra's gaze. "Are you sure you want to know?"

"Yes." What could be so terrible?

"Your sister probably had begun to work for Artie. In his escort service. Many women, before they become stars, turn to this type of work."

Victoria continued to talk, but Audra no longer heard her.

Rosemary wouldn't do something like that. Not in a month of

Sundays. She couldn't turn her back on everything they'd been taught. Not so easily and quickly. No, if she'd needed to stoop to something as terrible as working for an escort service, surely she would have called home for help first.

"You're wrong."

"I hope you're right. Truly I do. But you need to be aware it's a possibility. A lot of girls who never thought they'd do anything like it find themselves doing exactly that."

Audra's stomach felt like she'd eaten too much. Her mind turned sluggish. "I need to go." She didn't know where. The train suddenly felt confining. Why did everyone think Rosemary had been an escort? How many of the men on board had taken her with them for a night on the town? Too many. Suddenly all those names Audra had seen in Rosie's black book took on a new meaning.

One she hated.

Audra slid from the booth and lurched to her feet.

"Are you all right?" Concern laced Victoria's voice.

Audra couldn't answer. She hurried down the aisle and into the next car. Her feet didn't slow until she reached her berth. She simply needed to get into her room, away from prying eyes, and then she could process everything Victoria had said.

One thing Victoria hadn't said was that Rosie definitely was an escort. How could Audra automatically believe the worst of her sister? In a heartbeat? She needed to slow down and think. Treat this like she would if a stranger came to her with a story about a family member. Check out the details but reserve judgment until she knew more.

Her heart tightened at the thought Rosemary would have sunk so low.

Escorting was so far removed from the dreams that had driven her west. Though it would certainly explain Rosemary's vacillating moods and her high excitement over the potential role. One good role with good reviews and she could walk away from escorting.

But with that thought came the realization that everything she'd known about her sister in Hollywood was false. And a new world of people who might want to kill her opened up.

CHAPTER TWENTY

Wednesday, June 17, 1942

Robert's leg jiggled up and down in the bouncy motion he hated. He couldn't stop it, the energy bubbling through him. He had to get off the train and stretch his legs. Fortunately, in a few minutes the train would pull into Washington, D.C.'s Union Station.

This group wouldn't visit the White House like the first group of Hollywood Victory caravaners. That would have been an incredible experience, but the powers that be had decided not to bother the president. They would head straight to the National Theatre instead. Since 1835 the theatre had hosted great performances and stars, making it a fitting place to launch the caravan.

Somebody pounded on his door. "Fifteen minutes."

Dalia would take care of his tux. He just needed to make sure he had his shaving kit and other necessities. Getting ready was so simple, he almost felt like an interloper. How could he pull his own weight on a tour like this?

The acts had pulled together in ways no one had anticipated at the beginning. The show would be a hit. And the good press they'd get out of tonight would carry them through the rest of the tour. Two more weeks. Fifteen performances. The adrenaline surges would spike up and down. He'd better watch for the fatigue that would be the natural result of a tour like this.

He yanked the blanket on his bed straight then tugged his shirt sleeves down until they peeked from the bottom of his jacket cuffs. He rolled his neck and took a deep breath. Tonight he'd focus the audience on the theme of sacrifice. If he did that, their pocket books would fly open. The war bonds would roll leading to a satisfied Uncle Sam and happy studio.

He rolled his neck again, fighting the building tension. It had been years since his days as a kid in live vaudeville. What trick had his dad used when everyone got antsy before a show? Whistling? That was it. He could do that. Even that tune from *Snow White*. He puckered his lips and went to town on "Whistle While You Work."

"You coming, Robert?" Winston Portland's nasal voice carried through the thin door.

Robert stopped whistling and wondered how much Winston had heard. "I'll be right out."

The train lurched to a stop, and Robert two-stepped to keep his feet. His head collided with the top bunk. "Youch." He rubbed his forehead, wondering if the contact would leave a welt. Just what he needed on opening night. A growing lump on his noggin.

Guess it would be fitting justice for someone who had suddenly become so focused on himself. He forced a whistle out, trying to regain a moment of relaxation.

He opened his door and joined Winston in the hall. Winston wore the threads his role required. The ladies would love his get-up. Hobo pants, floppy hat, and holey boots competed with a bandana-red long undershirt. Winston even walked with a defined limp, a far cry from his typical rolling gait.

"Looks like you're ready."

Winston looked at him, then away. He peered at Robert from the corner of his eye. "You talking to me, mister?"

"Sure." What was Winston up to now?

Winston pointed at Robert's chest. "I'm sure I don't know you."

"Getting into character already?"

Winston straightened and clapped Robert on the back. "Method acting. That's what it's called."

Robert straightened his tie. "Must be another of your harebrained schemes."

"You haven't heard of it?" Winston stepped backward, a hand clutching his heart. "It's the latest rage for actors in New York City. Mark my words, it'll change the way we act."

"I'll take your word for it." The train ground to a stop, and Robert staggered against the wall. "For now, we'd better get with the rest of the gang."

"Time to get the show on the road."

"At least off the train."

"Say, what do you think of that Audra Schaeffer chick?"

The question caught Robert by surprise. He hadn't had much occasion to run into Audra, and the last day she'd kept to herself. Any hopes he'd had to spend time with her had disappeared with the clack of the wheels over the rails.

Winston socked him on the shoulder. "Methinks you're noodling a simple question hard."

"She's different."

"Of course. She's not a performer. But have you heard her grill folks about her sister? "

"Can't say I blame her. I'd want answers too."

"Why ask us? She can't think we had anything to do with the murder."

"I don't know." All Robert knew was he liked her hair down in that short fashionable cut but hated the way her mouth drooped. There might not be a lot to make her happy right now, but he wanted the chance to see her smile like she had at the USO fundraiser and occasionally since. She'd surprised him by letting a glimpse of joy escape.

"People are growing leery around her. What if the whole reason she's here is to grill us?" Winston opened the door for Robert. "That's just wrong."

"Look, there's the rest of the group." Robert stepped off the car onto the station platform, relieved to have a reason to change the conversation.

Audra stood to one side, dressed in a simple suit. She held her bag and a stack of papers.

Mark called everyone together. "We've got a few limousines, enough for everyone to fit if you squeeze together as though you like each other." He glanced at his watch. "We've got four hours until show time. Just enough time for rehearsals and setup. Let's go."

Letting everyone push into a limousine in front of him, Robert waited, hoping to board Audra's. She caught his glance, and a rush of color warmed her cheeks until they resembled roses. The innocence of the color captured his attention.

"Garfield, climb in a car. We can't wait forever." Quincy's words brought a chortle from the Lester twins.

"I'm coming." *But not in that car.* Robert sauntered to the next vehicle and stooped to look inside. Fortunately, a couple of vacant spots remained. "If we all act as though we love each other…"

"Like. I swear Mark said like each other." Winston made a face that resembled a mask of horror. "If it's love, you'll have to go elsewhere, my fine man."

"You'll never grow up, will you?" Annabelle Kelly pulled her long legs away from Gene Costos. The action didn't slow him down. Robert winced as Gene edged closer to Annabelle. "Stop it." She pushed him away. "This won't work if you don't leave me alone."

"My co-stars like to get cozy." His words sounded innocent as the purest lamb.

"Not this one and not this time." She leaned against Gene then scrambled from the vehicle. "You can have my seat, Robert. Maybe he'll keep his paws off you."

"I'll be glad to give it a go."

"You do that." She huffed to the next car.

"How do you plan to dance with her tonight after acting like that? Think she'll snuggle up for your cheek-to-cheek number?" Robert shook his head, disgust boiling in his gut.

Gene grinned wolfishly. "Ah, it's just part of our warm-up. I get her mind off the fact it's a live audience and there are no takes. She gets to call me a lecherous old man. We're both happy."

"If you say so."

"I do." He waggled his eyebrows. "You have no idea how wonderful it is to rub up to her, even if it only gets her ire up."

"There are some things I'll never understand." Robert left it at that. What else could he say? He'd tried before to tell Gene that he should treat women better.

"Is this seat taken?" Audra leaned into the car and pointed at the seat across from Robert.

"He's held it for you, ma'am." Gene had transformed into a Southern gentleman, accent and all. He held his hand up to his mouth as if to share a secret then stage-whispered, "He's got a thing for you."

Robert shook his head. "Gene."

"See, it's true."

"You're way out of line."

Gene ignored his warning, so Robert tuned him out. Once Gene got started, the only way to stop him was to take away his audience. Fortunately, Audra seemed even less inclined to listen to Gene's banter. Instead, she stared out the car's tinted window, a lost look cloaking her face. Her face looked taut, like she'd lost weight in the few days they'd been on the train.

Suddenly she startled. "Ouch!"

"Are you all right?" Robert leaned across the narrow space.

She rubbed her thigh a moment then pulled her hand away as she caught Gene staring at her. "Fine, other than the fact that one of you fine gentleman pinched me." She wrinkled her nose, as if she smelled something foul.

The Lester twins and Quincy were in the other car. Winston didn't seem the type to pinch. Jim Collins was the only other man in the car, but he wouldn't do something like that unless it was scripted and in front of an audience. He was too happily married—a rarity in Hollywood—to risk doing anything with anyone not his wife.

Robert caught Audra's eye and shrugged. She frowned then settled back against the window. In another moment they reached the National Theatre.

"Guess we'll be back in plenty of time to catch the train tonight."

Audra looked at Robert. "The train has to wait for us."

So his attempt to engage her in conversation fell flat. He'd better find the charm somewhere or tonight would be a long one.

The cars pulled in back of the theatre and deposited the performers at that entrance. The stone façade befitted a building set on Pennsylvania Avenue. Audra climbed from the car and then pirouetted, a look of wonder on her face. "Do you think we'll have any time to see the monuments?"

"Maybe." Robert watched her delight. "Have you been here before?"

"No, but I've always wanted to see the sights. If I could catch a glimpse of the Supreme Court…" She stopped abruptly. "Well, it wouldn't matter."

"Let's see if we can't find time after the show to take a quick taxi tour. You've come this far. Seems a shame to not at least wave to Mr. Lincoln and drive by the Court."

A faint smile curved her delicate lips. "I'd like that."

"Then let's get inside, make the show a hit, and break away for a few moments of freedom."

As soon as they entered the backstage area, chaos reigned. Sets, curtains, props, and costumes cluttered the area, yet it pulsed with the energy of performers eager for their shot to wow a live audience.

"This is nothing like the movies." Lana walked backstage, a look of fear warring with excitement.

"You'll be great. Remember they all think you're a star already."

"Thanks for that ridiculous pep talk, Robert." She shook her head and walked away.

When would he learn? Leave her alone. Don't respond. The pain only deepened when he looked up to find Audra's gaze on him. What must she think of the mess with Lana? Not too highly of him. No one from outside Hollywood could understand how artificial the world was. Maybe he should forget about taking Audra on a tour of the city. Who was he kidding? A tour of D.C. at night evoked romance. And the last thing he wanted—should want—was romance. He groaned. He knew the thought he didn't want romance was a bald-faced lie.

Audra moved upstage, and a shadow followed her.

Robert squinted. Maybe his eyes deceived him. Why would someone follow her? But as he watched, the shadow stuck a hand in a coat pocket. The shadow pulled something out, something that looked like a gun. Pointed at Audra.

CHAPTER TWENTY-ONE

The backstage world formed a confusing maze. Everywhere she looked, Audra saw ropes, pulleys, people, and acres of sets—some for tonight's show but others left from previous performances. Mark had sent her off to locate Jim Collins. At the rate she traversed the theatre, she'd be lucky to find her way back to the main stage. Though she'd attended many theatre productions in Indianapolis, she'd never considered everything that happened behind the scenes.

A yelled word carried indistinctly above the din of activity. She paused but couldn't understand it.

She'd better concentrate and find the missing Mr. Collins.

It didn't matter that she'd get lost in a heartbeat. She needed to locate him and get back to the million and one other things on her list that must be accomplished before the curtain rose in two hours. At this rate she'd be breathless and still not done.

"Audra." The word was faint, but she stopped. As she looked around she couldn't tell who wanted her attention. In fact, she'd left people behind and was surrounded by abandoned sets stacked against the walls.

A footstep echoed off the wood floor. A shiver trembled up her spine. Surely whoever had called her name wouldn't sneak up on her. She couldn't let her imagination get overactive.

She took a deep breath and a few steps forward. Something bumped followed by a clatter of something falling. A muffled curse followed, and Audra shuffled behind a curtain. She felt oddly protected in its shadows even though its thick layers prevented her from seeing anything.

Words breezed past her, the voice muffled. "You think you'll save Audra?" A thud reached her, followed by a moan. She burrowed deeper into the curtains, praying they hid her and the tips of her shoes. Her heart tripped to a rapid beat until she thought she'd faint.

"This isn't a script from one of your movies. I'll get her and I'll learn what she knows about Rosemary."

Father, help me.

Rosemary's killer was on the train. There was no other reason someone would be here, now, mentioning Rosemary. Or did someone want to upset her? She hadn't hidden her interviews. It didn't take a genius to figure out what she wanted. Nor figure out how to rattle her.

Audra quivered and waited as the minutes slipped by. After what felt like an eternity, she eased the curtain to one side, half afraid of what she'd find on the other side. Only emptiness stood beyond the curtain. She shook free of the heavy brocade and eased through shadows down the hallway. Ahead a form lay on the floor. She hesitated a moment.

"Ohhhh." The groan barely reached her.

She slipped forward, slowing again as she neared. In the dim light she could tell it was a man. Based on the dapper outfit, could it be Robert? He moaned again, and she hurried to his side.

"Robert?" She rolled him onto his back. His left eye looked swollen and would need ice if he didn't want to sport a black eye the rest of the tour. She brushed a strand of hair from his eyes. "Robert, wake up. What happened?"

He opened his eyes and groaned again as they sagged shut.

Why hadn't she hurried from her hiding place? How seriously

injured was he? It looked like just his eye, but what did she know about things like this? "Come on, Robert. We've got to get you up." She added a cajoling tone to her words. "You know Mark's in the throes of a fit, wondering where his star emcee has gone."

Robert's eyelids cracked; he started to push up then sagged back down. "That smarts."

"I imagine. Can you sit up or should I get someone?"

He groaned again then gingerly touched his cheek. "I need a minute." He swallowed then seemed to pull reserves of strength from deep inside. "How long until the show starts?"

"About ninety minutes."

He struggled to a sitting position and closed his eyes again. "I'll need some aspirin and an ice pack. And a bunch of pancake makeup."

"Maybe you should see a doctor."

He started to shake his head then stopped abruptly. "No, the show has to go on."

"Why were you back here?"

"Following you."

Audra frowned. "Why would you do that? And that doesn't explain your bruise or being knocked out."

"I saw someone following you. Whoever it was didn't look like they had honorable intentions." He frowned as if holding something back then staggered to his feet, leaning from left to right like a palm tree swaying in the breeze. "We need to get back to the others."

"Are you sure you should move?"

"I have to. We've got a show. I'm not going to let whoever did this keep me from my job."

"Then lean on me, and we'll get you something for that eye."

* * * * *

Robert leaned against Audra's slight frame. The thought of getting near her had crossed his mind over the last few days, but he'd never imagined it happening like this. His head pounded, and he knew it would take a miracle for him to do his job. Coffee, ice, and aspirin would have to be sufficient. And somehow he had to find a quiet place to tell Audra about what had happened. She had to understand she'd been in real danger.

He glanced at her, seeing a cloud shadow her delicate features. "How did you find me?"

"I heard something. After hiding like a ninny, I finally came out and saw you."

"So much for being a knight in shining armor. I don't remember them getting knocked around when trying to rescue the damsel."

"You were trying to protect me?" Audra supported him as a wave of dizziness rolled over him.

"Yes. I saw someone following you with what looked like a gun. Guess I wasn't as stealthy as I thought. He turned on me and bashed me in the face with a quick hook. I fell down on the job." Robert straightened, bearing his weight, relieved to find the fog lifting from his mind.

She paled as she searched his face. "Thank you." He could almost see the kaleidoscope of images that must play in her mind at his words. Pictures that had been impossibilities before her sister's death. She touched his cheek, her fingers light and cool against his skin. "I'm glad you weren't hurt more seriously."

"That makes two of us." He eased away from her. He needed some distance between them if he was going to stand on his own in an hour. Might as well get started now, no matter how good her soft touch felt. He tried to shake the thought from his mind. He needed to focus, but his brain felt muddled, and her presence took what little was left and shook it to bits. He slowed his steps before they reached the main stage. "Audra, I'm not sure what's going on, but be careful. Someone tried to sneak up on you tonight. I'll stay close, but I'll have to be onstage."

She looked at the hive of activity, tugging her lower lip between her teeth. "I guess I'll stay close to you, Victoria, and the other gals."

"Be careful not to wander off on your own, or let Mark send you on an errand by yourself. I don't like the fact that someone here tried to threaten you."

"I don't either." Her fear now held a tinge of annoyance, but that was okay. As long as she took him seriously.

The closer they walked to the main stage, the more the buzz of activity accelerated.

"Where have you kids been?" Mark stormed up to them. His brow knit and his torso thrust forward. "Now is not the time to sneak away. The show starts in seventy minutes." He cocked his head to the side as if trying to see Robert better in the dim light. "What happened to you?"

Robert opened his mouth, but Audra spoke first. "He ran into someone who was following me. We need to get a steak or something on his eye before it swells shut."

Mark shook his head. "Let's get him to Dalia. Maybe she can work some makeup magic. But if your eye swells shut, you're pulled." He stomped off. "Of all the lousy timing…"

Robert forced his back to straighten as he followed Audra toward Dalia's workspace. Curious gazes followed them. "This will be fun to explain."

"Let's focus on your eye and the show right now. Later we'll figure out what happened and what we should say, if anything."

Another sign his brain had been muddled by the punch. He should have thought of that himself. "Something to drink and some aspirin. That'll help."

Dalia swooped up to him. "My, my, my. You go lookin' for a fight?"

"It came hunting me."

"Well, let's see what I can do." She um-ummed and shook her head. "It's gonna take some magic to keep yous from lookin' like you fell on the losin' end of a bar brawl. Sit."

Robert collapsed in the folding chair then accepted the glass of water and swallowed the aspirin Audra gave him. He leaned back and allowed Dalia to place a poultice of some sort on his face. It smelled foul but soothed deep into his sore eye.

"Buddy, what did you get into?"

Robert cracked an eye to find Winston standing over him. He licked dry lips, considering what he should say. Like Audra'd said, best to leave things vague. "No time to get into it. Run over the line-up with me again."

"Whoever did this must have rattled more than your pretty mug." Winston frowned. "Good thing there's lots of space between you and most of the audience. You'll be the bad boy of Hollywood if too many people see you with that shiner."

"It can't be too bad yet. Just tell me my face looks swell."

"Sure." Winston chuckled wryly, running a hand over his hobo hat.

The next twenty minutes passed in a blur while Winston filled his ear with the agenda. Dalia hovered over him, working on his eye. A soothing coolness spread from his eye to his cheek the longer the poultice stayed in place. Maybe he could hide the damage for one night. Show business didn't stop for a black eye.

No, what really concerned him was the uncertainty of who had cold-cocked him. The shadows had made it hard to get more than a fleeting image of a large man sneaking up on Audra then rounding on him in an instant. He should have been prepared, hands up to defend. At the least he should have tackled the man first, but he'd hesitated.

Whoever had hit him had packed a wallop. Maybe mystery man had used the gun? He'd said something to Robert as Robert had faded into darkness. Something about Audra. The uncertainty of what had been said ate away at Robert. His sense that he needed to stick close to Audra, protect her from whoever didn't like her investigation, solidified.

Someone didn't like Audra's questions and drive for answers. Robert didn't like where that reality left him. Someone on the train had something to hide about Rosemary's murder. While his fellow travelers likely had secrets, he didn't want to imagine which one had something to do with Rosemary's death. Now he had no choice.

"Fifteen minutes to curtains."

The activity outside Dalia's door pushed to a more frenzied pace.

"Out of my way," Quincy shouted as he raced by. His shirttail hung out and a layer of pancake makeup waited to be blended on his face.

Robert eased Dalia to the side. "Thanks. This will have to work. Time for me to finish getting ready for the show, and I know others need your help."

Dalia held him by the shoulders a moment and looked up into his face. She nodded curtly after a moment. "It'll do. Yous be careful, Mr. Robert. Come see me in the mornin' and I'll see what else that eye needs."

Robert stood, relief coating him that his head didn't spin. The aspirin must have taken effect, and now he'd manage to emcee the show. He walked to the men's dressing room, found his clothes waiting on the rack, and pulled on the tuxedo after slipping out of his jacket and pants. It had seemed over the top in Hollywood, but tonight as he slipped on the tuxedo, it looked great. He straightened the bowtie in the mirror and then examined his makeup. In the bright light, all looked fine. If anyone looked too closely, they'd see a shiner developing, but whatever potion Dalia had applied had delayed the effects and would keep the audience from noticing.

Now to protect Audra while keeping the show moving.

If only he knew who on the tour waited in the shadows, poised to harm Audra.

CHAPTER TWENTY-TWO

The murmur of an audience settling into its seats hummed backstage. Audra held her clipboard and felt useless. The actors and stagehands seemed to know their individual roles precisely.

Rosemary had always glowed when she talked about the theatre's chaos.

Audra stood there, all thumbs, in the way and inept.

"Audra, over here." Mark's sharp bark pulled her from her thoughts. Pre-show jitters had given her boss more prickles than a porcupine. She stepped over ropes lining the floor. "I need you here. Line the performers up. Follow along with Robert and send them in at the right time." He seemed to sense her nerves because he halted a moment. "You can do this." He turned away, and she vaguely heard his next comment. "Or you'll be on the next train home. Artie owes me for hiring that dame. What does she know...?"

Her spine stiffened at his words. She might not have any theatre experience, but she could follow an outline.

She stepped back into the flow of activity. In moments, her energy surged as she issued orders.

"Curtain goes up in ten minutes. Time for final touches."

People who five days ago were strangers now did what she said. Victoria Hyde strolled past, wearing a rich sapphire gown that emphasized her curves without looking melted to her like Lana's gowns.

Annabelle played with a fake flower pinned to the waist of her flowing gown. She would look like Cinderella dancing across the stage.

Audra studied the rundown of acts. She'd watched the hodge-podge of practicing and wondered what the total package would look like. The show kicked off with Robert welcoming everyone, and then Victoria would sashay out to join him for some witty banter. Next came the first skit with Quincy and Lana. She hadn't seen much of their skit yet. Just enough to know it should be a crowd-pleaser.

Victoria rolled her neck and then her shoulders. "I wonder if it ever gets easier."

"Performing?"

"The live audiences. Movie sets are completely different from the stage."

"Did you…" Audra's words died as Robert walked by. Her heart stopped at the sight of him in the tailored tuxedo. Dalia had somehow made the time to perfectly iron and starch the pleats down the front of his shirt. Audra swallowed and tried to pull her attention back to what she'd meant to say, but the thought had abandoned her.

"He looks swell, doesn't he?" Victoria winked at Audra.

Color rushed up her cheeks. "Yes, he does. Good thing I'm not an in-betweener or I'd swoon."

Victoria laughed. "He's worth it. Robert is different from many men around Hollywood. There are good eggs, but a lot of smelly ones too. It's too bad Lana broke his heart and ruined him to women." She shrugged. "I'd better find a glass of water."

Audra glanced at her watch then startled. It was time to get Robert on the stage and get the show on the road. "Robert?"

He turned, his smile dazzling her. "Yep?"

"Go find your mark. Mr. Feldstein will wave you on any moment."

He nodded, and Audra searched his face for any sign of tension. The only one she spotted came when he stuck his hands in his pockets and coins jingle-jangled. He must have noticed, because the noise stilled and he pulled his hands out. "Nervous habit. Thanks for the reminder."

"Here, give me your coins. I'll hold them for you." He gave them over, and she cupped them in her hand. Their gazes locked and she swallowed. "You'll do great." How could he not? With his dark good looks, any woman in her right mind would adore him. And all the men had to do was open their checkbooks and wallets. She looked at her list. Victoria stood in the wings, ready—as Audra expected. Based on the line-up and lack of Quincy and Lana, she'd better hunt those two down. She'd spotted the Lester twins off left stage, ready and waiting to go on at their time. "I'll be back." She looked down at her clipboard again, uncertain what to say. Without thinking, she stepped closer and leaned up to kiss his cheek. "Good luck."

Charlie Lester ran a finger inside his large polka-dot bowtie and made a show of fanning his face. "Whoo-whee. Do all of us get a smack before going on stage?"

Danny wolf-whistled. "Better check your cheek for lipstick, Garfield."

Easing away, Audra felt mesmerized by Robert's gaze. He studied her, and his serious expression collided with her muddled thoughts. Did he regret her unchoreographed move? She tried to clear her mind with a tiny shake. "I need to go—somewhere."

Victoria touched her arm lightly, and the spell broke. "Slide on out of here. Robert and I are set." Her words sounded innocent, but a tone of something underlay them.

Had she encroached on some relationship?

Shuffling backward, Audra tripped over a rope and then spun and hurried from the area, cheeks aflame.

* * * * *

Robert rubbed his hands together as he stood behind the curtain, waiting for it to part. He inhaled deeply then rubbed his wet palms down his pant legs. Show time.

But his mind kept turning to Audra and this crazy day.

Between her peck and the punch he'd taken earlier, he could hardly string one thought to another. And he had to string the entire show together.

Lord, help me.

He hadn't felt this out of his element since he'd signed his first studio contract. And that for a walk-on part.

This fell into a different ballgame. New ballpark. No, it was a different league altogether.

A shadow moved beside him. The light floral scent Victoria Hyde wore announced her before she spoke. "What was that all about?"

He shrugged and shoved his hands in his pockets. Mark hadn't reappeared, so he must have at least a moment to pull his head back in the game. "I've got to get ready."

"I'd say." Victoria shook her head. "You know I like you. And I like Audra. But this—whatever it is between you—it's sudden."

"Peck him on the cheek, Tori. He's on a roll with the ladies." Danny cackled at his joke.

"Yeah, enough already." Robert longed for one moment to let the others know what he really thought of their shenanigans.

Instead, Victoria reached up, her gloved hand sliding down his cheek lightly. "You had a dab of color." She winked at him and stepped back, leaving him alone at the center of the stage.

Robert straightened his shoulders and tried to imagine what Cary Grant or Jimmy Stewart would do to prepare for the moment. Even Humphrey Bogart's style would work at the moment. Suave. Cool. Collected. That's exactly what he needed to portray. Not some bumbling kid who grew up on the vaudeville circuit doing whatever stunt would get the audience to laugh. That didn't fit the image he had to build and maintain.

Mark walked by, tapping him on the shoulder. "Ready?"

Robert nodded.

"Curtains." Mark hurried off stage.

In one smooth motion the red velvet curtains whisked toward the vaulted ceiling. Well-heeled men and elegant women filled row after row of seats. Some of the ladies' hats were so large that Robert wondered if anybody would be able to see around them.

He strode to the standing microphone and nodded to the left then the right. "Good evening, ladies and gents. Welcome to the Hollywood Victory Caravan. We're thrilled to begin this jaunt across the country here in our nation's capital."

Hoots and hollers filled the air from a section of seating loaded with G.I. Joes.

Robert smiled and shook his head with a wry grin. "And you boys haven't even seen the girls yet."

More whistles erupted.

"Not only will you hear some whiz-bang singing, you'll also get the chance to see some bang-up Hollywood stars entertain you with their feet and a little acting. Quincy Cambridge. Victoria Hyde. The Lester Twins. Royce Reynolds. Lana Garfield." Robert had to wait as shouts and hollers erupted at her name. He kept the composed smile on his face. "You think any of these folks can bring a little light to your night?

"Let's get this show started."

Victoria peeked out from around the side of the stage. "Yoo-hoo."

Robert made a show of looking around before stopping, hand over his heart, at the sight of her. He pointed at his chest. "Me?"

"Of course, big boy." She glided onto the stage, elegant as a ballerina. She'd swept her brunette hair up in some kind of twist. The tongues of the boys in uniform were practically lolling out of their mouths.

"How can I help?"

"I'm looking for a spot to sell some war bonds. I started in Hollywood but seem lost."

"I'd say you've taken a detour."

She walked along the edge of the stage, hand shielding her eyes as she searched the audience. "You think I can find a place?"

"These good people look like they're eager to help you out."

"Then I'd better find my supplies."

"Supplies?"

"Photos. Pen. Lipstick." She puckered her lips and kissed the air.

"Whooeeee." Robert fanned his face and watched as she sashayed offstage. He swept the audience with his gaze. "And the show's barely begun." He rubbed his hands together. "Just wait until the end of the show. If you're ready to meet any of the stars tonight, make sure you buy your war bonds."

He hurried from the stage as a couple of stagehands ran on with a table and two chairs. Quincy brushed past him, dressed in tennis clothes with a dashing jacket thrown on for good measure. He looked ready for a country club. A woman in the front row sat up straighter. Robert eased into the curtains, keeping an eye on the stage while wondering where Audra had disappeared.

Lana hurried toward the stage, her cheeks flushed with color.

Robert stepped in front of her. "Everything okay?"

"Someone's been through my things." She sucked in a breath and then eased it out. "Out of my way. I need to get on-stage before Quincy forgets this isn't a monologue."

She straightened her navy skirt then walked with mincing steps on stage. Her hips swayed like a metronome, and Robert averted his eyes.

Audra hurried by, and he stopped her with a light hand on her arm.

"Can I get you something?" The words were polite, but Audra looked harried.

"Do you know anything about someone getting into Lana's things?"

Audra looked down at her list, a frown clouding her face. "No. I'll try to check on that—when I catch a moment."

"Okay." The Lester twins hurried up, ready to rush out the moment Quincy and Lana finished their skit.

A roar of laughter erupted from the audience. Robert glanced out, surprised to watch Lana sway as if caught in a gust of wind. The star never faltered. Instead, she was a performing machine.

She hurried off-stage the moment the skit ended, not even taking a moment to soak in the audience's applause.

Gene Costos and Annabelle Kelly swept onto the stage, moving past the Lester twins. The twins watched with thunder-struck expressions and the local orchestra hurried to flip their music sheets. Challenge number one of live theatre without enough rehearsals. Audra hurried up, a dark expression on her face as she glanced toward the stage then back at her rundown.

"What do I do about them?"

Robert shrugged. "Let it go for now, and make sure the Lester twins are ready to zip out. After the show will be early enough to deal with the confusion. Look at the crowd." He gestured toward the stage, and Audra's gaze followed. "They're entranced."

Annabelle mesmerized in a flowing dress that swayed around her in a lyrical manner with each beat of the music. The audience settled back as the two pros danced in a beautiful style. The twins relaxed, arms crossed over their chests, waiting for the next opening to get on the stage.

Lana staggered backstage, looking out of breath and drained. Before he could stop her, she pushed into the dressing room she shared with a couple of other women. The door closed but not before he heard a loud crash followed by a bang.

CHAPTER TWENTY-THREE

The music reached a crescendo as Gene and Annabelle tapped off the stage. The Lester twins hurried out before anyone else could slip in front of them. Audra wiped her forehead with Robert's handkerchief, the one she'd had since that fateful flight to Hollywood. She glanced at her run-down to see who should stand ready for their act.

"Did you hear that, Audra? The crowd loved us." Annabelle squeezed Audra into a quick hug.

"Just keep showing me that style and the next movie is ours. Move over, Fred Astaire and Ginger Rogers. It's time for the Gene and Anna-belle Show." Gene squeezed the blonde to his side and then led her down the hall with a quick dance step.

A door banged open, and Dalia ran out of Lana's dressing room. "Lawd have mercy. Mizz Garfield just dropped. Weak as a newborn kitten."

Audra spun to hurry into the room, but Mark stopped her. "Keep the acts moving. The audience can't know anything's happened. And get everyone back to the original line-up."

Glancing at the assembled performers, Audra waved them away from the dressing room door. "I'm sure she'll be fine. Next up are Con-stance and Frank. Let's hear all the high notes, Constance." The group dispersed slowly, the women taking a second or third look back, hesita-tion and fear painted on their faces.

Constance gargled some water then spit it out. "This is terrible."

"What do you mean?" Audra picked up the pitcher and sniffed it. She couldn't smell anything unusual. "It's just water."

The singer looked like she was winding up for a fit, something Audra didn't have time to figure out now. She grabbed a passing stage-hand. "Johnny, can you get Constance a fresh cup of water?"

The young stagehand jumped to comply and hurried back with a cup. Constance accepted the cup and swallowed the water then handed the glass back to him. She warmed her voice over an octave. A couple of the notes quavered and she frowned. "Nerves. More water, Johnny."

Audra chewed on the end of her pencil. The dance number was about over. She had to get Constance prepped to run on stage. "One minute."

"I can't go out there. Not before I run another octave."

"Doesn't matter. You'll have to do that as you waltz on stage. Come on, Frank, take her with you."

"All right, baby cakes. It's show time." Frank swept Constance onto his arm and marched her to the curtain. Johnny hurried back with the cup of water.

"Thanks, Johnny, but she's already on stage." Johnny walked off with slumped shoulders. Audra eyed the pitcher then found a clean glass and poured some water in it. After a sip she decided nerves must be bothering Constance since there was nothing wrong with it.

The Lester Twins hurried behind the curtain, Charlie rubbing his hands together. Audra gave them hand towels from a stack resting on a table.

"Thanks. That audience was really following us tonight." Charlie grinned and fanned his face.

Danny slugged his brother in the shoulder. "It's me they like, you big lug." The grin splitting his face took the sting from his words.

"You two'd better get changed. Your next number will be here before you're ready if you don't hurry."

The brothers bickered good-naturedly as they hustled to a dressing room. There didn't seem to be much activity coming from Lana's dressing room, so Lana must be okay. Audra wanted to check on her but felt tugged in too many directions. A creaking note in Constance's song yanked Audra's attention back to the stage.

Johnny rubbed an ear. "With a voice like that how'd she get on the tour?"

"First night. She'll smooth it out."

The strains of the song wafted to the last notes, the saxophone carrying the melody as Constance's voice collapsed. She barely waited for the curtain to fall before hurrying toward the dressing room, a storm cloud developing on her features. She stopped in front of Audra. "Tell me Mark didn't hear me sing. Please."

"I didn't see him."

"I'll die if he sends me home." Constance's eyes were huge in her face.

Audra smiled at Constance while waving the next act on. "He wouldn't do that."

"You don't know Hollywood or the rumors about that man." Constance hurried toward the dressing room she shared, her wails carrying back to Audra.

"What a diva," Winston Portland muttered while waiting for Robert to finish his shtick so the now dapper fellow could hurry out with his little skit based on the day's headlines. The man had abandoned his hobo costume for the role of professor. He'd scoured at least half a dozen papers, circling headlines and throwing wadded-up sheets in heaps around him on the floor of the theatre.

Dalia hurried from the dressing room, her hips swaying as she jogged.

Audra hurried up to Dalia. "Is Lana all right?"

"Smellin' salts worked like a charm. She got herself a headache from collapsin', but she gonna be good as new in the mornin'."

"That's a relief."

"Sho 'nough. I gots to get her somethin' to munch." Dalia hustled into the labyrinth of rooms.

Robert waved Winston onstage, and Audra's mind spun as she watched the buzz of activity. So many people coming and going, overlapping, yet she'd kept them straight and organized so far other than Annabelle and Gene. And the longer she spent time with them, the more she hoped none was involved with Rosemary's death. Nagging suspicion lingered from that afternoon's attack.

Rosemary would have loved every moment of this tour. From the time she'd stepped on the train, Audra had known the wrong Schaeffer sister worked the caravan. Now, as the chaos of the first show proceeded, she felt the bleakness of missing Rosemary cloak her.

* * * * *

"Now, Winston, rumor has it you're something of a professor." Robert angled his stance so that both of them could keep their bodies open to the audience.

Winston made a show of examining his coat, his pockets, even his tie. "I'm not sure what you mean."

"You're a student of history."

"On occasion. Especially if she's blond—about this tall"—he held his hand up to his chin—"and only a year or two older than me."

Robert did a double-take. "I'd heard more in the-study-the-headlines kind of way."

"Oh that." Winston straightened his bowtie. "I guess I'll accept that title if you think the coeds find it attractive."

The audience tittered while Robert stared at him. Winston was supposed to comment on headlines, not the female population. Had he seen all the uniforms in the crowd and decided to alter course? If so, how could Robert pull the interplay back to current affairs? Guess he and Winston would have to talk more before the next show. "While women are fascinating…."

"You bet they are." A soldier stood up a dozen or so rows back. "In fact, why don't you bring a few more out here. We'd rather watch them than you two."

Several men hooted and clapped. "That's what we like."

Robert folded his arms and pivoted away from Winston. "Sounds like they've got some opinions, Mr. Professor."

Winston shrugged and gestured like he was making a note on his hand. "Next time I'll bring someone with me."

"Make sure she's prettier than you, with Betty Grable legs," a soldier hollered at them, hands cupped around his mouth.

Robert shook his head and gave in to a grin. "Well, for now, professor, why don't you fill us in on the headlines?"

A groan rose from the men in the audience while Winston moved into his planned routine. In a few moments, he had them eating out of his hand, laughing and snorting as he rattled off jokes like a Bob

Hope in training. Robert had to admit, Winston had a humorous take on the headlines as he moved from topic to topic. But as he stood just off stage watching the audience, Robert knew much work remained. The haphazard nature of the caravan and its program needed to be smoothed out to ensure the audience got the polished performance they anticipated.

Robert imagined Mark would crack the whip on the train until they reached their next stop. It wouldn't take long to get to Norfolk and the naval installations near there. Not enough to give them down time to polish the acts.

The audience roared.

"That's telling it." A man's voice shouted approval above the crowd.

What had Winston said that tickled their funny bones? Maybe Robert should take notes. The man had a comedian's sense of timing.

Winston bowed then hurried off, and Robert squared his shoulders before walking back on stage. A woman in the front row looked at him expectantly.

Robert laughed and shrugged. "Don't know if I can top that, folks. So instead of trying, let's get the next act out here. Are you having a good time? Enjoying yourselves?"

The roars of approval and clapping could have lifted the roof from the National Theatre.

"All right. That's what we like to hear." Robert clapped along for a moment then stepped back up to the microphone. "I think you'll like this next act. These gals sing in a way that makes you think you're in heaven."

"Do they look like angels?" A man in the fifth row stood up and searched behind Robert.

"Yes, indeedy." Robert stepped back and motioned to the curtain. "Put your hands together for the McAllister sisters."

The three beauties jitterbugged onto the stage as Robert exited. The soldier in the fifth row clasped a hand to his heart and sighed dramatically. "That's more like it. Look at those dames!"

"Ah, be quiet." The airman behind him tugged the sailor down.

Soon the girls sang in a style reminiscent of the Andrews Sisters. Sweet harmonies wove around the auditorium and then they switched to another jitterbug number.

Robert turned and collided with Audra. He reached out to steady her. "Sorry about that."

"I guess I was distracted."

"The show's going well."

"Yes, but I haven't seen Lana." Audra's gaze darted to his ex's dressing room and back. "Her next number is coming up in a minute, and I have a feeling the audience will get antsy if they don't see her soon."

"It's not like she's Kate Hepburn."

"True. But she's the female headliner for this tour." A lock of her hair tumbled in front of her eyes. Robert considered brushing it behind her ear, but she did, before he could act. A pang of disappointment shot through him.

"Why don't you go check on her?" Robert reached for her clipboard. "Who's up next?"

"Jim Collins act. And then Lana and Royce."

"Then go find her. Lana's not a lot of things, but she is a professional. She'll do her part on the caravan." The pucker between her eyes told Robert that Audra didn't believe him. "Trust me on this. She'll make it work."

Audra nodded. "I don't have much choice. Does she snap people's heads off?"

"Only husbands'."

Audra scurried down the hallway. Robert watched her until she disappeared from sight. It wasn't like Lana not to be primed and ready when it was her time to appear before an audience or camera. She lived for the spotlight. No need to worry Audra about that. Lana would be fine. She always was. She had more lives than the proverbial cat.

Jim Collins hustled by.

"Hey, wait a minute, Jimmy."

The stout man stopped and turned with a frown. "No one but my mama, God bless her, calls me Jimmy."

Robert held up his hands. "Sorry. Just needed your attention. Soon as this group stops singing, you're up."

"I know. Too bad Winston sucked all the laughs out of the audience."

"Don't believe that for a minute. You have the touch. You'll have them eating out of your hand."

"I hope so. Do I ever." A bead of sweat trailed down his forehead.

"Better see Dalia and have your makeup touched up." Robert clapped Jim on the shoulder. "And hurry back. You've got three minutes by my count."

CHAPTER TWENTY-FOUR

The dining car rocked as the performers decompressed from the show. Audra sat at a table across from Robert, trying not to be disappointed their planned tour of D.C. had evaporated with Mark's shouted orders to return to the train as soon as the war bond sale ended. He'd been so abrupt she wondered if he'd feared losing stars on the D.C. streets.

Robert had looked like he wanted to sit next to her when he followed her onto the dining car, but Elizabeth McAllister slid in beside her before he could. Audra tried to cover her disappointment, especially since she was a fool to think anything could develop with Robert.

Watching him today, her first impression had been reinforced. His star would rise again. When it did, he wouldn't look to a nobody from the Midwest for companionship. Even if he might, the studio would line up the perfect starlet.

She'd do well to guard her heart. No matter how encouraging he looked, nothing was destined to develop between them.

Between that and the earlier attack, she couldn't shake a glum mood. She resisted a tremor at the thought someone had tried to harm her earlier. While she'd wanted to get to know some of the people Rosemary had known, she'd never really expected to find Rosie's killer. But after the attack, it appeared the killer was here, maybe even in this very car. Right now.

Nobody else shared the fearful direction of her thoughts. Instead, the performers talked over each other in their excitement. They quickly filled plates and cups from the refreshments Mark had the porters prepare. Even Dalia sat in a back corner enjoying the general excitement while keeping a close watch on Lana. Fortunately, the star had continued to improve, just as Dalia had predicted. Other than an underlying paleness, she carried herself with her customary elegance.

"Did you see the people lined up to buy war bonds?" Constance bounced on her seat.

"What a beauteous sight. Yes, sir!" Winston rubbed his hands together. "I think we'll be the talk of this town for a while."

"Maybe we should stay another day, Mark. Imagine all the bonds we could sell since people will talk about the show." Frank did a quick tap dance move. "We only thought people packed the theatre tonight."

Mark shook his head. "You must not have seen the show I did." He leaned against the bar and rapped the top with his knuckles. "We've got a trainload of work to do before we're ready for Norfolk. I've got half a mind to cancel tomorrow's appearances. The radio shows can wait. But rehearsals can't."

"What a wet towel." Winston brushed the air in front of him. "You're sucking the fun from this trip. Making us working stiffs."

"Besides, I signed on for those appearances, and I'm probably not the only one." Lana puckered her mouth in a pretty pout. Audra shook her head. She could try for a hundred years and never pull off that look without appearing petty and put out. "Last time I checked I wasn't getting paid for these weeks on the road except in publicity."

"She's right, Mark." Royce snuggled closer to the pale star. Lana pushed away, but he ignored her, almost pinning her to his side. She shot him a pointed look but stopped resisting.

Was everything all right there?

Maybe Audra should check. That is, if the star would let her.

Mark shook his head. "This is about more than you and your publicity, Lana." His gaze included every performer in the car. "We've got to give our best…"

"The 'it's your duty' line is getting worn, Mark." Quincy plunked a few keys on the piano, the discordant notes making Audra cringe. "We're all performers, stars on the rise…"

"Or fall." Danny Lester jumped in. "It's no secret some of us have to make this work or we might as well stay in Atlanta or some other city. Hollywood won't have much to offer us if we can't entice the studios to believe the public loves us."

"The audience seemed to eat out of your hand tonight, Danny." Constance put her hand on his leg and grinned at him.

"That's just 'cause they knew the sooner we got off, the sooner you and the other gals would get back on stage." He shrugged. "It's the same everywhere. Charlie and I aren't pretty faces like Quincy and Royce. If we can't make people remember our slapstick, we're done."

Charlie nodded, his red curls bobbing. "It's a dog-eat-dog world out there. Five people standing in line to take our spots."

"Some will fight for it, while others wait in the wings." Danny crossed his arms.

Quincy played a couple of chords. "You two might as well hop off now. Even Robert is more entertaining than you."

Robert glowered at Quincy. Charlie had always seemed so unmoved by everything, but now he looked rattled by the criticism.

Audra reached across the table, placing her hand on his. "Don't let him get to you."

"Aren't you sweet." Audra moved her hand at Lana's acerbic comment. Guess she felt like herself again. "I don't know, Royce. Wasn't Miss Schaeffer's sister more attentive to you gents?"

Audra bristled at the mention of Rosemary. She started to stand, wanting to ask Lana what she meant. The abrasive, snide tone had every instinct in Audra on alert.

Robert restrained her with a slight shake of his head. "She's not worth it." Still there was a worried pinch around his eyes.

"In fact I'm pretty sure I saw her around town with most of you. That Artie knows how to keep a girl busy while she waits for a contract. No idleness on his watch." Lana's smile was tight and mean.

Audra flashed back to Rosemary's black book where Robert's name had been prominently displayed along with several other men on the train. She shook off his hand, uncertain what to think about him or any of the other men. Her head hurt as she considered the images that everybody seemed to paint about Rosemary. She couldn't believe them. She knew Rosemary, the sweet kid before she boarded the train for Hollywood. Certainly a locale alone couldn't change a person as radically as the picture they all tried to fill in for her.

"Lana, you are so full of hot air." Royce leaned against the cushion. "You know it didn't mean anything. To any of us."

His words didn't make Audra feel better about the implications.

Lana stood with a languid stretch. She tightened her hold on the ever-present stole then brushed a hand along Mark's arm. "Hollywood can be a tough place unless you know people's secrets."

Mark stared at her then stepped to the side. "Sit down, Lana."

She met his gaze, chin tipped at a defiant angle. "After I get a drink."

Silence filled the car as she sashayed to the bar. Audra propped her forehead on her hand. Robert's strong fingers rubbed her elbow, his touch sending electricity racing up her arm.

"All right, folks. Enough sniping. We're all working together on this." Mark ran his hands through his hair. "I swear you are worse than toddlers. Mine, mine, mine." He shook his head. "It doesn't matter. We've got work to do."

He led them through the agenda. Audra held her clipboard in front of her and made a note or two, but couldn't part the fog that had descended. Her hopes of finding her sister's killer seemed foolish in light of her growing list of questions.

She should have waited in Hollywood or traveled home with Rosemary's body while waiting for answers from Detective Franklin.

Maybe he'd learned something.

In the morning, she'd call him and then let her parents know she was okay.

The trial her boss had offered her would be run by someone else in two weeks. With it, her opportunity to move from assistant to attorney slipped away. All on the foolish hope she could do something the police couldn't. If she'd hurried back to Indianapolis after identifying Rosemary, the opening might have still existed. But no, she had to believe she could do something the professionals couldn't.

A tear slid down her cheek, and she startled. She swiped it, hoping no one had noticed.

Robert's solemn gaze rested on her, almost as if he could read her mind.

Heat flashed up her neck at his scrutiny. She dropped her hands to her lap and tore her gaze from his. She couldn't be undone by him.

Elizabeth leaned in to her. "You okay?"

"If you don't mind…I need some fresh air."

"I know what you mean." She winked at Audra. "All this hot air in here…it takes it right out of a gal."

Audra nodded and slid from the bench. She brushed by Robert, ignoring his outstretched hand. The door at the rear of the car opened, and she sucked in a lungful of fresh air. A light breeze played with her hair as the train eased down the tracks. They must still be in the city or suburbs since they weren't moving like they would in the open country.

Audra turned her face toward the stars, fatigue warring with fear. How would she ever explain to her parents the awful things people like Lana insinuated about Rosemary? Her parents would never believe their precious daughter did those things. Maybe she didn't need to tell them and could let them retain their image of Rosie.

What options had Rosemary had?

Hollywood was a bleak place. Harsh and exacting. Short on opportunities and long on expectations.

Just look at the people on the train.

Each of them had talent. From her estimation, a great deal of talent. Yet they were the second or third tier in Hollywood. This caravan wasn't loaded with the talent and star power of the first caravan. If a tragedy befell this train, Hollywood would keep right on doing what it had done for twenty years: churn out motion pictures filled with stars.

And all the wannabes like Rosemary would keep right on dreaming in vain of someday joining those who routinely saw their names in lights.

"God, it's not fair." Audra balled her fists as her eyes searched the stars. "How could You let that happen to someone as innocent as

Rosemary?" She drew in a jagged breath, pain pounding her chest. "I was supposed to protect her but didn't."

The door opened behind her, and she jabbed at her cheeks, wiping the tears from them.

"You okay, Audra?" Robert's rich voice tore at her. She wanted to trust him, but he'd been in Rosemary's book. Was he any different than the rest of the men in there?

"I'm fine." She kept her face pointed toward the sky, praying he couldn't see her well in the shadows.

"You sure?" Robert took a step closer until she could feel the heat of his body. "The professional woman I know wouldn't leave a meeting in the middle. Not when she had a job to do. Not when Mark will wonder what's going on."

"Maybe I don't care about that anymore."

"Not buying it." Robert wrapped his arms around her waist. Audra stiffened, unsure what to do, how to respond. "You care too much to just walk away." He tugged her around until she had to face him. "Ignore Lana. She takes perverse pleasure in getting under people's skin."

Audra searched his face, wanting to believe him. "Why did you follow me?"

Confusion flashed, replaced in a moment by indifference. "I thought we were friends, and friends take care of each other."

"Is that what you did with Rosemary?"

He dropped his arms from her, and a wave of cold washed over her.

"Is that what you think?"

"I don't know." Her accusation echoed through her mind, leaving her heart hollow. "I don't understand anything that's happened." She closed her eyes, bracing for whatever came next. Somehow she would accept whatever it was.

A finger traced the contour of her cheek. She allowed herself to lean into the stroke for a moment then stiffened against the rush of emotion.

"You still don't get it, do you?" He cupped her cheeks and she opened her eyes to be captured by his gaze—and the sensation she could see straight to his soul. And despite her doubts, she saw nothing hiding in the shadows. Instead, his clear eyes studied her. "I've done nothing, Audra. As much as possible in Hollywood, I've lived a life that honors Christ. You can search and hunt all you want. Aside from that disaster of a marriage to Lana, you won't find anything I'm ashamed of. And if I learned anything from that experience, it's that I need to submit every decision to Christ's authority, not some studio's and certainly not mine." He stroked her cheeks and then took a step back and released her. "But nothing I say can convince you. You'll have to decide whether you believe me. I promise I'm not the enemy."

Did he protest too much? Her mind swam. She so wanted to believe him, but none of this could be real.

"Life isn't a fairy tale."

"What?" He leaned in as if to capture her whispered words.

"Nothing. I have to go." She slipped past him and crossed to the next car. The no-man's-land where only the women were supposed to go. It didn't stop many of the other men, but as she entered the car, she knew Robert wouldn't follow. Her heart sank at the certainty of that truth and how much she wanted him to come after her.

CHAPTER TWENTY-FIVE

Early morning, Thursday, June 18, 1942

The night blanketed her berth in heavy shadows and silence. Only the rocking of the train and clack of the wheels on the tracks surrounded Audra as she struggled to settle into a restful sleep. But every bump and turn pulled her back to wakefulness.

Finally, exhaustion won the battle over the noise.

A shriek and loud thump. Another thump.

Audra jolted up in bed. The distant stars provided the only light that penetrated the darkness of her berth. Even their faint twinkle felt cold in the darkness.

What had woken her?

Audra rubbed a hand across her eyes, trying to decide whether to lie down or get up. The middle of the night. She should sleep.

She began to lie back down, when she noticed something move along the floor, blocking the light trickling in from the hall.

Nothing good could come of someone sneaking. Must be another man trying to get to one of the starlets. Her mind on high alert, Audra reached for her robe and slipped her arms through the satin sleeves. She stepped into her slippers and prayed that whichever man thought he could slip past her to the women's berths would accept her correction easily. She didn't feel up to fighting. Not when most of the men were larger.

"Why did I think I could protect another's virtue?" She cracked open the door but saw no one in the narrow passage. She listened, but only the creaking of the car swaying on the tracks reached her. A door slammed, and she jumped. "Good heavens." Audra took a deep breath and tried to calm her racing heart. If she wasn't careful, she'd see evil in every corner.

She crept down the hall to the door that led to the dining and lounge cars. Nothing appeared through the misty fog outside that the train trudged through. The reverberation of a door closing carried across the distance. Even when she squinted, she couldn't see anything, so Audra turned from the door back to the hall.

Someone had been here. Even if she had doubts, the faint scent of musky cologne alerted her.

Audra tightened the robe's belt at her waist and gathered the satin at her neck.

Regardless of whether the intruder had disappeared, she needed to check on the performers. Make sure everything was okay. The challenge came in doing it without annoying everyone by waking them. From the silence that surrounded her, she might be the only one awake.

She passed her door then paused at Victoria's.

Silence.

Surely all was fine. Audra shivered and considered returning to the warmth of her little bed. No, she needed to at least walk the cars. She slipped past Constance's and Annabelle's berths. Nothing out of the ordinary reached her ears. All seemed as it should in the middle of the night.

As she passed the empty berth before Lana's, a low moan reached her ears. It sounded like the mew of a kitten struggling for breath.

Audra peeked her head into the empty berth, but seeing nothing, hurried to Lana's door and tapped on it.

"Lana?" She waited a moment then knocked again. "It's Audra. Is everything all right?"

That low sound came again. A tremor crept up Audra's spine. She moved to open the door but froze. What if this was like her sister's bathroom? The image of that poor woman filled her mind until she forced it away.

"Move, Audra." The words sounded loud and harsh, even though she barely whispered them. If something were wrong, she'd never forgive herself for standing in the hall like a ninny. After all, Lana hadn't told her not to enter. She pushed on the door, expecting it to resist her efforts. Instead, it moved at her light touch.

The barest shadows etched the room. Faint light from the hallway projected Audra's silhouette on the floor. She swept the room with her gaze. Lana didn't move from her position on the bed. Yet as Audra moved closer, nothing looked right.

A faint gurgle echoed from Lana, and Audra rushed to her side. Lana had slipped halfway off the bed, one arm thrown to the side at an awkward angle. Her scarf, which should have been wrapped around her curls to protect them as she slept, was askew and seemed wrapped around her throat. Audra reached for the fabric and loosened its silky hold on the actress. It slid to the floor in a pool.

"Lana?" Audra felt her cheek then touched her shoulder. "Please be okay." Panic welled through her. This couldn't be happening. Not again.

Help. She needed to find help.

How could she do that without abandoning the poor woman?

Torn, Audra rushed to the door then back to Lana. "I'll be back. I need to send someone for help."

Lana's eyelids fluttered, and then she opened her eyes. Her lips trembled, and Audra knelt beside her, leaning in.

"Yes?"

Lana mouthed a word. Robert?

Audra stared at the star's lips. That horrible gurgle came again. "I have to get help, Lana."

She rushed to the door and down the passageway. Who could she trust to do something more than shriek? Victoria? Audra rushed to Victoria's door and tapped on it before twisting the knob. Locked as it should be. "Victoria? I need your help. Now."

A moment later the lock slipped, and a sleepy-eyed Victoria cracked open her door, pulling out her earplugs. "What is it?"

"Lana's been attacked. Please go get Mark, the conductor, somebody. She needs a doctor. Immediately." Audra heard a gasp behind her and turned to see Constance clutching her robe.

"What happened?"

"Lana's been hurt." Constance gasped as Audra rushed to speak before she could wake the other girls. "Go get Dalia, please." When she turned back around, Victoria had shimmied into a dress and was buttoning it up. "Thank you."

Without waiting to see who else had heard, Audra hurried back to Lana's room, brushing past several people. What could she do to help the star? How she wished she'd taken any of the Red Cross classes offered in Indianapolis. She'd never had the inclination to serve at a hospital. Now—too late—she knew the value of that training.

"Lana, I'm back." She hurried to the star's side, watched her chest, but saw no movement. "Come on, Lana. You can't leave us. Not like this. Come on, honey, breathe." Audra pressed two fingers to Lana's throat. The silky fabric of the star's navy negligee brushed her fingers. Why would she be dressed like that? Especially when the rules said no fraternization?

Fear skittered over Audra. Earlier she feared she'd made a terrible decision by joining the caravan since she was no closer to finding her sister's killer.

Now as she stared at Lana's limp body, fear of another kind climbed her.

It was now undeniable that she was locked on a train with a killer.

And the only word Lana had mouthed was *Robert*.

* * * * *

Pounding feet echoed off the hall floor. Robert struggled from the depths of a dreamless sleep. Frenzied activity filled the area outside his berth as doors slammed open and shut and hushed conversations filtered to him. Robert sat up and ran his hands through his hair. He wouldn't return to sleep unless he saw what was wrong and if he could help. He felt along the floor for his slippers then put them on. Stumbling to his feet, he waited a moment until his body recaptured the rhythm of the moving train.

In two steps, he stood at the door and cautiously opened it.

His eyes popped open when he saw Victoria standing in the hallway fully clothed. There was no good reason for her to be on this side of the lounge car. "Victoria, what brings you here at this hour?"

She turned around and worried her lower lip between her teeth. "Someone attacked Lana. Audra sent me to get help."

"What?"

Victoria rubbed her hands up and down her arms as if chilled to the bone. "Mark needs to move, though. I got the sense it was serious."

"I'd better come too." He turned to grab clothes but stopped when she touched his arm.

"Are you over her, Robert? You need to be prepared…"

Robert swallowed against a sudden lump that formed in his throat. "She successfully killed any loving thoughts I harbored toward her."

Victoria looked at him then nodded. "I'm heading back. Bring Mark with you."

"Be careful." Maybe he should make her wait the couple minutes until he could escort her. He had to assume something terrible had happened, especially after the theatre attack. And if it had happened to Lana, it could to anyone. Despite her acerbic need to belittle others, he couldn't think of a reason anyone would hurt Lana. "Wait for me."

She looked at him then nodded.

Robert hurried to his suitcase and pulled out a pair of khakis and tennis shirt. After shrugging them on, he stepped into the hall. "Did Mark go by?"

"Finally." Victoria fell into step behind him. "I don't know what took him so long."

"Slow dresser." Robert kept his eyes open as they hurried from car to car. Hours earlier the train had been filled with good-natured competition and camaraderie. Now, every shadow seemed nuanced with evil. He needed to rein in his imagination until he knew for sure what had happened. "How's Audra?"

"Shaken, but holding it together." Victoria trembled next to him. "Can you imagine?"

"No." He couldn't embrace the idea that something horrible had happened on this trip. And that Audra had to find Lana after everything else she'd already endured.

They pushed through the lounge car and into the first women's car. Performers huddled outside the first berth.

Constance rushed to them. "Victoria, where have you been? It's just terrible."

"I can't believe she's gone. Like this." Annabelle brushed tears off her cheeks. "She might not have been my favorite person, but murdered?" Horror etched her words and dropped into Robert's thoughts.

"Murdered." The word slipped off his tongue. Lana had been so vibrant earlier today. Even after the show she'd seemed to have recovered from whatever ailed her during the program.

He moved past Victoria. A need to see for himself if there was anything he could do propelled him forward. He brushed past the other women. Eased toward the doorway everyone seemed intent on avoiding. Stilled when he saw Audra leaning against the frame. Defeat slumped her body over, curls brushing her cheeks. This was too much for one person to handle. He approached her, hands shoved in his pockets, longing to pull her into an embrace and shelter her from what she'd seen.

"Audra?"

She looked up at her name. Her face crumpled as if relieved to see someone she could trust. That relief quickly disappeared from her face. Replaced by something darker. Something questioning. Something hard.

Where she'd looked at him with trust—even just that evening—now bleakness edged her expression. The questions in her eyes shot through his heart and left him wounded. As if somehow he'd betrayed the hope and trust she'd placed in him.

What had she seen or heard that left her questioning him?

A flare of anger erupted in him. Lana had to touch everything good in his life and destroy it. Even in death she'd managed. Again.

Stomping on his heart and hopes hadn't satisfied her. No, she'd successfully spent the last year killing his career. And now this.

He didn't know what to do, other than refuse to walk away.

CHAPTER TWENTY-SIX

The pain in Robert's gaze flailed Audra. She braced herself against the wall. It was too hard to know who to trust.

Robert.

One word. Mouthed on dying lips. And with it, everything she thought she knew about Robert shifted. She hadn't felt so alone and surrounded by unknown danger since discovering the body in Rosemary's flat.

She closed her eyes and wished she could return to Indiana before all this horror occurred. Rosemary would be safe. She'd be in her job preparing for a new challenge. And her heart would be empty. She opened her eyes and saw Robert still standing in front of her. "What is going on around here?" Mark's panicked voice registered as he stomped toward them.

Robert glared at him. "Where have you been?"

"Around. Someone tell me what's going on."

Audra gestured to Lana's berth. "We've got to stop the train."

"No can do." Stubbornness edged Mark's tight stance.

"I think the conductor would disagree. We'll need the police, and I don't want to think what else." Audra closed her eyes against the thought of what would need to be done with Lana's body.

Mark stepped past Audra and Robert into the berth. He stared a moment then hurried back out. "You're sure she's dead?"

Audra stared at him. "You didn't check? I couldn't find a pulse when I came back. I don't think there's anything that can be done, but we should try—just in case." A shiver traveled over her at the thought. Robert placed a hand on her shoulder, and she forced herself to step away. Place some distance between them. The cold inside her settled deeper as she did.

Mark crossed his arms as if considering what he should do. Shouldn't that be easy to determine? "All right. I'll inform the conductor. Ask how he wants to proceed." He glanced back in the room. "Who's been in there?"

"Just Dalia and me."

"Where's Dalia now?"

"She headed back to her car. Seeing Lana upset her terribly." The woman had been nearly hysterical, as if somehow she had caused the death. Audra should check on her. See if there was anything she could do to console the sweet woman.

"I suppose so." He considered her a moment. "Guess none of us imagined this scenario when we signed on for the caravan. Robert, keep everybody out of the room until the conductor gets back here. Let's keep everyone in the lounge car. I can't imagine the headlines this will generate." He walked away, shaking his head, then gathered the starlets and other performers, taking them with him.

He stalked out of the car, marching like an officer given a distasteful task.

She knew she should leave Lana as she was until the police could arrive—whenever that would be. Yet it seemed in terrible taste to leave her sprawled like she was. Couldn't she at least cover Lana with a sheet or blanket? She stepped into the room that now had the stillness of a viewing.

"I'm so sorry I didn't get here in time to stop this, Lana." A tear trickled down Audra's cheek. She might not have formed a fast friendship with Lana, but she still couldn't imagine anyone wanting her dead. The malevolence required by this act staggered her.

"I don't think you should be in there." Robert stood in the doorway, uncertainty puckering his brow.

All the emotion she'd suppressed for weeks pushed to the surface. "I have dealt with more gruesome deaths in the last weeks than any person should in a lifetime. She should be covered, not gawked at like some horrible carnival sideshow."

And maybe if Audra took a quick glance around, she'd see something that pointed to the killer. Either way, she would not leave Robert alone with the body. Not if there was even a chance he'd harmed Lana. As much as she didn't want to believe it, she had nothing to point away from him yet.

Robert eyed her warily, as if wondering what would slip past her lips next.

She sighed. "Look, I hope someone would have given Rosemary this simple courtesy if they'd found her on display like this." She trembled as grief washed over her again. "This is a nightmare."

Robert nodded, his gaze settling on his ex-wife.

"I'm sorry. This must be hard for you too. Even after everything."

"It's hard to comprehend. She was so full of life."

"I know." Audra slipped the white sheet over Lana, watched the folds of the fabric settle over her face.

After a moment she looked up and found Robert watching her in the reflection of the small wall mirror. A haunted look cloaked his eyes as he searched her face.

"I didn't have anything to do with this." He said the words with conviction, but she had to remember he was an actor. One whose star would go far once the studios again matched him with the right roles. Could she take his words as truth? Or should she continue to guard her heart and mind from trusting him?

So little here was worthy of her trust.

She couldn't forget she'd met him in Hollywood, an artificial town.

Audra scanned the room. The space was comfortable, but really too small for entertaining. "Who would Lana let into her room?"

Robert shrugged, shoving his hands in his pockets and shuffling from side to side. "She didn't necessarily maintain the same standards you would. Lana embraced everything about Hollywood from the party life to the freedom from morals."

He stepped into the room and the space seemed to shrink. She wondered if she should be afraid since Mark had taken the others to the lounge car, but she wasn't. She might be a fool, but she couldn't find anything threatening in his posture. Or his invasion of the small space.

No, all she could think as he stepped closer was that she felt safe and protected.

She took a deep breath and tore her gaze from the mirror.

With that movement her thoughts cleared. She scanned the items in the small room. Clothes exploded from a suitcase thrown on the floor, and cosmetics spilled across the small table beneath the mirror. Perfume bottles mingled with the powders and leg makeup. Even stars had to sacrifice their silk stockings. She took care not to touch anything as she looked.

A thin black volume sat among the tubes. "Do you think anyone would mind if we looked at that?"

"If she were alive, Lana would have a fit. She's carried a book like that as long as I've known her and never let me look inside. Must contain her deepest, darkest secrets."

Audra arched an eyebrow at him. "That's what I'm hoping." She picked it up and flipped through the pages. It looked like a regular datebook. "Rosemary had one of these." Audra watched Robert out of the corner of her eye, waiting for a reaction.

"Nothing unusual about that. Most people carry one. Surely you have one in Indiana, filled with appointments and dates to keep."

"Loaded with activities." Audra turned another page and found it filled with names and phone numbers.

Robert reached for the book and flipped through the pages quickly. "She certainly kept busy." Robert closed the book and placed it back on the counter. "Don't you feel odd doing this while she's laying there?"

"When else will we get the chance?"

"Maybe that's the point. We're not supposed to do this."

Audra walked toward the small bathroom then stopped. Nothing seemed out of place. Audra backed from the doorway and walked into a hard, firm surface. Arms reached around her, to steady her, and she shrieked.

"It's me. What's wrong?" Robert's voice was modulated, meant to soothe her. But it did nothing of the kind. Instead, the knowledge that his arms were the ones encircling her caused a well of panic to bubble inside.

Robert.

He couldn't have killed Rachel Gibson in Rosemary's apartment. She knew that. Not when he'd been trapped inside the same plane she traveled in.

Yet his name kept appearing—tied to dead women.

Audra pulled out of the circle of his arms and backed to the hallway. "Did you know Rachel Gibson?"

He stared at her as if wondering if she'd gone mad.

"Did you know Rachel Gibson?" Her volume climbed as she waited for him to respond.

He put his hands up and backed away from her, stopping when he neared the bed. "I don't know who you're talking about."

"The girl found in Rosemary's flat." Her breath hiccupped and she stepped into the hall, trying somehow, some way, to reel in her emotions. "Just tell me. Did you have something to do with her?"

"I don't know. I may have met her. What did she do?"

"What do you think? An aspiring actress like every other girl who finds her way to Hollywood. Only, unlike Rosemary, she was ready to leave. To walk away from her dream." Audra took a step back. She had to get away. Put distance between her and this man and the body.

But first she needed an answer. The simple truth. "Did you kill her too?"

Robert furrowed his brow and a cloud formed on his face. His stance tightened as he studied her. "That's crazy. I didn't kill Rachel or anyone else."

She wanted to believe him. But nothing had been as it seemed since she reached that God-forsaken Hollywoodland.

The train braked, and Audra stumbled in an attempt to maintain her balance. She cracked her head against the wall, and her vision doubled before she sank into oblivion.

CHAPTER TWENTY-SEVEN

"This train is cursed. Lawd's sakes, it surely is."

Audra heard the words, mumbled in Dalia's sweet Southern drawl. "Dalia?"

"Yes, ma'am. Praise the Lord you's with us still."

Audra cracked an eye and peeked at the large black woman, who cradled Audra's head in her lap. "You had me fair worried. Yes, indeedy." She patted Audra's cheek. "The smelling salts done their work."

"Where am I?"

"I had Robert carry you to my room so's I could keep an eye on you. You ready to get up?"

"I'll try." Audra closed her eyes and took a deep breath. Other than a pounding in her head, she felt fine. Her thoughts traveled to Lana. "That poor woman."

"I knows it." Dalia's jowls drooped. "Someone evil is on this train."

Audra couldn't disagree. With Lana's murder, she had to believe evil followed her steps. Maybe she should distance herself from the train before anything else happened.

"That won't make no difference to nothin'. This ain't got nothin' to do with you, child."

"Are you a mind reader now, Dalia?"

"No, ma'am. Don't know what you mean. I's just answerin' ya."

Audra realized she had spoken her thoughts out loud. "Then I'm more addled than I thought." Audra pushed to a sitting position then looked around the small room. It was hidden in shadows and, from what she could see, looked like all the other berths she'd visited on the train. "Why are we stopped?"

"The conductor takin' care of Mizz Lana's poor body."

"Of course." Audra rubbed her forehead, praying her thoughts would cooperate. Lana. She needed to make sure the killer didn't do anything to change the evidence the police would find. "How long was I unconscious?"

"Long enough we's in the next town. I don't know what y'all gonna do."

"I imagine the show will go on." Audra shuddered at the thought.

"Hollywood sho can be cold sometime."

"Maybe."

"I hope you's wrong."

"Me too, Dalia. Me too." Audra slowly stood, keeping a hand firmly on the mattress. To her surprise, the room didn't spin. "Your smelling salts worked well." She turned to hug the woman but stopped at the tight lines around her eyes. The easy peace that normally surrounded Dalia seemed to have abandoned her. "Are you all right?"

"No, ma'am, I'm not." Dalia opened her mouth then firmly closed it.

"None of us is okay right now. Is there anything I can help with?"

The woman shook her head, her kerchief slipping forward a bit on her forehead. "I'll be just fine. You see to Mizz Lana. She was a misunderstood woman, yes, she was."

Audra took a step toward the door then paused and collapsed in the small chair tucked in a corner. "Why does God let evil win, Dalia?"

"It don't in the long run. Remember, we knows who wins at the end."

"But the last few weeks it hasn't felt like He's winning. I'm certainly not."

Dalia shifted her girth on the bed. "But we gotta look with our hearts' eyes, not what we can see. If we goes only by what we see, we miss God. His fingerprints is all over this world. Someday we gonna understand this. Yes, ma'am, someday we gonna understand."

"How can you be so sure?"

"He promised though we sees through a glass darkly, one day that gonna change. These weary bones looks forward to that day. Um-hmm."

Audra considered her words. She'd chew on them later. "Well, thank you for caring for me." Audra hugged Dalia then slipped from the room. She crossed the bridge between cars and hurried toward Lana's berth. It had become a hive of activity. Robert and Mark stood on the outskirts watching several uniformed police move in and out of the room. Audra looked for an unfamiliar man in suit and tie. He'd likely be the detective in charge, but she couldn't find one. Maybe he'd already slipped inside or had yet to arrive. There was only one way to find out.

"Audra! You're all right." Robert hurried toward her, relief lighting his eyes.

"Yes. I'm surprised Mark hasn't chased you off to the lounge car with everyone else."

"The police were waiting when we arrived at the station a few minutes ago. They asked me to stay until the detective arrives." He brushed her cheek, and warmth spread from the caress. "Are you sure you should be up?"

"If I've learned anything in the last few weeks, it's that the police will want to talk to me." Audra sank into his touch, unable to stop herself.

"Then let's get you settled so you can rest until he arrives."

"If they'll let me through."

"Wait here." Robert left her and hurried to one of the officers. After a hushed conversation, he returned. "You're cleared. We just can't talk to the others until the detective interviews us. Let's get you something to drink."

She followed him to the lounge car, surprised to see the light of dawn beginning to break on the horizon as they walked between cars. She stopped, letting the sun's first rays soak into her heart. *His compassions are new every morning.* She'd read the promise many times in her Bible. But this morning, after all that had transpired in the night, she clung to the promise. She sensed she'd need all the compassion she could get to make it through the day.

A bird sang nearby. She flinched. "It's Thursday, right?"

"Yes." Robert studied her curiously.

Audra gripped the railing and held on tight. "This afternoon is Rosemary's funeral." Bile rose in her throat and she trembled. A sob almost choked her as she tried to hold it back. Robert wrapped his arms around her and she clung to him. "I should be there, but I couldn't watch my baby sister be buried. I just couldn't do it."

He stroked her hair, each touch sending a shiver of comfort through her. "Your parents understand."

"It doesn't matter. When this caravan ends I'll return to Indianapolis, and then I'll have to face the truth. Even if I find her killer, Rosemary will still be dead. My baby sister will still be ripped from our family. And I'll always wonder how much of what I've learned is true about her." She muffled her sobs in the soft fabric of his shirt. "How can I ever forgive myself for not doing more to make sure she was okay?"

His hands stilled then moved to her shoulders, where he pushed her only far enough away to look into her eyes. "Audra, you cannot accept the lie that you are responsible for Rosie's death. She was an adult who chose to move to Hollywood. The actions she took after moving out there were her responsibility. Not yours."

She knew he was right, but somehow her heart couldn't accept the truth.

He wiped the tears from her cheeks then hugged her. "Keep reaching for God. He'll show you the truth."

Before she succumbed to the darkness that thoughts of the funeral brought, Audra nodded and tried to smile. It felt fake and taut on her cheeks. A hum of voices trickled from the car in front of her. "Is everybody in there?"

Robert nodded, his blue eyes solemn. "They'll probably be awhirl with gossip."

"And want me to add to it."

"Likely."

"They'll be sorely disappointed."

"I think they've noticed your propensity to ask questions rather than answer them."

Audra released her breath slowly. The truth in his words hit her. She'd need to be careful, especially after Lana's murder. The murderer, whoever it was, didn't feel the need to hide. She soaked in the sky another moment then nodded. "Let's go."

Robert leaned in front of her and opened the door.

"There she is. The woman of the hour. So how'd you do it? What a woman, taking out her nemesis. " Danny Lester stood to his feet and swayed, even though the train didn't move. How much alcohol had been consumed since the performers had been secluded in the lounge car? The piano remained silent in its corner, but it looked like at least some of the stars had made use of the small bar.

Audra settled into the first vacant booth, ignoring Danny and his words.

Royce looked like he'd tried to drown a lifetime of sorrows as he slumped forward over a table. Constance had snuggled next to him, but he seemed oblivious to her presence. Frank had an eagle eye on the pair, though. Audra could only imagine what he thought of Constance.

Victoria sat on the piano bench, fingers playing with the keys. When she caught Audra's gaze, she stood and hurried over. "Are you all right? I can't imagine what you've gone through tonight. On the heels of Rosemary. It's too horrible to consider. And ignore Danny. He's deep into his bottle."

A numbness settled over Audra. She didn't know who to trust. As she sat there, staring at the woman she'd begun to consider a friend, she fell mute.

Trust Me.

The words reverberated through her heart. A lifeline from a caring God. One she needed to connect with at a deep and desperate level. So little of her life made sense. At the moment nothing was turning out as she'd imagined or planned. Instead, her carefully constructed life, filled with intentioned moves and steps, had spiraled out of control.

She didn't like the feeling. Not one little bit.

Father, You have to show me what to do. Who to confide in. I'm flummoxed and uncertain. So uncertain.

"Audra?" Concern laced Victoria's words.

As Audra considered the woman, she knew she could rely on her. No matter how crazy and confusing life had gotten, God had planted a friend in her life. Gratefulness welled inside her, spilling out as tears on her cheeks. "It's been an unimaginable night."

"I'm so sorry." Victoria said the words, but they echoed in the shadows filling Robert's eyes.

Audra sensed he would have spared her finding Lana if he could. "We'll get through somehow."

"They don't think she died of natural causes?"

Audra considered Victoria's question. Could she state with certainty that Lana was murdered, or had her over-stimulated imagination gotten the best of her? "I really don't know."

A delicate shiver vibrated across Victoria's shoulders. "It terrifies me to think someone on this train killed her. These people are our friends. At least I thought…"

"I guess it shows you never really know someone." Annabelle leaned into the threesome. "Mind if I join you? This whole situation gives me the willies." She slid onto the seat next to Robert and leaned against him. "You'll protect us from whoever did this, won't you?"

Robert shuffled as far away from her as he could before nodding.

The door to the car opened, and Audra looked up to find a man wearing a suit striding inside. He stopped and observed the assembled group. When all conversation stumbled to a stop, he clasped his hands behind his back. "I'm looking for Miss Schaeffer. A Mr. Garfield as well."

Audra clenched her fists on top of the table. Could she endure another interrogation? It didn't really matter, since she had little choice in the matter. Robert placed his hand on top of her fists. She laced her fingers through his and studied their hands. This time she wouldn't be alone. She settled back, exhaling quickly, and then pulled free. "We're here." She looked around the packed car. "Where would you like to talk?"

"Mr. Feldstein suggested the dining car."

Audra nodded. That made good sense.

The detective eyed the room. "We'll have a bit of privacy there, so the rest of you stay here until I call you."

Victoria and Annabelle slid off the benches, making way for Robert and Audra to stand. He placed his hand at the small of her back, a surprisingly comforting gesture. The assembled performers parted like the Red Sea as she and Robert walked through the car and onto the deck at the end of the car. The swirl of colors from the sunrise had evaporated, replaced by increasing humidity that signaled they were in the heart of the muggy South. Audra was relieved to cross and enter the dining car, leaving the humidity outside.

"Why don't y'all have a seat at the table? I'll interview you separately. But we can address the preliminaries together." The detective gestured to the nearest table. "This will do. My name is Earl Brown. I'm with the Williamsburg PD. Looks like y'all stumbled into some trouble on your trip."

"Yes, sir." How else to answer such an inane comment?

Audra studied Detective Brown as he pulled out a notepad and pen from an inner jacket pocket. Where Detective Franklin had been wiry, giving the impression he could chase down any criminal, Mr. Brown gave the good-ole-boy impression of someone who enjoyed his time at the local diner filling up on pie and coffee. His girth indicated a definite lack of interest in physical activity, and Audra hoped that inactivity did not carry over to his mental acuity.

"I'll begin with you, Miss Schaeffer. Mr. Garfield, you can wait over there."

Robert looked at her a moment, as if asking permission to leave her alone with the detective. "Do you want me to get someone?"

"I'll be fine. I've been through this before and after all, I am an attorney."

Mr. Brown's ears perked up at her comment. "Been through this before. What's that mean?" He shooed Robert away as he stared at her.

"My sister was murdered in Hollywood a couple of weeks ago. And I discovered a body in her apartment when I went there to check on her." She clasped her hands in her lap and planted her feet on the floor. "It's been a horrifying period."

"So I see." He made a notation on his paper. "Who was the investigating officer?"

"Detective Franklin with the Hollywood Police Department. I think it's imperative you talk to him."

"That so? Can I ask why a pretty thing like you would think that?"

"Because I believe these murders are connected." Audra braced for his disbelief.

He quirked an eyebrow and let his silence talk.

Heat crept up Audra's cheeks. "Call it instinct, but please talk to him."

The detective jotted down a few notes but remained silent.

Even though she knew his silence was meant to encourage her to speak, she couldn't hold her tongue. "I don't ask you to believe me. But

Detective Franklin needs to know about Lana's murder." She paused and licked suddenly dry lips. "If I'm right, then my sister's murderer is on this train." Should she mention Lana's last word? If she wasn't 100 percent sure about it? And if her heart knew Robert couldn't be the killer?

CHAPTER TWENTY-EIGHT

Mr. Brown asked quiet questions of Audra. Robert tried to read his body language from across the room. If he were right, the detective was a highly skeptical man. Was it simply because Audra was a woman or due to a cautious nature? Guess he'd find out when his turn came.

Robert studied the floor as he waited.

He knew the people on this train. Some from working together on movies. Others on a purely social level. Still others by reputation. He'd always thought he was a good judge of character. Now he wondered.

Yesterday before they arrived at the theatre, if a detective had asked him, he'd have sworn no one on the train was a murderer. Then Audra'd been stalked, he'd been attacked, and Lana had been murdered.

Someone on this train had killed his ex-wife. Who? And did it have anything to do with him? He couldn't imagine it did. He wasn't a threat to anyone. Not with a career in need of a rebound. Still, the question remained embedded in his mind.

He guessed, from Audra's reaction, this incident was tied to her sister's death. That made little sense. Rosemary had been a sweet kid, but she'd barely blipped on most studios' watch lists. A contract could have changed that.

Lana had arrived. In fact, if she'd told him the truth, she was ready for some big negotiations with a major studio. Sign a seven-year contract with one of them and her star was as good as embedded in front of Grauman's Chinese Theatre.

Could this have anything to do with a film she'd worked on or was slated to appear in? His head throbbed at the implications. He must really need sleep if he thought her murder was related to some silly piece of celluloid that didn't exist yet.

He was right back where he'd started with the firm conviction her murderer couldn't be anyone on this train. And the equally concrete reality that it was. It wasn't easy deciding which of his colleagues he didn't really know. And which one to point the police toward.

* * * * *

"Mr. Brown, I'm sorry, but I don't know what else to tell you." Audra rubbed the base of her neck, noticing the tension flowing from there to the headache pounding her temples. "I only met Lana a week, maybe two, ago."

The rotund man settled back in his chair, posture closed as he crossed his arms. "Did you have something against the lady?"

Audra bolted upright. "No, sir."

"Well, if I'm to believe you," he eyed her warily, "someone else did. And you or someone else is going to have to give me insight into all these hoity-toity types here."

"I'm not the right person to help you." She felt weighted to the chair, the sleepless night catching up with her in a rush. "I don't know these people. Any of them."

"Really?" The detective smirked behind his hand. "Tell that to Mr. Movie Star over there."

The man meant Robert. "You're quite mistaken about him."

"I doubt that. But regardless of what's between you two, speculation doesn't help me find a killer."

"Robert's the better person to ask. He's known these people longer than me." As far as she was concerned, she couldn't wait to end this caravan and abandon that scary little city in the desert. Her life had gone horribly wrong from the moment she boarded the plane to find Rosemary. She reined in her thoughts, focusing on the words whispered in her soul that morning. *Trust Me.*

She glanced at Robert sitting at a booth, alone, across the car, and knew she didn't really wish she hadn't journeyed to Hollywood.

"Miss Schaeffer."

Audra pulled her attention back to Mr. Brown. "Yes?"

"There's something I still don't understand. You were surrounded by women. Why not scream for help rather than look for it, leaving Mrs. Garfield alone. To die."

Audra toyed with the charms on her bracelet. The point of the cross pricked her skin. "I wanted to keep as many of the girls from panicking as possible. And I knew Victoria, Miss Hyde, would act quickly and keep her head. She's very steady that way." Audra took a breath and looked into Mr. Brown's eyes. "I had to make a judgment call. You might have done things differently, but it was all I could think to do in the moment." A tear slid down her cheek, but she steeled herself from more. She didn't need this man thinking she was weak with waterworks she could turn on at her whim.

He jotted a couple more notes. "All right. Tell me what you know about the performers."

Audra spent the next twenty minutes telling the little she knew about each person. "I'm sorry I can't tell you more. There was an incident at last night's performance."

Mr. Brown leaned forward on the table. "Really? Tell me."

"Mr. Garfield saw someone following me. Then he was attacked."

He studied her a moment. "That's it?"

"Isn't that enough? Someone attacked Mr. Garfield; he has a bruised eye to show for it. That person said something about me, and now Lana's dead."

"I don't know how that helps."

Audra sucked in a breath, convinced he thought she was an idiot. "I thought you should know."

"Anything else suspicious or odd?"

"No, sir." She paused as a thought came to her. "I know you plan to talk to Robert, but I think you should talk to Dalia as well."

"Who?"

"She performs many roles but is primarily the costume organizer and helps with some makeup and hair for the gals. She's been around awhile and was very upset about Lana's death." His eyes hardened, and Audra held up her hands. "I don't think for a moment that she was involved or killed Lana. She's a gentle soul. But she can give you insight into everyone on the train."

"I'll find out what I can when I talk to her." The investigator leaned back in the booth and reviewed his notes. "So this Detective Franklin. What do I need to know?"

"He's the lead detective. Seems to be good at his job." Though he hadn't found Rosie's killer yet. "Please call him."

"As soon as I'm done with the dozens of interviews." He tucked his notebook in his inner jacket pocket. "I think you should have crammed a few more people on board."

The door to the car opened, and Mark stormed inside the dining car. The officer stood to his feet, shoulders back and legs braced.

"How much longer do you plan to keep us trapped on this train?"

"As long as it takes."

"We've already waited over an hour."

Detective Brown reached in his pants pocket and pulled out a stick of gum. He carefully undid the silver wrapper and then stuck the piece in his mouth and chewed. "Um. That's good." He chomped a couple more times. "What was it you huffed in here about?"

"I've got restless movie stars. From Hollywood. And we've got a show to perform. Tonight. In Norfolk." Mark accented each staccato sentence with a stab of his finger.

"That's real nice. But here's what I've got. A body. A trainload of suspects." He looked around then shrugged. "And last time I looked, I was the only one here to interview everyone. Cool your horses. I'll get to everyone as fast as I can. Maybe you can rehearse or whatever it is stars do to prepare for their audiences."

"That won't work." Mark sputtered and thrust his shoulders back.

"It will. It's my body and my investigation."

* * * * *

The exchange had an unreal quality to it. Robert couldn't believe Mark was so focused on the performance, though the others would likely give the detective a hard time too. They had to wait cooped up in that lounge car. And hearing Mr. Brown call Lana "his body" made the blood rush to his ears. He felt offended for Lana.

Sure he didn't love her anymore. But no one deserved to be treated so callously after death.

"Can you hurry things along?" Mark spit the words out.

"I'll see what I can do." Detective Brown stood, chomping his gum several moments after Mark stormed from the car. Then he turned toward Robert. "Your turn."

Robert nodded and tried to keep his expression open and non-threatened. Should be easy since he was an actor. But the environment was one he'd never imagined himself in. "What can I help you with?"

"You were married to Mrs. Garfield, correct?"

"Was. She divorced me about two years ago."

Detective Brown slipped his notebook back out. "How'd you like that?"

"It wasn't what I'd planned, if that's what you're getting at. I never imagined my marriage wouldn't be a forever commitment. I learned that it takes two to make that work. When one is convinced it's over and out the door, you can't force them back."

"Get along well?"

"Honestly, no. We avoided each other, or I steered clear of her. We shared an agent, though, and both ended up here."

"Did you get along during the caravan?"

"So far, but we kept our distance. Nothing unusual."

"So it didn't bother you that she was spending so much time with Royce Reynolds?"

Robert startled at the quiet question. How did the investigator know things like that? "Lana and Royce were new, but he's not the first man she's been seen with since our divorce."

"And it never bothered you?" Brown shed his casual air and planted his elbows on the table. "You watched without flinching."

"Sure." Robert studied his fingers clasped in front of him. "I won't lie to you. I didn't like it at first, but I learned to let go of her a long time ago. She'd chosen someone else. A different lifestyle."

"Were you in her berth?"

"Not before early this morning after she was already dead."

"Did you have any fights or flare-ups on this trip?"

"No."

"Did you kill your ex-wife, Mr. Garfield?"

"No." Robert fought the urge to stiffen and cross his arms as the questions and accusations punched into him.

"You're sure there isn't something you want to tell me? Like the truth?"

"No." Where was he going?

"Then maybe you can explain how this got in her berth?"

CHAPTER TWENTY-NINE

Robert stared at the handkerchief. The square of cotton had his initials embroidered in the corner. He had at least a dozen like it sitting in a dresser drawer in his condo. "I don't know why she had it, but it could be a relic of our marriage. She was forever borrowing a handkerchief then. Maybe she took a few when she moved."

Mr. Brown stared through him as if weighing his next words. "The thing is, Mr. Garfield, this was clutched in her hand. When we examined her."

An uneasy silence settled between them. Robert had nothing to add but refused to look away from the detective. The shifting of another booth brought his head around. Robert's gaze collided with Audra's. The hooded look had returned, with questions almost visible on her face. She must have overheard Brown's question and his "presentation" of the handkerchief.

I didn't do it. He tried to communicate the thought to her.

She looked down and studied her hands. "May I leave now, Mr. Brown?"

The detective turned in his seat and studied her. "Yes. Don't leave the train until we're through."

"Yes, sir." She stood and slipped from the car without once glancing at Robert.

"So you were left to guard the body."

"Yes."

"Did you alter anything in the room?"

"I entered it, but I certainly didn't kill Lana or put my handkerchief in her hand."

Brown rolled his eyes. "Even movie stars aren't dumb enough to do that."

"Look." Robert leaned onto the table, boring into Brown's eyes. "The divorce wasn't my idea. I loved Lana, and her leaving was one of the hardest things that happened to me. I looked for ways to make it work, but she'd have nothing to do with me. We were not the best of friends. But the last thing I wanted was anything to happen to Lana.

"Having my ex-wife die on a train I'm riding?" Robert looked at his hands, trying to find the right words. "That makes me an automatic suspect. But you'd be better served spending your time looking for someone who hated Lana."

"Thanks for the investigation advice. Like I said earlier, I'll follow this investigation to the end. Wherever the evidence leads. Regardless of fancy words from an actor." Mr. Brown rubbed his short neck, studying his notes. "Tell me about the others on this train. Who might not like your ex?"

"I don't like to think any of them is capable of murder."

"Yeah, Eve didn't want to think that of Cain either, but he was." The investigator quickly walked him through the people on the train, Robert filling him in on the details he knew about each and how they interacted with Lana.

"You have to understand we didn't move in the same circles the last two years." It had been too hard to see her surrounded by other men.

"Sure, sure." Detective Brown tugged his rumpled tie then closed his notepad. "That's all for now. Do not, under any circumstances, mysteriously disappear from this train or caravan. I expect to be able to find you the moment I need you."

Robert nodded and pushed up from the table. Mr. Brown clamped down on his arm.

"Mind telling me what happened to your face? And don't bother with 'I ran into a wall.'"

Robert tugged his arm free and eased back onto the bench. "It wasn't a wall."

"No kidding."

"Someone followed Miss Schaeffer last night during rehearsals at the National Theatre in D.C. I didn't like the looks of things, followed, and got popped in the eye for my trouble."

"Really?" Brown hitched an eyebrow as he stared at Robert.

"Yes."

"Any ideas who did it?"

"None. It wasn't especially bright backstage and the man who approached stood in the shadows."

"A man. Notice anything else about him?"

"He was large and had a mean right hook."

"All right. I'll have to take your word for it. Now remember, don't leave the train. I will find you if you leave."

"I understand." Robert left the car. The humidity slapped him when he reached the car's platform. What had just happened? Did the investigator seriously consider him a suspect in Lana's murder? While he didn't like the idea that one of his fellow performers could have turned violent, the idea that the police believed he might have done it left him shaken.

Why had Lana had his handkerchief?

It had been two years. There was no reason for her to keep a handkerchief with his initials and certainly no reason to bring it on the train. If it didn't mean having to pass the inspector, Robert would march to his room and count how many were in his bag. Even then, he didn't know if he'd remember how many squares he'd packed. That would still make it his word against Mr. Brown's gut instincts and investigation.

He had no choice. He had to find Lana's killer before her murder got pinned on him.

Robert wiped the sweat from his brow and entered the lounge car. Whatever conversations had been in process stopped at his appearance.

"What's going on?" Quincy Cambridge pushed up from his position by the piano and marched toward Robert. "Audra didn't say a word and disappeared."

"Surely Mark told you something." After all it was that man's job to keep the caravan running.

Quincy snorted. "Sure. The man's a wreck. One of his biggest stars turns up dead. His future's finished in Hollywood."

"And I'm hoping mine isn't." Elizabeth McAllister quivered dramatically. "This is so terrible, and now we'll all have the black mark next to our names of traveling with Lana when she died." Her eyes widened and her voice dropped. "Or was murdered."

Mark rushed back into the car, his normally well-groomed hair running in all directions as if he'd run his fingers through it repeatedly. "Calm down. Nobody else is going to die. And we don't know for sure what happened to Lana."

"Then you ain't too bright," Danny Lester stage-whispered from behind his newspaper.

"Enough. Mr. Brown, the investigator with the Williamsburg police, is on his way in to talk to each of you. Just tell him what you know. Answer his questions. Et cetera."

"Don't we need attorneys present?" Royce asked the question with a bored air.

Robert shook his head. Royce had enough experience with the law to have received his law degree on the side. He certainly kept his studio's fixers busy covering up his extra activities.

"If you want to drag things out and try to find an attorney in a town none of us has visited before, be my guest." Mark raised his hands in a how-could-I-stop-you-anyway gesture. "As for me, I want these officers off the train lickety-split, so we can get back to business." As several gasped, Mark hurried on. "I'm as upset as you are Lana's dead. But there's nothing we can do for her other than cooperate with the police. Once that's done, the best thing we can do is finish getting ready for tonight's performance."

"You're not going to postpone even a day?" Frank Crosby eyed Mark like he had lost his mind. Robert had to agree with him.

"We've got a dozen stops in the next two weeks. I don't know about you, but all I want to do is keep this show moving so we can get off this train. It's our duty to keep going for the war effort."

The words might sound right, but Robert thought Mark threw the word "duty" around a bit loosely. It wasn't like they stood on the edge of a battlefield hearing the tanks and artillery pounding around them.

Constance crossed her arms and planted her petite frame in front of Mark. "There is no way I can do anything tonight. What if whoever it was had stumbled into my room instead of hers?" Her face crumpled and large tears rolled down her cheeks as she sobbed.

"Here, here, kid. It'll be all right." Frank pulled her into a rough embrace. She melted into his side as he stroked her hair. "We're all glad it wasn't you."

"Which one of you was glad it was Lana?" Detective Brown stood at the end of the car, hands planted on his hips, a glare affixed to his face. Somehow he'd sneaked into the car.

Several folks sucked in a deep breath at Brown's crazy question. Robert looked at him, flummoxed. Did he really think someone would answer his idiotic challenge? He didn't know which interrogation training the guy took, but it lacked finesse.

Mark gestured to the detective. "This fine gentleman is Mr. Earl Brown, a detective with the Williamsburg, Virginia, police department. As I mentioned, I encourage you to fully cooperate with him." Mark hurried toward the dining car, muttering under his breath.

"Hey, don't forget we need something to eat." Charlie Lester pointed at his stomach. Robert shook his head. So Mark wasn't the only one fixated on strange things.

"Good morning." Detective Brown nodded to the group. He seemed unimpressed with those standing before him. Robert wondered if Cary Grant would garner a reaction.

"It's practically afternoon, and we've waited a long time for you." Charlie's belligerence grew with each word.

"It's a pleasure to meet you too." Detective Brown chomped on his gum hard enough to make Robert wonder if his jaw hurt. "Mr. Garfield, you're excused, since I've already talked to you. I need a few minutes with each of the rest of y'all." He surveyed the group then pointed to Constance. "I'll start with you."

Constance stumbled from Frank and moved toward the detective.

While he ushered her to the dining car, Robert looked around for Audra.

"So what do we need to prepare for?" Danny asked Robert, frown lines appearing around his eyes.

"Tell the truth and you'll be all right." At least he hoped.

"You sound like my mother. Parroting words that don't really help."

Robert shrugged. "There's not much more I can say. Has anyone seen Audra?"

"She hurried off to the women's car." Victoria considered him, as if searching to see how he'd held up. "Would you like me to get her?"

He would but didn't want to admit it. "That's okay. I need some fresh air after spending time with the good detective."

Birds squawked when he stepped outside. Robert sat on the edge of the platform, his feet dangling over the side. He studied the piece of sky he could see between the cars, the bright sunshine vastly different from the star-studded velvet sky of the night. Leaning forward, he waited—not sure what for—but needing a moment of peace.

Father, what's going on? I don't understand any of this.

While he and Lana didn't love each other anymore, a part of his soul grieved her death. And to think the detective thought he might have done it, all because of a silly square of cotton. Disquiet grew inside him.

God?

The words of the Psalm he'd read the prior day trickled through him.

He healeth the broken in heart, and bindeth up their wounds. He telleth the number of the stars; he calleth them all by their names. Great is our Lord, and of great power: his understanding is infinite.

He needed the thought that God was there in his brokenness and grief. Lana's physical death was her second to him; God had already walked with him through the days he grieved the death of her love. *He healeth the broken in heart.* To think God cared about his grief. The very same God who called the stars by name. Far more of them than the stars that had ever been in Hollywood or would ever hope to ascend there.

While he couldn't begin to understand everything that had happened, God already knew. And He even understood the mixed-up, muddled emotions Robert felt.

He bowed his head and prayed. For Audra and all she must feel as she relived Rosemary's death and the horror of finding Lana. For the detective and officers to have wisdom. For the caravan to proceed with safety. And for the killer to be identified quickly, because until he or she was, Robert doubted anyone on the train was safe.

CHAPTER THIRTY

Did Audra need someone guarding her?

She shook off the idea. She wouldn't give in to fear. Instead, she'd stay close to others, especially Robert. That and a good night's sleep were what she needed.

But if Mark had his way, she wouldn't sleep for another twelve hours. It didn't matter. She had to rest. Collect her thoughts. Even if for a minute. She lay down on the twisted sheets and pulled the thin blanket over her. She'd close her eyes—just for a minute.

A tap pulled her from her doze. Audra opened her eyes and took in her surroundings. All was quiet. No side-to-side motion or clack of the train wheels against the tracks. The train must still rest next to the station or wherever it had halted. The sun still shone so she knew she couldn't have slept long. As she yawned, she knew it hadn't been long enough.

The knock was insistent this time. "Audra."

Mark.

She sat up and stretched. Her neck and upper back muscles bunched painfully. "Yes?"

"We need you in the lounge car."

"Five minutes."

"Why does everybody need five minutes? We don't have time."

"Good-bye, Mark."

She heard his huff as he walked away. Guess he'd won in his insistence to proceed tonight. He might be crazy. Did he really expect the performers to ignore what had happened to Lana? What a cold-hearted man.

Approaching the mirror, Audra grabbed a tube of lipstick and touched up her makeup. Then she tried to brush the wrinkles from her skirt. There was little she could do without time and an iron. She slipped on her pumps and left her berth. The policeman no longer stood outside Lana's berth. In fact, she didn't see any officers as she walked to the lounge car.

Gloomy faces greeted her when she entered the lounge car.

"The police have finally released us so we can finish the last little patch of track to Norfolk. From there we'll hop in a fleet of taxis and make our way to the theatre. We'll have two hours until the show if all goes well." Mark clapped his hands as if that made it so. "The show's at Loew's State Theatre."

"A movie theatre?" Danny Lester's lip curled.

"Why not on one of the military bases around here?" Charlie Lester crossed his arms.

"Don't worry. The locals call the theatre 'Dixie's Million Dollar Dandy.'" Mark turned to Danny, pinning him with a glare. "And don't forget we're here to sell war bonds, not entertain the troops."

"Can't we at least sneak close to them?" Constance twisted a strand of hair around a finger.

Frank frowned at her. "Ah, you just want to sneak a kiss."

"Maybe." She winked and blew the red-faced man a kiss.

The train jerked into motion and a few of the performers cheered. Audra reached for the wall to steady herself and, with the next jolt, fell against Dexter Snow. The wiry man pushed her upright and stepped to the side.

"Excuse me." Audra studied him, rubbing her side. Dexter hadn't said two words to anyone that she'd heard since he'd hopped on the train. Even now, he simply stared at her, a cold look in his eyes. She refused to be cowed by the rude man.

Conversation took off among the performers, reaching a dull roar as they talked in clusters. Mark slapped a table and whistled. The sharp sound brought a quick halt to the discussions.

"Enough. You have ten minutes to gather whatever you'll need for tonight. Dexter, I need to see you pronto. Audra, you too."

The dark-haired man gestured in front of him. "After you."

His deep voice wasn't what she'd expected from such a thin man. He looked like he hadn't eaten a bite in days. And his clothes looked disheveled, like he hadn't had the opportunity to have them properly cleaned or ironed.

Victoria stopped on her way out. "Ride with me to the theatre?"

"Of course." Audra imagined she'd need the time with a friendly face. And anything would be better than riding in a cramped car with the Lester twins or philandering men with wandering hands.

"Audra." Mark sounded exasperated as he waited for her.

"See you in Norfolk then." Victoria squeezed her hand then slipped from the car.

Audra approached the two men, waiting for Mark to tell her what he needed.

"We need to get Dexter incorporated. Any thoughts?"

Audra mentally ran down the schedule. "Well, he certainly won't be effective filling in for Lana in a love scene with Quincy or Royce." She must be tired to have said that out loud.

"A tad scandalous."

Audra blushed. "Of course. But I think Annabelle could fill in on Lana's bit for one of those. Then Dexter…I'm sorry, what do you do again?"

"Cut women in half."

The color rushed from her cheeks at his words. "In light of what's happened today, I find that repulsive."

Mark placed a hand on her arm. "Calm down, Audra. Dexter's a magician, not a murderer."

Dexter stiffened at the word. "I beg your pardon?"

"Look, it's been a long day already—and we're all on edge." Mark looked from Audra to Dexter. "Dexter, maybe you should watch the show tonight, and we'll figure out where to add you in at the next stop. In fact, it might be best to use you when we go to the different military stops or in the pre-show entertainment. We'll have to work it out."

Audra nodded. "That could work. None of us is prepared to think hard now."

"Then maybe I should hop right off this caravan."

Mark glanced at the pile of papers in front of him, dismissing the man. "If you wish…"

With a harrumph, Dexter turned on his heel and stalked toward the men's cars.

"Is he always so…"

"Pompous? Yes. Mr. Snow there believes he's God's gift to this caravan. Frankly, I wish he hadn't joined us. A magician? What on earth are we supposed to do with one of them? On top of everything else?" Sweat poured from Mark's forehead, and he fidgeted with the top button of his button-down. "Good night, as if I didn't have enough egos."

Audra hurried to the small serving station and picked up a glass and pitcher of water and brought them to him. "Would you like a drink?"

"Indigestion. Get it something terrible and this job does not help one iota." Mark accepted the glass of water and gulped it down without pause. He rubbed his stomach then sat down. "Get on the first taxi headed to the theatre. I'll need you on the ground to check the layout. It's supposed to be a classy place, but we'll see for sure when we arrive. And make sure Dalia's ready to run. She'll have her work cut out for her when we get there." Mark looked up from the stack. "Why are you still standing there? We don't have time to lollygag, doll."

Audra hurried from him and knocked on each door as she passed. "We should arrive in five minutes. Pull your things together."

Mumbles and incoherent phrases were all she heard as she hurried to the next car. She rapped on a few more doors then slowed as she reached Dalia's room. Guilt washed over her. She should have made an effort to visit her earlier in the day. Especially before she layed down to rest. Poor Dalia. It had been uncaring to leave her alone while the others gathered in one place. Had the police even talked to Dalia? Audra knocked then paused.

"Dalia?"

The muffled sound of wails reached her.

Audra twisted the knob and hurried in. Dalia was sprawled at the foot of her bed, her large frame crumpled on the floor. Horror flashed through Audra at the sight, until Dalia looked up at her. Nothing seemed amiss with her other than the grief lining her face in twin rivers of tears.

"I sorry, child." Dalia began to struggle to her feet but couldn't get them underneath her.

"Are you all right?" Audra hurried to support her and help her to her feet.

"No. I can't rightly say I am. Such a well of grief in me at everthing I didn't say or do for that poor lost lamb who died today."

"Lana?"

"You ain't seen no other bodies lyin' around, has you?" Dalia's face contorted into a mask of horror.

"No, ma'am."

"Well, then, that's a good thing. It shorely is."

"But why are you so upset?"

"Because that girl never got things right with God. Leastways not before last night. I can only pray she did in the end." Dalia wiped her eyes with a hankie and then tucked it in a pocket. "What you need, Mizz Audra?"

"Mark wanted to see if you needed any help before tonight's show."

"Shore he did. He's never offered to help me. Not a single day of his life." She settled on her bed, rocking from side to side. "I'll be ready. I always is."

"I'll let him know."

"You do that. And pray nothin' else goes wrong with this here caravan."

CHAPTER THIRTY-ONE

The theatre lived up to its nickname. With turquoise velvet seats, box seats, and gilding, it didn't look like any movie theatre Audra had ever attended. Add the air conditioning, and she didn't think she'd want to leave when it was time to return to the train.

The show proceeded without a hitch. The performers amazed her as they pushed the last twenty-four hours' events from their minds. They pulled energy from the audience, and with each laugh, roar, or round of applause, they stood straighter and played their parts in a bigger way.

What was it like? Experiencing the energy of audience approval? From Audra's spot off-stage, it looked intoxicating.

After the show, Mark directed the fleet of taxis to an officers' club. The men groaned while the women preened. Audra tried to wash the exhaustion from her face but feared no amount of makeup could hide the circles under her eyes, the questions plaguing her, and her overall fatigue.

The thought of entertaining strangers…she shuddered. Maybe she could find a corner to hide in, a palm to shield her while she watched the pros at work.

She was all for contributing to the war effort. But she was an attorney. Not a Hollywood star. And frankly she wouldn't change that. Forget about the murder—as if that were even possible—watching the lengths these women went to, the pixie dust of longing for fame had not been sprinkled on her.

The taxis pulled to a stop. Elizabeth squealed and turned to Victoria. "How's my makeup?"

"Perfect, as always." Victoria's smile looked strained. "All we do is talk?"

"Of course." At least Audra hoped so. She couldn't imagine anything more being demanded of the women.

"Oh, I'm sure a kiss here or there is fine." Constance grinned and then winked at Audra. "Just to raise morale of course."

"Well, I think I'll stick to the talking." Victoria flipped through her purse's contents. "Looks like I misplaced my lipstick." She turned to Elizabeth. "Can I steal some of yours?"

Elizabeth handed the beautiful brunette a tube of red.

The stars hurried from the cab, giggling and talking like sorority sisters. Audra lingered long enough to pay the driver then stepped from the car. Swing music drifted from the open windows. A saxophone wailed through a solo, and then it pitched to a sour note.

A soft breeze blew off the ocean, bringing the scent of salt water. Maybe she could stay outside, enjoy the evening without anyone noticing she hadn't entered the club.

Officers walked by in their dress whites, then paused at the door to remove their hats and tuck them under an arm. Then they paused long enough to remove their hats. One spied her in the shadows and stepped away from the others.

"I'll catch up with y'all inside." His Southern accent sounded like slowly dripping honey. Audra stepped farther into the shadows, hoping he'd walk a different direction. "There you are." He stopped in front of her. He pointed toward the club. "I understand the good times are in there."

"Not my idea of fun."

He grinned at her, an air of Clark Gable in the smile. "You haven't attended with the right fella. Let me escort you."

He seemed harmless enough, and she supposed she should play the part while with the caravan.

"I've never been good at things like this." Another taxi pulled up and she imagined Mark watching her. Or worse yet, Robert seeing her. The thought made her stomach plummet. Was it worse to be alone with one man or with a herd of them? Her quiet moment had already disappeared, might as well get inside that club.

A door to the cab opened, and Audra looked that direction. Mark stepped out, his expression hidden in the shadows. He glanced around then started walking toward her. Something in the set of his shoulders caused her to stiffen. The lieutenant looked at her with a question in his eyes.

Audra took a deep breath and smiled at him. "All right. You may escort me, though I've been told not to let one man dominate my time."

"We've received similar warnings." He studied her face as they walked into the pool of light that slipped through the windows. "I see every movie that comes to the station. I'm surprised I don't recognize you."

"I'm a lawyer rather than a star."

His mouth quirked to the side as he studied her. "Then they've missed a beautiful opportunity."

Heat climbed her neck at his words. She hoped the shadows hid the blush. "I see they teach flattery in officers' school."

He rubbed the back of his neck. "That awkward, huh? Guess I'd better get you inside." He slipped a hand under her arm and led her inside. Audra looked over her shoulder and found Mark approaching.

She smiled, but he didn't smile back. For someone who'd insisted the performers attend, he didn't look happy about being here.

Audra shook off the thought and took in the club. She didn't know what she'd expected, but this smallish space wasn't it. Wood floors tapped with the heels of dozens of women's dancing shoes. Couples jitterbugged across the front part of the floor. Along the walls men in naval uniforms mixed with women. At least five or six men already surrounded Victoria. Despite her earlier misgivings, she looked at ease.

"Shall we get something to drink? The refreshments are usually pretty good."

"I'd like that, but only if you tell me your name."

"Lieutenant Charles Midlan at your service. And yours, Miss Attorney?"

"Audra Schaeffer."

As they squeezed through the crowd, she realized she might be with Lieutenant Midlan, but her heart searched for a certain tall, dark-haired movie star. The one who sent her pulse racing even as she refused to acknowledge the questions her mind pondered.

"Here you go." The lieutenant handed a cup of red liquid to her.

"Thank you." She accepted the cut-glass cup and took a sip, relieved that it tasted like plain punch.

The music started again, this time a slower waltz.

"Would you like to dance?"

One couldn't hurt. Then she could plead fatigue. "I'd like that." She set her now-drained cup on a waiting tray and stepped onto the dance floor, his hand at her back.

Lieutenant Midlan turned out to be a good leader, and Audra relaxed in the circle of his arms. She kept an eye on the caravan members as they danced. Mark slouched in a corner, lips pulled down in a frown and his gaze firmly fixed on her. The lieutenant startled, and she saw a wonderful, tall man from Hollywood tapping him on the shoulder.

"Pardon me, may I cut in?"

The officer looked at her. "Would you like to dance with him?"

"I've very much enjoyed our time, but yes, I would."

Lieutenant Midlan released her and gave a slight bow. "Miss Schaeffer."

Robert stepped into Lieutenant Midlan's spot and took Audra in his arms. "I'm sorry it took me a bit to work my way over. Are you all right?"

"I don't want to think right now." She wanted, no, needed, to forget everything. In his embrace, it was easy to do.

The way his gaze caressed her face, she wished she could read the thoughts he hid. Then his gaze traveled to her lips. She licked them self-consciously. What did he see when he studied her like that? Could he really want her, a Midwestern girl without the finesse of a beautiful actress?

The drums banged to an end. Robert leaned forward, and Audra's breath caught in her throat. She didn't think she could breathe and at that moment didn't need to. Not while he looked at her like that. Then a young woman Audra didn't recognize approached, eyes fastened on Robert with a doe-eyed, star-struck glaze. "Are you Robert Garfield?"

He nodded, looking from Audra to the young woman.

"It's all right. I'll go get a drink." And find that palm tree she'd meant to find when she arrived.

* * * * *

Audra slipped away from him and into the void stepped this kid he didn't know. Robert pasted on a smile, the one Lana had made him practice ad nauseam when they first married.

"You have to be prepared at any moment to greet a fan."

"Don't I first need some?"

She'd stared into his face, the mole on her cheek bobbing as she smiled and then straightened his bowtie. *"Not if you want to be a star, my dear. Not if you want to be a star."*

Back then that's all they'd wanted. Matching stars in front of the Chinese theatre. Now, as he bowed to the woman in front of him, he wondered why they'd chased the illusion so hard. Look where it had gotten them. Him fighting for a role so he didn't have to become a car or insurance salesman—see how the smile worked then. And Lana murdered.

"I can't wait till I tell the girls at the office that I danced with a bona fide movie star. How amazingly romantic." She laid her head on his chest with a contented sigh. A moment later her head popped up again. "How many movies have you been in?"

Robert wondered when the song would end. He didn't appreciate having a woman he didn't know plastered to his side. The berth on the train sounded wonderful. Even his toes felt tired and no one had stepped on them yet. Ouch! Guess he'd been premature. "Probably two dozen."

He didn't add that many had been small roles she probably hadn't noticed. Even his mother had missed him in one of the films.

"Two dozen." Her smile almost reached from ear to ear. "How wonderful."

As they continued to dance, Robert could only imagine what tall tale she'd weave in the morning. *You should have attended. I danced with a world-famous movie star.* The office gals would join her in swooning until one thought to ask her which star.

The song swung to an end, and Robert bowed to the gal. "I'm off to get a drink."

"Don't mind if I do."

He tried to pay attention to her chatter as he searched for Audra in the sea of people. Wherever she'd found to hide worked. She had disappeared.

In spite of her accomplishments, she apparently longed to avoid crowds. Where Rosemary seemed to thrive in large settings, with an abundance of social graces, Audra flourished in smaller settings. It formed part of her charm. So unlike the women he spent his days around.

He groaned when they reached the line for the refreshment table that wound around a corner.

"Don't be surprised." The girl grinned up at him. "Many of the officers come so they don't have to cook. Mighty lonely life for many of them. Some had to leave their families behind. Can you imagine?"

"It wouldn't be my choice."

An older lady walked by and gave the girl a pointed look. Her back stiffened and a defiant look flashed across her face before dissolving. "I enjoyed our dance. Now back to mingling." She looked so downcast that Robert reached out to stop her.

"Wait. Do you have anything I could autograph? Something to show the girls?"

Her eyes widened and she grinned. "Would you do that?" She reached into her small purse and pulled out a pen and slim notepad.

With a slight bow, he accepted the pen and scrawled his signature on the first blank page. After reclaiming the book, she clutched it to her chest, batted her eyelashes, and then reached up and pecked him on the cheek. "Oh!" She flushed red and pirouetted before racing toward a group of girls watching with interest from their place along a wall.

Robert scanned the room again for Audra. He didn't like her wandering in the crowd where he couldn't protect her. Finally, he spotted her near Victoria with a couple sailors standing near. A few of the actors stood a bit beyond the two women, Mark keeping a sharp eye on them. Robert's shoulders lost their tension at the sight. He was being overly nervous. Especially when other men were standing by to help if Audra needed it.

Part of him felt relief at that knowledge. The other part resented it. He didn't want others stepping into that role.

No. He'd protect her for a lifetime if she'd let him.

CHAPTER THIRTY-TWO

Monday, June 22, 1942

The next several days passed in a blur. Audra tried to keep up as Mark seemed intent on making them all work doubly hard in a convoluted effort to keep them from thinking about Lana. The caravan played to packed crowds in the cities of Raleigh, Charlotte, and Columbia, moving so fast all Audra remembered was the thick accents and sweetened tea. Mark finally gave them a couple of hours to relax when they hit Atlanta.

"Why are we stopping in Atlanta?" Charlie Lester asked the question he seemed to ask at every stop.

This time everyone chimed in to answer. "We're here to sell war bonds, not entertain the troops."

"Though you'll likely do that too. Atlanta's a hub for troops stationed within a three-hundred-mile radius. And don't forget there's money here too. We're in the heart of the old South, and these folks are waiting for an opportunity to open those old pocketbooks and buy bonds. Tonight you'll help them do that." Mark paced in front of the group in the lounge car. The area under his eyes bore a purple tinge, the stress of his job wearing on his health.

"I've got it on good authority they're shipping men up from Fort Benning and other military installations for the show." Mark leaned on a chair, a pinched look closing his face. "Take a few hours. Shop on Peachtree Street or wherever it is folks shop in Atlanta. You can even sleep in a hotel tonight. The Winecoff is a good one, and right in the middle of any action. Then tomorrow we'll rehearse and have a show."

A murmur floated through the room at the unexpected freedom. After a week on a train with Mark controlling her every movement, it seemed odd to Audra to suddenly have unscheduled time to do whatever she wanted.

The performers rushed from the meeting to get off the train, most not even stopping to pack a bag.

Victoria hooked arms with her. "I think we should get our bags and head to Peachtree. Surely whatever cab we hop in, the driver will direct us to the right store. Go pack an overnight bag and let's escape before Mark changes his mind."

The idea sounded wonderful to Audra. "Give me ten minutes."

"You've got five."

After getting caught in a conversation with a porter, Audra hurried toward her berth, barely noticing the hot, heavy air when she stepped between the cars. The quiet led her to believe the others had escaped. She hoped she could still catch Victoria if she hurried. The thought of spending the night on a full-sized bed sounded glorious. She stepped across to the sleeping car but felt something tug at her shirt. Before she could regain her balance, a shove sent her flailing to the iron platform. She tried to catch her breath but felt a weight press firmly between her shoulders.

"Keep your attention where it belongs." The deep words hissed into her ear.

The air was forced from her lungs by the weight, and she desperately tried to breathe. Her mind raced as she tried to glimpse whoever pinned her, but a hand pushed her face into the rough grillwork. Just when she knew she would pass out, she felt the vibration of footsteps. Someone was coming. Maybe they could help her.

Audra gave a desperate twist as her lungs screamed for oxygen. She caught an image of a trench coat, polished Italian loafers, and a hat pulled low to meet the upturned coat. Then her face was pressed once more into the floor and everything went black.

"Miss Audra, Miss Audra." Dalia called to her while stroking her cheek. "Come on, sweet child. Come back."

It felt like a wet, damp blanket enveloped her. Audra struggled to open her eyes.

"Thank the Lord. You had me worried again, Mizz Audra."

Audra opened her eyes and met Dalia's soulful gaze. She opened her mouth to speak but only croaked. Licking parched lips, Audra tried again. "Did you see anything?"

Dalia's eyes widened, and she sucked in a quick breath. "No, ma'am. I didn't see nothing. Just you layin' here like some poor hurt bird. I didn't know what to do, what with seein' poor Lana in my mind's eye. Can you get up?"

"Yes, or everyone will be staring at me."

In fact, she was surprised Victoria hadn't headed back to check on her.

"Everybody else gone the other way. Wantin' to get off this here train."

"I was too."

"You still be gettin' off. Just wearin' a bit of pancake makeup."

Audra felt her cheek and groaned. It felt like the cross-work of the platform had been permanently embedded in her skin. "I think I'd like to get as far away from this train as possible."

She needed to get away from whoever had attacked her. The quick glimpse of the person didn't give her much to go on. It might be a man, but she wasn't certain—though the Italian loafers seemed to indicate that. Her mind spun, and she decided the safest thing to do was abandon the train and head to the largest group of people she could find. Shopping, like Victoria had suggested, sounded like just the ticket. If Victoria hadn't decided Audra had stood her up. Audra needed to find her then somehow act like nothing had happened.

"Let me helps you up." Dalia creaked to her feet then offered Audra her hand. "Here you go."

Audra stumbled to her feet, a large pain settling between her shoulder blades. "Whoever it was, I've probably got his knee imprint on my back."

Dalia clucked her tongue. "I just don't understand people. Hurtin' each other, murderin'…" She shivered dramatically. "Mebbe it's time to get away from these here folks for a while. After this tour be finished."

Audra nodded. Yes, she'd be headed far away if she survived. Indianapolis looked more appealing every moment. "Thank you again, Dalia."

The woman watched her as she hurried to her room. Her attentiveness felt protective and left Audra with the urge to hurry and get off the train while Dalia still stood guard in the passageway.

When Audra heard Dalia's plodding footsteps move down the hall, she doubled her efforts to get out before something worse happened. She tossed a dress and nightgown in her smaller bag then added face cream, cosmetics, shoes, and stockings. She paused in the bathroom, studying her face. From her right jawline up to her eye, a discolored area spread.

She touched her cheek, wincing at the pain. Maybe she could find a cosmetics counter with someone who could help her hide the forming bruise.

Until now the attacks hadn't seemed personal. Anyone could follow her. But this… She shook at the realization that something had changed. Someone—the person who killed Lana—had decided she needed a warning.

Should she abandon the train? In Atlanta? She had the perfect opportunity right now. Get off when Mark gave permission for time off—and never return. She doubted anyone would miss her. They didn't need her to get people on stage at the right moment. In fact, why would they really need her, unless someone wanted to keep an eye on her?

Mark?

She quickly discarded the idea. He wouldn't sabotage his precious caravan by killing Lana. And why would he attack Robert? Not when he'd needed the actor ready to emcee a show in two hours.

Move.

The urgency hit her by surprise. She abandoned the mirror and grabbed her bag. Then she hurried from her berth and off the train. She walked the platform without seeing any familiar souls.

* * * * *

Robert shoved his hat on. Almost twenty-four hours of true freedom. The concept sounded fabulous, but what could he do in a strange city with that kind of time?

From what Mark had said, the Winecoff Hotel sat in the heart of downtown. If all else failed, he could hop on a trolley or stroll the area, taking in the sights and sounds of the Southern jewel.

He picked up his suitcase and lugged the thing off his bed. He hadn't thought to bring a smaller bag, so he would have to haul the full case along. Once he checked in, he'd be free of the weight. He stepped from his small berth.

"See you tomorrow." He saluted the space and closed the door.

A full-sized bed. He almost groaned at the thought of sleeping on one tonight. Luxury defined after sleeping on that tiny bunk. At least the train had rocked him to sleep, but he remembered how to do it on his own.

The heat assaulted him when he stepped off the train. Then the humidity swept across him like a tidal wave, and circles of sweat formed under his shirtsleeves. He'd thought it was sticky in Virginia and North Carolina. But nothing had prepared him for this. Now he knew why the air conditioning on the train hadn't kept up for the past couple of days. How could it against this humidity?

He hurried across the platform to the inside of Atlanta's Terminal Station. In the coolness of the station he adjusted his hold on the suitcase. People bustled through, but what caught his attention was the solitary figure seated on a bench as if trying to hide in plain sight. Something about her posture put him on edge.

What had happened now?

Robert wound his way through the pedestrians and travelers. "Audra?"

She barely looked at him, instead averting her face as if hiding from him. The action punched through him.

"Aren't you headed to the hotel?" He crouched in front of her, trying to see her face.

"Please leave." The words were weak and hesitant, without any of her normal strength.

"Not until I know you're all right. What kind of white knight would I be if I left you without ensuring that much?"

Her head popped up at his words. Her eyes made round circles on her face, and she covered her right cheek with her hand. Something was most definitely not okay.

Robert reached up to touch her fingers. He slowly tugged them away. When he saw what lay beneath, his blood began to boil but he held it in check. "Who did this to you?"

"I don't know."

He sucked in a quick breath and then stroked her cheek with a light touch. "Audra."

"I only have an impression, but whoever it was sat on my back and shoved my face into the grill." Her pupils loomed large in her eyes as she stared at him. "I wouldn't call me as a witness."

"Did he say anything?"

"All he said was to keep my attention where it belonged." She shrugged, steeling her spine. "I don't understand what that means. I haven't talked about Rosemary since Lana was murdered."

"True." He tugged her to her feet and then pulled her into a light embrace. She trembled like a terrified kitten. How could he remove her fear? "I won't let anything happen to you."

"But it already did." The muffled words pierced him.

Somehow he would keep that from happening again. He'd once had true feelings for Lana, but as the fear and rage battled inside him, he realized that what he felt for Audra made the former a faint shadow.

"Let's get checked into the hotel. Then we'll make a plan. We'll find a way to identify who's doing this."

"When the police haven't?" Audra pulled away from him, sinking back to the bench. "I really thought I could after Rosemary's death. That's why I signed on for the caravan. I didn't have any strong patriotic notion of serving the war effort. I wasn't even interested in spending time with stars."

He slumped next to her, acting as if she'd shot him through the heart. "Not even me?"

"No." She smiled apologetically then hurried on. "But I've enjoyed our days together. We'll return to Hollywood, you'll go back to movies, and I'll leave for Indianapolis. I'm a diversion. That's all."

Robert grabbed his bag and pulled her back to her feet. "Do you really believe that?"

She stared at him blankly, as if the last emotion had been drained from her.

"You are no diversion. What's growing between us is much deeper and something I want to explore. What if God brought us together?" He studied her, watching a flicker of light brighten her eyes. "Right now we're going to the hotel." Any talk of their future would have to wait.

CHAPTER THIRTY-THREE

"There you are." Victoria hurried to take Audra's bag when she entered the hotel lobby.

"You've joined the bell service?"

"No, silly. You had me worried sick, though. I checked in almost an hour ago." She stopped talking long enough to take in Audra's cheek. She covered her mouth. "Good heavens, what happened to you?"

"Long story."

Robert stepped to the counter. "I'll get your key, Audra."

"Thank you." She sank to one of the lobby couches, all energy drained. "I could sleep for a week."

"Only after you spill what happened." Victoria sat beside her, studying her with a troubled expression. "Now."

"I'd rather not."

"You'll need some kind of cover story for that bruise on your face unless you want me to believe Robert did that to you." Victoria quirked an eyebrow and crossed her arms. "I've got all day to wait."

Audra leaned her head against the couch. If she closed her eyes, she could almost imagine she'd reappeared at her parents' home in Indianapolis. The comfy cushions embraced her like their old davenport. If only it were that easy to disappear and pretend none of this had happened. The throbbing in her head and on her cheek made that impossible. "I was attacked."

"Any person with two good eyes can see that."

"That's all I know."

Victoria studied her, eyes blinking rapidly. "Well then, let's get you settled, find some aspirin, and locate some makeup to hide the damage. Did you know one of Atlanta's largest department stores is next door? Davisons is waiting for us to explore."

Shopping? Audra stared at Victoria. "I think I'd like a nap."

"Trust me. A distraction is exactly what you need."

Robert walked up to them. "Here's your key, Audra. The bellboy can take your case up if you like."

"No, thank you." Audra patted her satchel. "I can handle it." She stood and hitched the bag over her shoulder. "I'll see you later."

Victoria and Robert exchanged a look that Audra chose to ignore. She moved toward the elevator that stood in a corner of the lobby, its wrought-iron door adding a decorative feature.

"Oh, I'm coming with you." Victoria hurried after her. "There is no way I'm leaving you alone. Not after this." She patted Audra's cheek and winced in sympathy. "So consider me your shadow. Anyone tries anything I'll swing my bag at them." Her large purse hung at her side. "That should make them think twice."

A giggle pushed up Audra's throat, one that seemed oddly out of place. She tried to stifle it, but it erupted anyway.

"What?" Victoria eyed her with a frown, though her eyes twinkled. "You don't think I'm very scary looking."

"No, I think I'd need a knight on a white horse to race to my rescue."

"Reporting for duty, mademoiselle." Robert stepped closer and then saluted with a crisp motion. "All bad guys will be duly impressed and stay far away."

Audra grinned as Victoria shook her head. "Your service is accepted, young man. Don't let me down."

He stiffened at her words and nodded. "I never will, Audra."

She stood mesmerized by the intensity in his gaze.

Victoria cleared her throat, and Audra snapped toward her. "How's this? I'll give you thirty minutes to rest, as long as you place something cold on your cheek. Then we'll distract ourselves with shopping. No sense sitting around waiting for something to happen that might not."

"You're right. A bit of rest and some ice should work wonders."

"I'll drop my bag in my room, then meet you in yours." Robert picked up his suitcase and hefted it as he headed for the stairs.

The elevator doors slid open. The employee inside smiled. "Which floor?"

"I'm not really sure."

Victoria took her key and wiggled it in front of her. "Room 1204, please. And fast. This girl needs some rest."

When they reached the twelfth floor, Victoria led the way. The actress slid the key into the lock and turned. The door swung open into a clean room. While not large, it felt spacious after the berth on the train.

Audra walked to the bed and collapsed. The firm mattress supported her, and she closed her eyes, allowing her muscles to relax for the first time since the attack.

Victoria rummaged in the closet and brought a blanket to her. "Thirty minutes. That's all. I'm going to find some ice."

Exhaustion weighted Audra down, and she sank into a deep sleep. An icy coldness on her face jolted her back to reality.

"I know you don't like this, but later you'll be glad you iced that cheek."

Audra pulled herself to a sitting position at the head of the bed and held out her hand. "Give it to me."

Victoria handed the towel-wrapped ice to her. "Hold it for ten minutes if you can. I had lots of practice with a brother. He always landed in some scrape or another."

The cold seeped through her skin until her cheek was numb. If only her memories could disappear with the pain.

* * * * *

Robert strode toward Audra's door. Victoria had made it clear he had half an hour to get up there before they'd disappear. Maybe he'd be the knight who protected Audra while she shopped. He'd do it, even if it meant he ended up burdened down with their bags. If they only went next door, he should be okay. How much damage could they do in one little store?

He walked up to 1204 and knocked.

While he waited for a response, a few muted sounds filtered through the door.

"Who could that be?" Audra's voice?

"Mark or Robert. Maybe housekeeping. Who knows? I'll check."

"Be careful."

Someone pushed the door from the other side as if peeking through the peephole. He stepped back and waved.

The door pulled inward then stopped as a chain released. Victoria held on to the door while leaning against the doorframe. "Yes?"

He looked past her shoulder to where Audra leaned against the headboard. "Are you beautiful ladies ready for some fresh air?"

Victoria winked at him and mouthed "About time." Aloud, she said, "I think we are. Come in."

A soft blush colored Audra's cheeks as she watched him enter. "Playing the protector?"

"I hope it's more than that." Yes, he wanted to ensure she stayed very safe, but he wanted to do it for more than the length of the caravan. He examined her cheek and frowned. "That looks painful."

"Victoria's insisting I get some professional help."

"It doesn't look like it's worse than a bruise." Robert looked at Victoria, trying to read her expression.

"Professional cosmetic help, silly. Come on, Audra, make it snappy. I'm tired of waiting." Victoria stepped in front of the full-length mirror and touched up her lipstick. "Let's see what Atlanta has to offer."

"Will you humor me a minute more? Can we stop in the lobby? I want to call Detective Franklin and my parents. I haven't talked to my folks since the funeral and need to make sure they're holding up. We haven't had good phone access for so long."

Robert shrugged. It made sense that after what happened she'd want to know if Franklin had made some sort of progress and let her parents know she was still okay. "I'm sure Victoria can hold off on shopping a bit longer."

Victoria sighed and flopped on the bed. "I guess I might as well stay here another thirty minutes."

"It won't take that long. A couple of minutes to route the call and we're set. The detective probably won't even be available." Their agreement sparked an energy in Audra that had her ready to leave a couple of minutes later, after a stop to grimace at her image in the mirror. She turned away and urged Robert to open the door. "We need to do something about this quick."

Victoria continued to lounge on the bed. "I'll follow you down in a minute—give you time to place your calls."

Robert followed Audra into the hallway and placed a hand on her back as he guided her down the hallway. "Sure you're up for all of this?"

"Activity is better than lying there on the bed wondering who attacked me. The questions are too hard to tolerate. I need answers. Pray Detective Franklin has something for me." As soon as they reached the lobby, Audra hurried to the telephone booths along the wall. She slipped into a vacant booth and began to slide the door closed before pausing and motioning him closer. "I don't know if we'll even be able to talk…"

"Understood."

Audra dialed the long-distance operator. "Detective Franklin with the Hollywood Police Department." She gave the operator the police department's exchange and then settled back into Robert's arms while she waited.

Robert studied Audra, enjoying his role as protector. She twisted a strand of hair that had slipped in front of her ear. Her uncertainty made her even more attractive to him. She had no idea that when he held her he wanted to protect and shelter her—not just now, but for the rest of her life.

"Have dinner with me tonight?" The words popped out before he even knew he'd thought them.

She looked at him, startled eyes wide. She swallowed then considered him before opening her mouth. He braced for her rebuke, sure it would come.

"Yes? Detective Franklin, please." She placed a hand over the mouthpiece. "They're looking for the detective. Do you really want to?"

"Want to what?" Did she want him to beg? He could, but he didn't like the idea.

"Go to dinner tonight?"

He nodded. "I wouldn't ask otherwise."

"Of course." She held a finger up and then pointed at the phone. "Detective Franklin? This is Audra Schaeffer, wondering if you have any sort of update for me on my sister's murder." She waited a minute. "Yes, we have had trouble this week. It's been terrible, and I really wish you'd been here to compare Lana and Rosemary. Did Detective Brown contact you?" Her frown deepened as she listened. "I'm not trying to do the police's job. Believe me, I'd like to avoid dead bodies for the rest of my life. But I was there. I found her. I couldn't walk away and pretend I didn't." She took a deep breath. "Now someone attacked me again today...."

"I'm sorry, Detective." She perked up. "You did? Isn't that good news?"

Robert leaned closer. He heard the detective's faint voice. "Rachel, Rosemary, and Lana tried out for the same movie."

Audra looked at Robert, a look of mute appeal as she slouched forward. "The same movie?"

"Yes." Static invaded for a moment. "That's the only tie we've found other than the friendship between Rachel and Rosemary. Looks like the producer and director liked Rosemary for the lead, Lana for the second female lead. Rachel would have had a smaller role, unless something happened to Rosemary."

Audra gazed at Robert without seeming to see him. She wore a glazed look that concerned him. "Then why was Rachel leaving town?"

"Not sure. Maybe she was disillusioned in spite of the role. Maybe she never knew." The detective paused. "Has anything else happened that I should know about? Anything Detective Brown wouldn't know or might overlook?" Detective Franklin's voice, though scratchy, managed to have authority even across the miles.

Audra filled him in on the attacks.

"That concerns me. You must be closer to an answer than you think."

"I suppose." Audra's brows pulled together in a worried pucker.

"Keep people around you at all times. No wandering off on your own." He sighed. "I'd like to order you off the caravan, but I know that won't do any good. Remember most of the men on that train are on the list of names in your sister's book. And think about what these three women had in common. You might come up with something we've missed. Watch your back though. I don't want you next."

His words sent a chill through Robert. He didn't want her next either. What did the three women have in common? He'd be in a better position than Audra to figure that out.

"Yes, sir. Thank you." She hung up and turned to Robert. "There's not much there to help us." She turned back to the phone and asked for the long-distance operator again. Silence settled over them as they waited for the call to connect with her parents. He held her against him as she chatted for a couple of minutes with her mother, managing to keep a light tone and spin a few stories about her adventures on the caravan. Audra glazed over Lana's death, downplaying what had happened but hurrying off the call after that.

She hung up and stayed within the circle of his arms. "Mother's worried."

"She should be—imagine how worried she'd be if you'd told her everything."

"Which is exactly why I couldn't. I need to see this through and then go home knowing I've done everything I could."

"Come on, you two. No looking glum and down in the mouth." Audra jolted to her feet at Victoria's words. Victoria bounced toward them across the lobby, looking immaculate in a smart suit with a striking hat topped by a long plume. She linked arms with Robert and Audra. "We're going to forget everything for a bit. Anything Detective Franklin told you can wait. Well, unless he told you I'm the killer." Victoria laughed, but Robert didn't find anything amusing in her statement.

Together the three walked out of the Winecoff and went next door to the department store. It overflowed with people perusing goods of all sorts. Reminded him of a Macy's or other nice store. The floor was marble with jewelry and cosmetics stands in the center. Behind it a sweeping set of escalators led to the mezzanine level.

Audra allowed Victoria to lead her to a cosmetics counter. A woman quickly approached them, clucked when she saw Audra's cheek, and brought another woman over to assist her. They started pulling out cosmetics in an assortment of tubes and containers. It looked like torture to him.

"I'll be over there and will keep an eye on you."

Audra smiled apologetically as she climbed on to a stool. "Time to get beautiful."

He chucked her under the chin. "You already are."

"All right, you two love birds." Victoria pushed Robert away. "You have a mother, right? Go shop for her."

CHAPTER THIRTY-FOUR

That night Audra stumbled into her hotel room. While shopping with Victoria had diverted her, she'd never forgotten Robert stood in the background ready to come to her aid.

The fact that she needed a bodyguard horrified her.

Yet she'd also felt safe and protected.

So when he'd suggested again that they have dinner together, she'd quickly agreed. Now, as she collapsed on the bed, she considered ordering room service instead. Anything to avoid moving. A long soak with lots of bubbles and a good book sounded like a recipe for forgetting. Although, an evening staring into his gorgeous blue eyes would be better, even if it meant she'd have to freshen up and prepare for an evening out.

All she wanted to do was forget everything but Robert. Then maybe she could return to Indianapolis and be content. As much as she wanted to believe that her time in Hollywood and on the caravan hadn't marred her, she only had to look at her face to see the truth. And that didn't begin to address her hidden scars.

Audra tugged open the drawer on the bedside table. A Gideon Bible nestled inside. She pulled it out and held it to her chest. *Father?*

The one-word question was all she could murmur.

He was God. He was everywhere, could be with her anywhere. Yet His presence had been so hard to find. Was it something she'd done? Was it where she was? Her heart ached for His presence. All she felt was empty.

She set the Bible in her lap and it fell open in the Psalms. With a few flipped pages, Audra turned to Psalm 126. She reread verses 5 and 6. *They that sow in tears shall reap in joy. He that goeth forth and weepeth, bearing precious seed, shall doubtless come again with rejoicing, bringing his sheaves with him.*

Would those days come for her? She touched her cheek and thought of all the tears she'd cried. For Rosemary, for Andrew, even for Lana. She thought of the fear that threatened to overwhelm her.

Father, please give me wisdom. Keep me and everyone on the caravan safe. And can You bring that time of rejoicing? Please. The words throbbed in her mind, matching the pounding of her pulse.

Audra closed the Bible and slid it back into the drawer. She needed to hurry if she wanted to be ready when Robert called for her. Her satchel didn't contain clothes appropriate for dinner, and she hadn't found anything at Davison's that she could afford on an assistant's wage. Hopefully Robert would be equally ill-prepared for an elegant dinner, and they'd eat somewhere informal. She dabbed more of the foundation on her face and topped it with powder. She eyed her cheek in the mirror, and it looked like the cosmetics had done their job. Only the faintest discoloration showed.

Grabbing her handbag, Audra took the elevator to the lobby. As she entered the area, she spied Robert sitting on one of the brocade-covered couches, reading a newspaper.

"Any news I can't live without?"

He lowered the paper, and a slow grin crept onto his face. "Hey, good-looking." Robert folded the paper and placed it on a glass coffee table. He winked. "What do you say we ditch this popsicle stand?" He held out his elbow, and she wrapped her arm through his.

She wrinkled her nose, unsure exactly what he meant. "I'm ready for that dinner you promised."

"Right this way. I checked with the bell station. They had some great recommendations. But since we're keeping tonight relaxed, we'll try a café that made the list."

Audra relaxed, relieved to follow Robert's lead. This surprised her. She'd spent so much time in college and then law school trying to show she could compete with the men in her classes. Then, when she graduated from law school, all of her efforts had been for nothing when she could only find work as a glorified secretary. At that point, she'd buried her head in her work, hoping and praying for a chance to show she'd learned everything the men had. Now she walked Peachtree Street in downtown Atlanta on the arm of a star, content to let him set the direction for the evening.

For the moment, she would ignore the reasons and events that led to this point. Instead, she would enjoy every minute of the evening.

Cars crawled up and down Peachtree. The sun still shone, but the humidity had faded a bit after a late afternoon shower that left the sidewalk damp. Audra soaked in the scene as Robert wound their way through pedestrians and other couples strolling in the early evening.

"I've been thinking about who could have attacked you this afternoon."

Audra stopped walking and placed a finger on Robert's mouth. "Shhh. Let's forget all that for a minute. Please." She smiled up at him, quirking her head at an angle.

He stared at her, electricity zinging between them. "I don't know that I can."

"For a moment. At least until we reach the restaurant."

"I need a distraction." His gaze traveled to her cheek, in a gesture so soft she could almost feel the caress, then traveled to her lips. She closed her eyes, wondering if she should break the moment, let him talk about whatever he fancied. Instead, when she opened her eyes, she found herself lost in the depths of his eyes. People moved around them, vague images at the edges of her vision, but she focused on Robert.

His arms circled her, and she longed to sink into them.

Slowly, ever so slowly, until she thought the moment would never come, he lowered his mouth to hers. The hint of a promise flowed between them, until her breath nearly disappeared. He eased back, eyes searching hers.

"I'm falling in love with you, Audra Schaeffer." The sincerity of his words wrapped around her.

Did she want him to love her? What would that mean for her plans of returning to Indianapolis? The questions paralyzed her.

"Don't, Audra. Let's enjoy tonight and leave the future in God's hands."

Someone jostled her, pushing her deeper into the circle of Robert's arms. His stomach rumbled, and he flushed. "Guess it's time to get to that café."

Audra grinned, almost relieved at the break in mood. "Lead away. I think your stomach has voted for a quick filling."

"Before I do, there's one little thing I need." Robert leaned down and gave her a peck on one cheek and then the other.

"I think that was two." Audra touched her cheeks where he'd kissed her.

Robert shrugged. "I never was good at math. Come on, Good-looking, let's see if this restaurant lives up to its billing."

The inside was cheerful, each café table covered with a blue-and-white checked oilcloth that was topped with a tiny vase containing a daisy. Some tables held small white candles as well, soft light flickering from them. The scent of roast and something savory swirled around them as they waited for a waitress to seat them. The two gals ran among tables, busy enough to make Audra wonder why they didn't have help. Could so many people already be working in factories that it put the pinch on businesses like this?

After waiting several minutes, one of the waitresses ran by them. "Help yourselves to a vacant table. One of us will get with you as soon as we can."

Robert chuckled. "We should have done that when we arrived. Where to?"

"How about a window table?" She'd love to watch the pedestrians and enjoy Atlanta's energy.

After they'd settled into their seats and the waitress brought them cold sweetened tea, Robert studied her. "All right to bring up our mystery?"

Audra studied her Mason jar. The amber liquid looked as cloudy as the tangled events. "I suppose."

Robert reached for her hand. "I want to find whoever is behind this before something worse happens to you."

"Or you." She winced as she took in the faintest outline of a bruise still discoloring his face. She touched the fading spot. "I'm sorry you had to take that punch for me."

"It wasn't enough. And I wasn't there when you needed me today."

"No one could have predicted another attack."

"That's the thing. I think we should have. The first attack happened before Lana's murder. But I shouldn't have assumed everything ended with her death."

Audra shook her head. "The last few days passed quietly. They lulled me to a sense of well-being." She rubbed her temples, pushing against the building pain. "Lana's death must be linked to Rosemary and Rachel's. The question is how? But it's too much to be a coincidence. Isn't it?"

Robert put his menu on the table. The waitress hurried by, stopping long enough to take their orders. After she picked up the menus, Robert drummed his fingers on the table. "Didn't Detective Franklin ask you to think about how the three women intersected?" Audra nodded, and Robert's fingers tapped faster. "Have any ideas?"

"Other than the movie Detective Franklin mentioned? No. Rosemary only mentioned Rachel once, and I don't remember her ever talking about Lana. First, Rachel was killed, then Rosemary." Audra ticked the events off on her fingers. "After I join the caravan, someone attacks you when you follow him following me. Then, Lana's murdered, and I'm attacked."

"And the police have no leads?"

"That's what Detective Franklin tells me." Audra nibbled her lower lip. "Could this have anything to do with Rosemary accompanying men around Hollywood?"

Robert shook his head. "I don't see how that would tie to Lana. She's never been involved in that—at least not that I'm aware of."

"You went around with her?"

"Rosemary?" At Audra's nod, he shook his head. "No, the only time I should show up in her calendar is when Artie set us up to attend an event together like the USO fundraiser. It would be like Victoria and I appearing at the same fundraiser. Nothing to get worked up about."

"It could be possible, right? We know all three shared an agent. And if Artie had Rosemary and Rachel serving as escorts…" The word felt like gravel on her tongue. "…Couldn't he have forced Lana to do the same?"

Robert crossed his arms and leaned back. "It's possible. What about the men on the train? Why would any of them be involved with an escort service? You've watched women approach them at every stop. Even the Lester twins. And that cuts out Dexter Snow. He's rarely in Hollywood anymore."

"Why not?"

Robert shrugged. "I don't know. His show's on the road, I guess."

"Then why is his name in her book along with all the others? I'll never believe Rosemary happened to spend evenings with all of Hollywood's eligible bachelors." Tension crackled in the air between them.

The waitress set plates of steaming food in front of them. "Can I get y'all anything else?"

Audra inhaled the aroma of fried okra and fried chicken. "No, thank you."

Robert nodded at the waitress. "Thank you, no." He reached for Audra's hand. "Let me pray. Father, thank You for this food and the hands that prepared and served it. Bless it to our needs, give us wisdom and clarity, and keep us safe. Lord, we're in over our heads and need Your protection and wisdom to solve this puzzle. Help us and guide us. In Your Son's name. Amen."

As Robert prayed, a peace settled over the table, and Audra felt the tension dissipate. Even though she had no flashes of insight, tears filled her eyes.

"Amen. Thank you." Audra met Robert's gaze and then lowered hers at the realization that a new intimacy had formed between them with Robert's prayer. Is this what her mother felt when Daddy prayed? She'd always wondered at the connection she sensed between them after one of their prayer times. This glimpse left her longing for more.

She picked up her knife and fork and cut a piece of the chicken and took a bite. "This is wonderful." A moment passed with the two of them enjoying their plates of Southern delights before she returned the conversation to the train. "Who do you know the least about?"

"On the train?" At Audra's nod, Robert paused with a forkful of food midair. "Dexter. Elizabeth McAllister is new, as are Frank and Constance. Jim isn't well known, but still, I can't see him killing three people. Besides, he's one of the few people I know in Hollywood who is happily married. He wouldn't use a service, let alone follow us around to deliver threatening messages."

"Then we're missing something. Somebody on the train living and working with us did this." Audra wanted to throw her arms up in the air and shout "Who?" Instead, she popped a piece of okra in her mouth. "What about Mark? He assembled everyone who's on the train. Made sure Lana, you, and I were all on board. You became a natural suspect when your ex-wife died, and he could watch me if he had me working closely with him."

Robert considered her words then shook his head. "Sure he's stiff and uptight, but why would he have known Rachel and Rosemary? There's got to be someone else."

CHAPTER THIRTY-FIVE

The soft candlelight didn't ease the discomfort Audra felt as she stared at her food.

The oppression weighed on her, making her wonder how much more she'd be asked to bear. She prayed it wouldn't be much.

"Hey." Robert reached across the table and brushed a strand of hair from her forehead. "I think it's time we changed the subject. Tonight we're supposed to relax."

"Do you think Dalia got the night off too?"

"Maybe. But where would she go? This is the deep South. I doubt she'd be welcome as a guest at our hotel."

The realization bothered Audra. "Guess I'm not as savvy as I thought."

"You're still pretty spectacular."

Her cheek throbbed as the aspirin she'd taken wore off. "I really appreciate dinner, but my cheek hurts as much as my mind's spinning. Can we stroll back to the Winecoff?"

"Before dessert?" His smile faltered. "I'm sorry I'm boring you."

"It's not that. I'm just exhausted." And she needed distance from the man her heart longed to love. The thought made her head pound. She could not live in the city that murdered her sister. It wasn't an option. Her father's reaction alone would ensure that.

"Let me pay, and we'll get on our way."

"Thank you." She closed her eyes, trying to block the pain reflected in his. She felt the attraction he did but didn't have the freedom to chase whether they could have a future. Surely he understood that. Yet, when she opened her eyes and found herself drowning in the depths of his blue gaze, she knew he didn't.

A few minutes later Robert helped her from her chair and then offered his arm as they walked down Peachtree.

"Did Rosemary mention Rachel more than that first time?" Robert's words startled Audra from her thoughts. He must have decided discussing the murders was safer than broaching their relationship.

Audra wracked her mind, trying to think if Rosemary had ever talked about a roommate or Rachel. "Yes. She mentioned her in passing once, but never as a roommate. Instead, she always painted a picture that things were good in Hollywood and improving. Maybe she wouldn't have mentioned a roommate if she thought she would sound like a struggling actress."

"Pride?"

"Maybe. I know she wanted to show Mama and Daddy she could make it. They weren't supportive of her cross-country move." Unfortunately, they'd been right. Didn't Rosemary know she could share her struggles with Audra, if not with their parents? Audra had let another sibling down. The weight of that burden overwhelmed her. Her steps must have slowed because Robert stopped and turned to her.

He stroked her cheek, comfort flowing from his touch. "You can't carry this, Audra. Your sister made choices, like you and your brother did. But you can't walk under the burden of what-ifs and what-might-have-been. It's too heavy and not yours. They each made their own decision." The sincerity in his expression touched her.

"But I could have done something."

"What? Rosemary had to make her own choices, and you were more than half a country away. If my sister had come to Hollywood, I'd hope to steer her away from trouble, but even then she'd make her own decisions. How could you do that from Indianapolis, even if she shared the truth with you?"

"Am I supposed to ignore the pain? Pretend it doesn't exist?"

Robert looked across the street toward a small park. He studied it for a moment. "Don't you think that's a weight God is better equipped to handle?"

"Along with all my tears." She nodded, trying to give the words time to soak deep. "Yes." Could she throw the burden on God's strong shoulders? She tipped her face toward the sky, staring at the few visible stars. The God who hung the stars in the heavens and called her by name could carry the burden of her grief and shame.

Father, please do this in my heart. Help me trust You completely. I turn it all over, surrender it to Your care. Please help me leave it at Your feet. Slowly she felt a bit of peace replace the numbness she'd walked in since identifying Rosemary. *Thank You.*

Audra took a breath, letting the humid air settle in her. It felt like an embrace as every fiber of her being was coated.

"Watch out." Robert's words caused her eyes to pop open. "You look like you're at peace."

"Working on it." She smiled at him. "I'm sure God and I will have more to talk about."

"I don't doubt it." Robert started walking again, and she hurried to match his stride. "The connection we have between the three women is Artie and that movie."

Audra wrinkled her nose. "What do you think of Artie?"

He stared down the sidewalk at nothing in particular. "He's got a good reputation in Hollywood as a man who can spot talent. I don't like all his tactics or the way he pressures some of his clients to enter the escort service. I hate to think about what has happened to some of them." He turned to enter the hotel but paused to wait for people exiting. "I don't see how he's involved, though, since he wasn't on the train."

"Unless he hired someone to kill Lana."

"That would mean someone on the train is a hired killer and not just an actor."

Audra fought the urge to lash out at the horrible nature of the mess. Her peace threatened to evaporate again. "We're right back to who would want to kill Lana." She pulled away from Robert and stalked down the sidewalk, only to bump into somebody. She shook her head and looked up. "Mark?"

The man's usually immaculate look had given way to a disheveled appearance with his shirttail pulled out of his khakis. Even his shaggy hair looked like he hadn't brushed it with anything more than his fingers. He held a paperback in one hand and a satchel in the other.

"You kids enjoying your time?"

Robert caught up and tucked her protectively to his side. "It's been nice. What are you doing?"

"Last-minute details for tomorrow night. There's always something to wrestle down." He scanned the street as if searching for a trolley or cab. "Say, you might be interested to know Artie's on his way to town. Decided he wanted to observe his clients working together. And check on you, Robert, after what happened to Lana."

Robert's arm tightened around Audra, and he pulled her under the hotel's green awning. "That's quite an endeavor for someone who's never flown."

"Sounded like he wanted to get out of Hollywood." Mark waved for a cab, and one slid to the curb. "Don't forget rehearsal first thing tomorrow." He stepped into the cab and closed the door.

Robert stared after him.

Audra nudged him as another group exited the Winecoff and walked around them. "Ready to get inside?" The cool air that flowed out of the open door felt wonderful to her heated skin.

Robert stared after the cab as it pulled from the curb. "Sure." Once inside, he led her to a vacant couch. "Do you mind if we sit here a minute?"

"All right." She gave him a moment then couldn't contain the question. "What's bothering you?"

Robert rubbed his face. "It's probably nothing, but Artie hates the idea of flying. I imagine he'd be even more anxious up there than you."

Audra bumped her shoulder against his. "Thanks."

"I can't see him flying out here to check on us or follow up on Lana. He's much more likely to wait for a full report when we get back."

"Mark wouldn't have any reason to lie."

"And Artie doesn't have any reason to come." Robert shook his head then straightened the pleats of his trousers. "This whole situation has me second-guessing everything. I'm seeing issues and motives where they don't exist."

"And we can't find the ones right in front of us."

Robert clutched her hand and squeezed it. "Thanks for dinner."

"My pleasure." She tilted her head up, memorizing his face. "Wait until the girls find out how much time I spent in your presence."

"Don't you want to reconsider where your home is?" He kept his expression flat though his tone betrayed his hope.

"I think there are a few things I have to resolve first." She stilled as he leaned closer. "Not here." The words scraped from her throat in a raw whisper. "What if there's a photographer around? Can't have our photo taken together, can we?"

"Why not? That's already happened." He held his pose a few inches from her face, his breath warm on her cheek.

The memory of their escape from the photographers at the Roosevelt during the USO fundraiser made her lips curve. He closed the distance between them, brushing her mouth with a kiss. When he leaned back, Audra stood before the electricity of that night reappeared.

"Good night, Robert."

He winked at her, bringing a rush of heat to her cheeks. "I'll see you up. Even Detective Franklin said you shouldn't be alone."

"I don't think he meant I'd need an escort in a hotel like this."

"Lana probably didn't think she needed someone…"

As the intensity between them increased, Audra knew his taking her upstairs was a terrible idea. Especially since Victoria wasn't around to serve as accountability and chaperone. "Good night, dear Robert."

Audra slipped toward the elevator, but not fast enough to avoid the satisfied look on Robert's face. Did she really call him "dear"? More evidence showing she needed to leave. Soon. The doors opened and she stepped inside the elevator.

"Floor, miss?"

"Twelfth please." Audra stood against the back wall of the elevator and felt the swoosh of its ascent. It chugged through the floors without stopping before sliding to a stop at her floor. "Thank you."

Even though she'd assured Robert she didn't need him to escort her, she scurried down the hall toward her room. She slipped the key from her purse and into the lock. Once she'd entered the room and locked the door, she took a deep breath. Her nerves jangled, and she placed her purse on the small writing desk. She scanned the room and the bathroom to make sure she was alone then settled onto the chair.

A pad of paper and pen rested on the desk and she picked them up. She tapped the pen against the paper. Doodling three circles, she then placed each murdered woman's name in a circle. Drawing lines between them, she stared at the image. Rachel and Rosemary were aspiring stars. Lana had already reached B status, with A in reach. She wasn't sure where Rachel was from but doubted that connected them, since Rosemary and Lana hailed from different states.

Next, Audra pulled out her list of names from Rosie's book. As she studied them, nothing new came to her. Many had joined the caravan, but that didn't mean anything. Even if Rachel had lived with Rosemary, Audra knew Lana hadn't lived with her. There was no way Rosie would have kept that quiet, and Audra had visited the star's apartment.

No, all that connected the three was Artie Schmaltz.

She studied the name. Her time with the man hadn't been long, but he simply didn't seem the type to hurt anyone. And strangulation? It was an intensely personal and physical act of violence. If Artie were to kill anyone, she thought him more likely to use a gun or other weapon that provided distance. That also didn't get around the fact he wasn't physically here to kill Lana.

A yawn stretched her jaw again, and she threw the pen down.

She didn't know enough.

She lived with a killer she couldn't identify, and there was nothing she could do to stop him.

CHAPTER THIRTY-SIX

Tuesday, June 23, 1942

The roar of a crowd's approval served as an intoxicating sound.

Robert stood shoulder-to-shoulder with the other performers, drinking in the sight as the people filled the Fox Theatre. They bowed in unison, and then he stepped to the microphone as he did at the close of each performance.

"Thank you again for joining us this evening. While we hope you were thoroughly entertained, the evening won't be complete without you joining us on the terrace as the performers sign autographs after you purchase war bonds."

A voice shouted, "How do I get a kiss from Miss Elizabeth?"

Robert looked over his shoulder toward the young woman. A beautiful rose color climbed her cheeks. "Elizabeth?"

She glided out of the line and stood next to him. "Well, it is a good cause."

"Absolutely." He watched her as she settled into the banter.

"The other gals and I have discussed it."

"I ain't interested in the others." Wolf whistles practically drowned out the man's words.

She tilted her chin and wagged a finger at the crowd. "As I was saying, if someone purchases at least a hundred dollars in war bonds, one lady will be happy to kiss the lucky gent."

"And for the ladies?" Robert couldn't wait to hear her response to this question.

"Why, I suppose they'd want to kiss you." Elizabeth winked at him and then sauntered back to her place in line.

"Guess I've been told." Robert turned back to the audience and shrugged. "Seriously, folks, this is your opportunity to make an important contribution to the effort. So give us a few minutes then join us out on the terrace."

He moved back into the line for the final bow before the curtain fell. Audra waited immediately off-stage when he exited. He pulled her close as the Lester twins hooted.

"Kisses for bonds?" Her eyes flashed as she teased him.

He put his hands up. "Not my idea."

"Nice try, buster." She pulled away from him. "I'm headed back to the train after I pack the last items. Did you see Dalia?"

He shook his head. He hadn't seen the woman all day. "Maybe she's sick."

"I hope not. I'm a bit worried though because no one I've talked to has seen her."

"Maybe you should wait to go back until the rest of us go…"

"Robert, my boy." Artie Schmaltz moved through the performers, nodding and patting shoulders as he came. Guess he'd made it in time for the show after all. "I wondered when I'd see you. Top-of-the-line job. Just what this ad hoc group needed."

"Thanks." Something about the gushing didn't sit right. "I didn't realize you'd arrived. How was your first flight?"

"Not as terrifying as I'd anticipated. Airplanes are the wave of the future. Time I tried the contraption out. Still, I think I'll stick to trains after this trip."

"Does that mean you're riding back with us?" The thought of Artie monitoring the caravan raised the hairs on the back of his neck. Audra stepped away, and the bad feeling intensified.

* * * * *

Artie's loud voice filtered over the top of everything else. Audra took his arrival as her opportunity to slip away. She didn't like the fact that nobody had seen Dalia. While Atlanta hotels might not have been friendly to the black woman, hopefully she didn't stay on the train by herself. Even as she thought it, she knew Dalia didn't have a choice. If Dalia couldn't stay at the hotel with the rest of them, where else was she supposed to stay?

An unsettled feeling gripped her stomach and wouldn't let go. *Father, please keep Dalia safe. Me, too.*

It might not be safe—no, it probably was a truly crazy idea—to go to the train by herself, but she couldn't wait until Robert could leave to check on Dalia. Who else could she ask? Her options were too limited. If Dalia had been Rosemary, Audra would have wanted someone to check on her. She had to make sure Dalia was okay. Surely, she'd find a conductor or someone at the station who would accompany her to the train once she arrived.

Peachtree hummed with traffic but only a few cabs traversed the street, most of them with fares. It seemed like she stood outside forever waiting for one to accept her hail.

A car finally slid to the curb. She slipped inside. "Terminal Station, please."

Once she reached the station, she paid the driver and then hurried to the ticket window. "Where would I find the Hollywood Victory Caravan train?"

The man looked at her with a blank stare. "I don't know what you're talking about."

"The chartered trains. Where do they wait?"

"Off the platform. You'll have to ask one of the staff there which one."

Audra hurried across the large station, her heels clicking against the stone floor. The station hummed with activity, even at the late hour. She saw a conductor and asked for his assistance. He pointed her toward a far track, one unlisted on the departure and arrival board. As she neared the train, her prayers intensified. Should she grab a patrolling police officer to go with her on the train?

An Atlanta officer strolled near one of the platforms. She walked up to him. "Sir, would you mind going with me to the train over there? I'm with the Hollywood Victory Caravan and had to come by myself to make sure everything is okay since we've been off the train for a day."

He studied her before thrusting his shoulders back and patting his stick. "All right, little lady. Let's check it out."

"Thank you. I promise it won't take long. The others should join me soon." They boarded the train, starting with the men's cars and seeing nothing out of the ordinary. It was the same story with the dining car and the lounge car. At the first women's car, Audra hesitated.

"You all right, miss?"

"A tad gun shy."

"That's why I'm here." He patted her shoulder as if she were his granddaughter or a flighty woman to be reassured. Normally, she would bristle at such an impression, but today, she welcomed his presence.

Audra sucked in a breath then forced a smile and stepped onto the car. "This is my berth." She pointed it out as they passed then peeked quickly into the others, her shoulders slowly easing as she made her way to the end. "One more car."

"Shouldn't be anything amiss on it, either."

"I hope you're right."

The first few berths looked as they should. They pushed past to Dalia's room.

"Dalia?" Audra felt the tension return to her neck when the woman didn't answer and wasn't in her berth.

"Who's Dalia?"

"The seamstress and much more. No one's seen her since we disembarked yesterday. Maybe she's in the last area with the sewing machine going." Audra prayed that was the case.

But as the police officer pushed her behind him and opened the final door, she knew that hope had been false. All she could see was a leg splayed on the floor.

* * * * *

Robert gripped the cab's door handle, feet pressed into the floor, urging the car to greater speeds. Why hadn't he followed Audra, bonds be hanged? Others could sell them. But he was the only one who could protect Audra.

"Come on, come on, come on." Robert leaned forward, willing the vehicle to get him to the station—now.

"Hold your horses. We'll get there presently." The cabbie glared at him from the rearview mirror.

Robert couldn't explain why that wasn't good enough. Had Audra foolishly walked onto the train by herself? He hadn't seen Mark at the Fox when he'd left. Would the man head back to the train and find Audra there? Alone?

As the cab zipped through downtown toward the terminal, Robert wondered about Mark. Of all the men on the train, he knew Mark the least. The man worked for a studio and wasn't an actor, so they didn't move in the same circles. All he knew about Mark came through rumors more than anything. Mark liked the ladies and was often seen with a different one on his arm. He'd heard talk that Mark had gotten rough with one or two, but that had died down a year or so ago. As much as Robert tried, he couldn't remember hearing that Mark had been seen with Rachel, Rosemary, or Lana. He almost snorted at the thought of the large man with Lana. Mark certainly didn't fit her type.

Even if he was, why would he kill the women?

The cab braked in front of the station. The looming structure pierced the night sky, twin towers poking into the darkness, separated by the terminal's main body. Robert paid the cabbie and then hurried through one of the arches and into the building. As he moved, he prayed that he could find the train quickly.

An overwhelming urge to find Audra washed over him. She needed someone with her to protect her.

Jostling around a man who stepped into his path, Robert continued toward the platform. A line wound from the ticket counter as if a fifth of Atlanta had decided tonight was the night to abandon the heat and humidity for any point north of the Mason-Dixon Line.

"Excuse me. Pardon me." Robert pushed his way through the line. Finally, he could see the trains along the platform. Just a bit farther and he should find the Hollywood Victory Caravan train. The caravan's logo should hang off the last car, providing the clue he needed to find the right train.

The tracks each carried a train. Some engines were silent, while others huffed in an eagerness to leave the confines of the station and return to the open tracks. He wound from platform to platform, beads of sweat dripping down the sides of his face.

He had to find Audra.

Finally he spotted the red and orange cars of the caravan's train. He picked up speed until he sprinted the length of the platform and up onto the first car. Changing his mind, he hopped down and hurried to the lounge car. All seemed quiet when he climbed aboard. Then he heard pounding farther in the train.

His breath hitched. "Audra!"

He ran to the next car, hopped across the small divide, and hurried through the first car that housed the women. Every door was closed. The car was eerily quiet other than his own footsteps and breathing. Then he heard voices. Men's voices. They got louder as he approached.

"Freeze." The word was a sharp command.

Robert put his hands up and pivoted on his heel. "My name is Robert Garfield. I'm a passenger on this train."

An officer boarded from the front of the car and approached him, while he could feel the vibrations of steps behind him. "That may be, and we'll sort it out in a moment. Right now, we've got a body to contend with, and anyone we find on this train will be detained."

A body? The blood drained from his face and Robert sucked in air. It couldn't be Audra. Not Audra. He kept his hands in front of him where the police could see he had nothing in them. "Is Audra Schaeffer on the train?" He didn't know what he wanted the answer to be. If she were on the train, it could be her body. If she weren't on the train, then he had no idea where she'd gone or how to keep her safe.

The officer in front approached and patted him down. "No weapons, Chuck."

"Good." The officer behind him drew nearer and indicated Robert should follow him.

"Back to the lounge car with you. Chuck, you go get the girl, while I stay with him." Once they reached the lounge car, the officer considered him. "Mind explaining what you were doing on the train?"

"Audra Schaeffer left the Fox earlier to come back. The more I thought about it, the more uncomfortable I became at the thought she came here alone. You've heard about what happened to Lana Garfield earlier?"

The officer nodded.

"I didn't want something similar to happen to Miss Schaeffer."

"Any reason to think it could?"

"Other than the fact she was attacked yesterday in her car?" Robert shoved his hands in his pockets, trying to look non-threatening and cooperative when all he wanted to do was race down the train and make sure the body wasn't Audra's.

"Tell me more."

Robert filled the man in while they waited for the other officer to return.

Chuck stepped onto the car. "Here's the lady."

Robert sagged when he saw Audra follow the officer into the lounge car.

She lifted her head, and a cry broke from her. "Robert." Audra raced toward him. "They've killed Dalia too."

CHAPTER THIRTY-SEVEN

The sight of Robert being interrogated by the police almost destroyed her. She couldn't have another person ripped from her. Not like this. She ran to him and held on tight, as if he were an anchor keeping her hooked to this moment.

"He was at the hotel last night and at the theatre with me today. He couldn't have killed Dalia."

The officer who'd accompanied her to the train considered her. "You two don't go anywhere. Chuck will wait for the detective outside the car in case you need anything or we need you. Promise you'll stay put until the detective arrives."

"Yes, sir. Thank you for coming with me."

"Glad I did, though I'm sorry about your friend." Warmth and concern radiated from his expression. "You're all right here?"

"Now that Robert's here, I am."

The officer nodded. "I've got to get back to the scene. Stay put." He left, taking the other officer with him.

Robert stroked her back, murmuring words she couldn't understand but that brought comfort. "Are you okay?"

She shook her head against his chest. "No. I had that officer come with me and when we got to the last car—and found Dalia—he pushed me to the side and called for help. The other officer is all that came. I could only watch as they worked. Dalia—she'd been murdered like the others."

Audra burrowed deeper into Robert's embrace, pulling strength from his presence even as she tried to get the image of poor Dalia out of her mind. "Why Dalia? What could she have done to anyone? She was so gentle. When will this end?"

"When we find who's behind it all." He pulled a bit apart from her. "Was Mark in your sister's book?"

Audra tried to imagine the pages she'd seen. Mark Feldstein… She could almost see her sister's scrawl and the odd doodles she'd drawn next to his name. "Yes."

"Certain?"

"As I can be." She closed her eyes and studied the image. "I think he last appeared a few days before someone found Rosemary." Why hadn't she remembered that before now? Had the idea that he'd murder someone seemed so remote?

"All right."

Something in his tone worried her. "Do you really think he's behind all this? He's a nice enough guy, but I haven't seen a hint of passion in him. Everything's about the job." The image of Mark strangling the four women left her cold.

Robert led her to a bench and eased next to her. "He's got a reputation of being seen with different women every night. Each one is beautiful, a star in the making. And he uses his position with a studio to entice them to believe he can help them. You and I know he isn't a producer or director, he's more of an administrator. But naïve young women wouldn't know that. I wonder if he owed somebody."

Audra studied him, letting his words filter through her mind. "Could he owe Artie?"

Robert thought a moment, looking across the car. "I suppose. Artie likes to have people in his debt."

Something still didn't fit. "Why?"

Robert turned and stared at her. "Why what?"

"Why would Artie want to kill the girls and why would Mark agree to kill them?" Audra rubbed her arms, trying to remove the chill that had overtaken her. "It's a big leap to go from owing a debt to committing murder. And why would Artie want them killed? Lana was appearing in movies. Isn't that what agents want? And Rosemary had about made it. Even Artie told me that."

"And that still leaves Rachel outside the picture." Robert reached for her hand and held it, heat shooting up her arm as he did.

The image of poor Rachel returned to Audra's mind. "You said she signed with Artie?"

Robert nodded and continued stroking her hand. Peace flowed through his touch. She wasn't alone.

She tugged her hand free. She needed to think, not get swept away by the electricity between them. Robert pulled back, not breaking eye contact.

Audra licked her lips and tried to smile. "What could Artie have on Mark?"

"That's an excellent question." Robert rubbed a hand through his hair. "And what would tie him to Rachel? The link to Rosemary and Lana is clear."

"If Rachel were an aspiring starlet, can we assume Artie would have forced her into the escort business?"

Robert nodded. "It seems to be his pattern."

"So Rachel and Rosemary worked for him. Lana worked in the movies. Rosemary told us she'd about made her break." Audra tried to remember anything Rosemary had said about the part. "She said the script was titled *Enemy from Within*."

Robert nodded slowly. "But that was Lana's next role. Filming starts when we get back to Hollywood. At least it was going to, until Lana died."

"Does Artie usually send his clients to try out for the same part?"

"Detective Franklin mentioned it."

"Victoria mentioned he only did it with that movie."

"What are the chances Rosemary got the part first, but Artie was trying so hard to keep Lana as a client, he promised her she'd get the role?"

Audra shook her head, trying to clear the murkiness. None of this made sense. Would someone really kill over a role? "That might explain withholding the contract from Rosemary, but not murdering her. And why kill Lana?"

"She'd decided to sign with Rochester Blanks."

Robert stiffened, and Audra searched for the source of the voice. Framed in the doorway behind them, Artie Schmaltz posed.

"Mr. Schmaltz?" Audra couldn't keep the tremble from her voice.

"Miss Schaeffer. Let me extend my condolences again on the death of your sister. It's always sad when someone finds herself in the wrong place at the wrong time." He stepped into the room but kept distance between them.

Robert stared at the man. "Her signing with another agent was enough?"

"It is when your ungrateful lead star abandons ship." The agent studied each of them. "I was surrounded by ungrateful hopefuls. Lana switching sides as her star is ready to peak. Rosemary poised for success, but trampling on my star's path. I couldn't let that happen. In fact, I could have found her another role. One better suited to her."

"Then why didn't you? Why did you have to kill her?" Audra couldn't comprehend Artie's callous attitude toward the dead women. Toward her sister.

"Oh we did—when she stumbled on Mark taking care of Rachel. That girl was ready to bring down my escort business, which is much more lucrative than agenting. Sad to lose two of my girls in one night, but some things can't be helped."

"Why make Mark do it?"

"No sense bloodying my hands, especially when I knew he'd already killed one woman. I didn't go to the police with the information but let him know I'd collect. That gave me the leverage I needed. Too bad that you will now join them. I liked you, Robert, really I did. I flew out here with an offer for a good role for you. Unfortunately, you couldn't let things lie. So I'll find someone else for the part." Artie pulled his fedora from his head then ruffled the flattened hair beneath.

"How did you get here with the police outside?" Robert stared at the man, contempt filling his eyes.

"Simple matter really. Just told the officer one of my stars is on board. When he stepped up here to confirm it, Mark gave him a quick punch. The officer won't bother us for a while." He beckoned behind him. "Getting Mark on didn't take much effort either."

Mark filled the space over Artie's shoulder, an officer slung over his shoulder. He dropped the man to the floor where he moaned but didn't regain consciousness.

"You'll have to do something with them." Artie flicked a hand toward Robert and Audra.

Mark studied the two then looked back toward the door as if listening for movement. "All right. We need to hustle. What did you have in mind?"

"Use that devious mind of yours to take care of this minor problem." Artie looked over the car a moment. "Time to get you two away from here before reinforcements arrive."

Minor problem? Audra didn't like the way he said that. Her mind raced through options. There had to be some way to get away. *Father*. She couldn't imagine the pain her parents would feel if she died. Her breath came in short bursts, and blood pounded in her ears.

"I'll go down on the platform and make sure no one's arrived. When I give the signal, get them off and take care of them. Then we're on the next train out of town. Doesn't matter where it's headed as long as it gets us away from here."

Mark eyed Artie. "You sure that will work?"

"Trust me. We didn't see anything."

The dominos lined up in her mind. Audra looked at Mark, recoiling from his grim smile. "You gave us the night off so that you could have the train to yourself. You knew Dalia wouldn't be welcome at a hotel in the deep South." Her voice rose, and she realized if she was loud enough someone outside might hear. "What did Dalia do to you? She had one of the kindest souls I've known." Her voice clogged on tears she refused to cry. She swallowed, determined to keep Mark from seeing her weaken.

Robert rubbed her hand. Had she pulled him into this too? She glanced at him. His eyes had widened while his cheeks paled. However, there was a sure set to his jaw and he squeezed her hand. He wouldn't go down without some sort of plan.

"Dalia didn't have to die." Robert's words were resolute.

"You want the firsthand dope? Fine. I had no choice. That's what happens when you stumble onto something you should avoid. If she'd stayed in her car away from the performers she'd have been all right." Mark's lips curled with disgust. "Instead, she had to come check on Lana one more time that night. I'd just left when I heard her footsteps and couldn't be sure she hadn't seen me."

"I would have seen her. And she never said anything." Audra was certain Dalia would have spoken up if she'd seen anything. "Maybe you heard me." Horror filled Audra at the thought he'd killed Dalia by mistake.

"At first I thought you were right." He stalked two steps toward them before Artie grabbed him by the collar and hauled him back.

"Not yet. You want to get them away from here first."

"You're right." Mark straightened his collar and shook his shoulders. "Dalia began to cower in front of me. Each day she acted more odd."

"That's why you killed her? You didn't like how she acted?" Bile crawled up Audra's throat at his callous attitude.

"I didn't know when she'd decide to talk to police. Couldn't risk that with her or with you."

"Enough talking." Artie glanced out the window. Whatever he saw made him stiffen. "Time's moving. Get going and make it snappy. Create a car accident or something that will explain how these two could die together. Far away from this train. They had the day off after all. It will be tragic how they ran from the police after sneaking back here.

You get the idea." Artie straightened his tie and slapped his hat back on. "I'm off to distract an officer or two."

Robert held her hand as Mark pushed them to their feet. "We'll make you look all cozy. It's no secret you're a couple."

As they walked toward the door, Robert eased her in front of him, shielding her from Mark.

"Stop." Mark slipped ahead of them at the door. He turned back around and opened his jacket. "I'll have friendly Bertha here trained on your backs. I haven't had to use her yet, and would like to keep it that way. But if you so much as make a peep, I'll fire. I don't think you want to gamble on whether I'm a good shot." He slipped the gun from his belt to his pocket.

The gun looked ominous, and Audra's hope of screaming like a mad woman the instant she hit the pavement died. She couldn't risk Mark shooting Robert. Robert pulled her close the moment they stepped off the car.

Audra stumbled and considered collapsing.

"No, you don't." Mark hissed. "Walk down the platform."

Robert put his head next to hers. "We'll find a way out. Keep your eyes open and keep praying."

"That's enough, love birds. Pick up the pace." Mark looked over his shoulder then slipped the gun from his pocket and prodded Robert in the back with it.

"Ease up. We're cooperating."

Audra moved forward blindly. Everything merged into tiny splashes of color until it looked like she'd entered a Seurat painting. She floated amid the swirling mass. Closing her eyes, she fought a surge of dizziness as they worked their way down the platform and through the station. Few people were around, and none seemed to see their three-some. Audra's steps faltered at the realization no one would bother to notice them, let alone help. Robert's grip on her arm tightened, and she looked up as they left the terminal. The night was so dark, it wrapped around her like an oppressive presence. How could they escape?

"Where are y'all going?"

Audra felt hope spark as she heard Charlie Lester's affected Southern twang. Then Mark stepped closer and shoved that horrid gun into her back. She jolted but kept moving.

Jim Collins approached, watching them with a curious gleam in his eye. "Robert, we wondered where you'd disappeared. Should have known you'd be here with the little lady."

Charlie winked at them and nudged his brother. "I told ya."

"No time to chat. Get on the train, and we'll see you in a bit." Mark's voice tightened, a sharp edge on the words. Audra's eyes widened as he shoved the gun deeper into her back. She tightened her grip on Robert's hand and prayed.

Jim eyed Mark, his jaw clenching. "I know you can be good for my career, but I'm really tired of taking directions from you. Thanks for the day off, but I'm not your servant."

Audra mouthed *help*, not knowing if they'd see the motion in the dim light. Danny studied her, confusion on his face.

"Did you say something, Audra?"

"No." The word squeaked from her lips. *God?*

Robert lurched to the side, knocking Audra off balance. She bit back a scream as she collapsed on the cement floor. Where was Mark's gun now? Had the others seen it?

"Audra, get up." Mark's voice held a steely edge.

She tried to get her feet under her, but her skirt bound her legs. Her breath came in shallow sips as Robert reached down for her.

Mark held his gun, no longer trying to hide it. "Step back, boys."

Robert released her hand, and Audra tried to melt into the concrete while keeping an eye on Mark and the gun.

Danny put his hands up and stepped back. "Whoa. What's this all about?"

"You shouldn't have interfered."

Robert crab-stepped to the side. Mark whipped the gun toward him then back at the other three men. "You'll have to choose, Mark. You can't shoot us all."

"Then maybe I'll start with you." The gun swung toward Robert. A shot exploded and the sound seemed to ricochet off the concrete.

Audra screamed and crawled toward him, the concrete scraping her knees. Her chest tightened as red spread across Robert's shoulder. A drop of blood fell on her cheek as she scrambled to her feet. He clutched his shoulder, pain twisting his lips.

A snarl tore from Danny and he threw himself at Mark. The gun fired again, and Danny crumpled at Mark's feet, but not before Charlie and Jim raced toward him. They tackled the gorilla of a man, and he crashed to the ground with a sharp *oof.*

Audra stood and touched Robert's face. Sweat glistened on his forehead. "Let's get you down." She helped him ease to the ground and then looked for something to press against his shoulder.

"Here." Jim handed her his jacket, from where he sat on Mark's back. "I never liked it anyway."

Charlie lurched to his feet and hurried to Danny's side. "Hang on, buddy. Don't go anywhere." He rolled his brother over.

Danny's face was pale and blood seeped from his side. He moved his mouth but no sound escaped. Police ran up and trained their sidearms first on one, then another, of the men. It looked like a dangerous game of ping-pong.

"Someone want to tell me what's going on?" A plainclothes officer stepped up. He pointed at a uniformed officer. "Let's get an ambulance here."

An officer knelt beside Danny and evaluated his wounds. "Better hope the ambulance is close."

Audra swallowed and pressed the jacket tighter against Robert's shoulder, her hands shaking. "That man on the ground just shot these two men. We also think he's killed four women, including the one who died on the Hollywood Victory Caravan train today. The man behind the killings is somewhere around here. Artie Schmaltz from Hollywood."

Charlie reached for Danny's hand and growled. "Artie did this? I'll get the man."

"We'll handle that part. Nobody move." The detective barked the words as he studied the group. "Handcuff the guy on the ground and the guy sitting on him until we can figure out what's going on."

An ambulance rumbled toward them, siren piercing the night.

Robert grimaced but pressed a kiss to Audra's cheek. "It's all over." He kissed her other cheek then her nose. The trembling built inside her until she felt like a leaf caught in a storm. "You're safe."

"Shh. Let them work on you." She eased away as the crew rushed to his side and Danny's. She watched them load the men, hands pressed to her chest.

She might be safe, but as she watched she knew her heart wasn't.

CHAPTER THIRTY-EIGHT

Friday, June 26, 1942 – Tuesday, June 30, 1942

The police had concluded their investigation, releasing the train to continue on its trip to Hollywood. The members of the caravan had regathered on the train after spending more time at the Winecoff and now sat in shell-shocked silence in the dining car. Danny still lay in a hospital room, his condition hovering between serious and critical. Charlie had refused to rejoin the caravan without his brother. Robert had insisted the doctors release him, which they had just that morning. Even though police had Mark and had caught up with Artie, he had stuck close to Audra since his release from the hospital.

The gentle motion of the train rolling down the tracks threatened to lull Audra to sleep. She leaned her head against Robert's uninjured shoulder, enjoying his close presence.

"What's next?" Victoria voiced the question that hung unspoken. "Are we headed to our next stop or back to Hollywood?"

Audra sat up, instantly missing the connection with Robert. "The studio heads have decided the train's going home. The publicity hasn't gone exactly as they'd hoped and we're far enough off schedule that it's time to return to Hollywood."

Jim's face pinched in a pained expression. "What if we want to stay? Finish what we set out to do? It's not like I'll ever get to wear a uniform. With my bum knee I couldn't even get through the physical. This is my chance to be a part of the effort and something bigger than a movie."

"I agree. We can't let Artie and Mark win by canceling the tour." Elizabeth's cheeks flushed and then she slumped over. "After all, not all of us have roles lined up when we get back. Especially now that it's known our agent was a homicidal maniac."

"I'm sorry, but the men I've spoken to were adamant. The caravan is over."

The return trip was somber. By the time the train pulled into Los Angeles's Union Station on Tuesday, many performers lingered on the platform as if reluctant to separate after all they'd experienced together.

Jim stared at the assembled stars, his cheeks weighed down and eyes heavy. "This caravan was an amazing experience. You are so much more to me than colleagues now. Promise me we won't let this die."

With a hiccup, Constance hugged him. "Let's stay in touch."

Audra watched the good-byes and hugs from the side. While she'd touched their world, she hadn't truly entered it. She'd distanced herself the final days, preparing for her return to Indianapolis.

Robert had stayed close, his shoulder bound with bandages and his arm held in a sling, telling stories and probing into her past. He had even pried stories about Rosemary from her. It had been a sweet release to laugh and cry.

Now that they were back in Hollywood, reality set in. She needed to stop by Rosemary's apartment, clean it out, and board the next flight to Indianapolis. Her daddy had demanded that she return without further delay, and she knew he was right.

She needed to leave but wanted to stay. Robert stood next to her on the platform, their shoulders touching. She memorized the feel of him next to her and the scent of his spicy cologne.

"Is this the little lady?"

Audra jolted from her thoughts to find a man in a tailored three-piece suit striding toward her. He commanded attention and respect in the very way he carried himself. Then there were the two men and a woman trailing behind him. Even Robert jerked to attention beside her.

"Miss Schaeffer? I'm Samuel Mayer." He stuck his hand out, and she shook it. "I've heard good things about you and your role in catching the men behind the murders. You have my thanks." He snapped his fingers and the woman stepped toward her, extending a card. "Here's my card. If you're ever looking for work, contact me. I want people like you working at my studio."

"Thank you, sir." She took the card and tucked it in her purse, though she doubted she would keep it.

"All right. I've got cars waiting up front to deposit you at studios or apartments. Good job, everyone. Way to push through tragedies to help with the war effort." He clapped his hands, and Audra had to stifle a laugh as the others hopped to attention and grabbed their bags.

Victoria hurried up to her. "I wish you'd stay. Please promise you'll stay in touch?"

"I'd like that."

"Then do it." The star winked at her. "I have a feeling we won't have to do it from across the country either. Not if a certain someone has his way."

Audra laughed then hugged Victoria. "We'll see. Good-bye, Victoria."

"For now." Victoria strode after Mr. Mayer, the eyes of every man drinking her in. The reaction left Audra no doubt that Victoria's star would rise to top billing soon.

She leaned down to pick up her bag but stopped when she noticed the masculine fingers that grasped the handle. Her gaze traveled up Robert's length, savoring the sight of him. Could she love him from a distance? Walk away and let others enter his heart?

She stood, shuddering at the thought.

"Let me come with you." Robert studied her, his face wearing a hang-dog expression.

Audra stared at him then shook her head. "The problem with a relationship with an actor is I could never know if you're sincere."

"Trust my heart. Trust my intentions. Trust my love."

Oh, how she wanted to.

"But if you come with me to Indianapolis, it doesn't mean I'll come back here."

"Maybe. But I still want to come." Robert shrugged. "I can't do anything on screen for a while anyway. And I want to meet your family, share my condolences. And see you in your home."

She studied his face, trying to gauge his sincerity. "All right. I hope to get a seat on tomorrow's flight."

"Take care of Rosemary's apartment. I'll arrange the tickets and come by tomorrow to get you." He carried her suitcase to a waiting taxi and opened the door for her. Before she slipped inside, he kissed her cheek. "See you tomorrow."

Audra collapsed against the seat and gave the driver Rosemary's address. Her emotions buzzed in a troubled, confused mix. If Robert really came home with her, what would her parents think of him? And would he like what he saw? The palm trees flowed past the window, standing stark against the bright blue sky. The cab pulled to the curb in front of Rosie's building, and the driver pulled her suitcase from the trunk. She paid him and then tugged the case toward the side entrance. After unlocking the door and putting the bag inside, she stared. Boxes were stacked against one wall, the contents of the wardrobe and kitchen area packed for her. She left and went back around to the front where she rang Mrs. Margeson's button.

The landlady hugged her. "My dear, what a trip you had." She stepped away and studied Audra. "We need tea. Follow me." She bustled to the kitchen and filled the teapot. "Tell me all about your trip."

Mrs. Margeson prepared their tea as Audra related a few stories. Audra took a sip then touched Mrs. Margeson's hand. "Thank you. For packing so many of Rosie's things."

"It was nothing. I had a few spare moments and needed to fill them. I left her desk for you, though. I thought there might be private things that should be left to family to sort."

"I'll do that tonight. Tomorrow I'll fly home."

"Leave whatever you don't want, and I'll see they go to people who can use them."

"Thank you. For everything." They hugged, and then Audra returned to the apartment.

The evening passed as she worked her way through the stacks piled on and around Rosemary's desk. Much of it she pitched into an empty box so it could be put out with the garbage. She sorted the final stack and stopped when she reached an envelope with her name scrawled across it in Rosie's handwriting.

Audra stared at it then turned it over. The envelope had not been sealed, and she slipped out the sheet of paper.

Dear Audra,

Hollywood hasn't been quite the adventure I imagined. I'm sure you've noticed in my recent calls. You always read me like one of the books you enjoy. I don't regret coming, but I do regret some of the decisions I've made. I'm in over my head, but don't worry about me. I'll find a way out. Maybe I'll follow my friend Rachel and come home, but first I have to see if I can land a role in a movie. I'm giving it another three months. Then...well, we'll see what happens.

Don't worry about me...I know you are. I'll be fine. You always worry too much, especially about things you can't control, like me. I love that about you.

Much love,

Rosie

Audra folded the paper and slipped it back in the envelope. She tucked it in her purse. Rosemary knew her well, knew she'd worry about all the things Rosie wasn't saying. Audra wiped her eyes. She'd always wonder what might have happened if she'd flown to Hollywood earlier, but for now she surrendered that burden over to God again.

Robert came by with a cab the following morning in time to catch an early afternoon flight from Los Angeles. After another long series of flights, but before she'd mentally prepared, her daddy met them at the airport the next morning. He hugged Audra then studied Robert. "This the actor you mentioned?"

"Yes, sir."

"It's nice to meet you. Thanks for escorting Audra home." He pumped Robert's hand once. "Well, your mother is waiting at home.

Let's get your bags and go." He led them to the Buick, shoulders slumped and face holding a lifetime of grief. They loaded the luggage and then she and Robert slid into the back seat as her daddy started the car. He eased out of the parking lot and pointed the car home.

"Can we stop at the cemetery?" Audra grasped Robert's hand, realizing she'd never even asked where they'd bought a plot.

Daddy clenched his jaw then released it. "Now you want to see her?"

"Please."

He turned the car onto 38th Street and eventually turned in to Crown Hill Cemetery. The car eased through the rows of graves until he reached Rosie's area. Stopping the car, he turned to look at her. "She's at the top of that rise. You'll see a small white marker with her name. Your mama wants to plant a rose bush there, but hasn't yet. Go say your good-byes." He swallowed hard and rubbed an eye. "I'll wait here."

Audra opened her door and Robert moved to open his, but she shook her head. "I need a minute alone with her. Please."

He considered her then nodded. "I'll be here when you're ready."

"Thank you." She slid out of the car and walked up the hill in the direction Daddy had pointed. Tears clouded her vision and she stumbled among the markers until she found one with her sister's name. ROSEMARY ELAINE SCHAEFFER. Audra sank to her knees beside the mound. She pulled Rosie's letter from her purse and reread it. Carefully she folded it and returned it.

"I'm so sorry, Rosie. I just couldn't come back for the service. But I did it. I found your killer and the man behind it. It looks like Artie will go to jail for a very long time, and Mark will likely get the death penalty." She tugged one of Robert's handkerchiefs from her pocket and studied it. "I'm sorry I didn't get to you in time. But I'm not sorry I went to Hollywood. I've met the most amazing man. His name is Robert Garfield. You knew him. He makes me feel beautiful and like I'm the only person in the world. Can you imagine that? I'm still amazed he notices me. He talks about a future, but I don't know what Mama and Daddy will think. And I don't know that I can live in Hollywood, not after what happened to you." She wiped her cheeks with the handkerchief. "I miss you."

She heard footsteps and turned to see Robert walking up the hill. He paused a few feet away.

"May I join you?"

"Please." She patted the grass next to her.

He sat next to her and tucked her against his side. "I could get used to you sitting next to me like this."

Audra toyed with the charms on her bracelet. "Thanks for coming with me."

"Glad to do it. It could be a bit before the next contract since my agent's implosion."

"What if you don't get another contract?"

"Then God will have something else for me." He tipped her chin up until she met his gaze. "I enjoy acting and transporting audiences into a story, but I don't have to do that for the rest of my life." He shrugged. "I try to be open to what God has for me."

Audra snuggled against him and watched the sun play across Rosie's grave. After a few minutes she leaned away. "Time to go see Mama."

The car had barely pulled in front of the house when Mama rushed through the front door and clasped Audra in a hug. "You're home." Warm tears fell on her as Mama held her. "I've missed you." She released

Audra and turned to Robert. "I do believe you have someone to introduce me to."

Robert laughed and stuck out his hand. "Robert Garfield, ma'am."

Confusion flashed across Mama's face as she shook it. "Lana Garfield's husband?"

"Not anymore. She divorced me two years ago."

Mama looked from Audra to Robert. "I see. Well, welcome. I've got brunch ready to go on the table."

Throughout the meal Mama and Daddy pumped Audra for information about Rosie, sending an occasional question Robert's direction. After the meal, Daddy patted his stomach.

"Thanks for the good meal, Mama. Robert, you have a minute?"

Audra played with her bracelet while watching them leave the room.

"Help me with the dishes."

"Yes, ma'am." Audra cleared the table while Mama filled the sink.

"What is going on with you and that man?" Mama kept her tone neutral but her eyes probed Audra.

Audra sighed and leaned against the counter. "I think he's serious about us, but I wasn't sure what you and Daddy would think."

Mama chewed her lower lip. "The divorce bothers me."

"It is unusual here. I've learned Hollywood is a very different place. And he's made it clear he wanted to make the marriage work. Lana wouldn't hear of it. He's got a good heart."

"Does he have faith?"

"Yes."

"Then we'll have to pray for clarity. How long is he staying?"

Audra shrugged. "I haven't asked. The house feels so empty without Rosie."

"She hasn't lived here for a year, but I understand. Something is missing."

The men rejoined them, Robert looking a bit pale. Audra frowned at her father. "What did you do to the poor man?"

"Only what a good father does. Checking his intentions."

"Daddy!"

After spending a week with the Schaeffers, Robert returned to Hollywood, and Audra tried to settle back into her life in Indianapolis. Mr. Clarion allowed her to return to her job but told her she'd have to wait for another case that would be appropriate for a woman to try. Audra tried to be content, but something important had disappeared from her life. Robert called a couple times a week, but that wasn't the same as sharing a table with him. She missed looking into his eyes, reading his heart. After a few weeks, Daddy asked her to join him for a walk after dinner. They walked a couple of blocks toward a city park, a comfortable silence between them.

When they reached the park, he led her to a bench and they sat.

"What's on your mind, Daddy?"

"You and your young man." He pulled a handkerchief from his pocket and swiped his forehead. "Indianapolis isn't your home anymore."

"Why would you say that?"

"You've been dutiful, doing everything as you always have, but you light up when that young man calls." He shoved the handkerchief back in his pocket and turned to Audra. "Your mother and I are not thrilled that he's been married and divorced. However, we've prayed about it and feel peace. You are a grown woman, and I know from watching you that you don't easily give your heart away. If it is your desire, you have your mother's and my permission to see what develops with Robert."

"What if he asks me to marry him?"

"Then we trust you to say yes only after you're certain you know God's heart on the matter." He put an arm around her shoulders and gave her a lopsided hug. "You are my only remaining child, Audra. I don't want to get in the way of what God may have for you. Robert seems like a good man. All we ask is that you know your heart before you proceed."

"I will. I think I already do."

He squeezed her hand. "I thought you'd say that."

They made their way back to the house. A man waited on the front porch for them, a glass of water sitting next to him. He stood as soon as they turned up the walk to the house.

"Robert?" Audra froze, uncertain her eyes weren't deceiving h

He hurried down the steps and wrapped her in an embra
breathed deeply, the scent of his spicy cologne smelling won

Daddy cleared his throat, and Audra felt her cheeks
forget our conversation."

"Yes, sir."

The screen door closed behind Daddy, and R
chairs on the porch. "What was this conversa
know?"

"First, what are you doing here?"

"I have a contract offer. It's a seven
before I sign it, I had to see you. H
you, Audra." He ran his fingers

"It's been the same way he
around."

He tweaked her no
Hollywood."

"I don't know. What's waiting there?"

"I am." Robert's expression was serious as he looked at her. "We have a future together, but not from across the country."

"How can you be sure?"

"Remember Sam Mayer? He doesn't offer jobs to just anyone. Besides, only God could have put the two of us together. A girl from Indiana and a boy from Arizona meeting in Hollywood. That has God ~itten all over it."

~~ked down then took a breath and stared into the depths
"The only way I'll come is if it's forever."

~aze. "I will promise you forever,

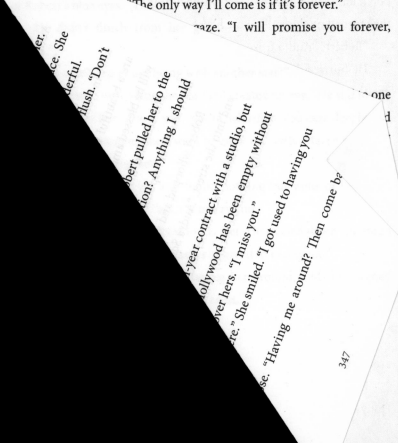

...one
...d

...er. She
...ce.
...derful.
...lush. "Don't

...obert pulled her to the
...tion? Anything I should

...-year contract with a studio, but
...ollywood has been empty without
...ver hers. "I miss you."
...re." She smiled. "I got used to having you
...se. "Having me around? Then come b~

347

ABOUT THE AUTHOR

 Since the time she could read, award-winning author Cara Putman has wanted to write her own stories. In 2005, she attended a book signing at her local Christian bookstore. The rest, as they say, is history. There she met a fellow Indiana writer, Colleen Coble. With prompting from Cara's husband, she shared her dream with Colleen. Since those infamous words, Cara has been writing books.

Cara Putman is an active member of ACFW and its conference committee. She served as the ACFW Publicity Officer for 2007-2008 and Membership Officer in 2009. She has also been the Indiana ACFW Chapter President and currently serves as the Area Coordinator for Indiana.

Cara is also an attorney, lecturer at a Big Ten university, and active in women's ministry, and an all-around crazy woman--crazy about God, her husband, and her kids, that is. She graduated with honors from the University of Nebraska-Lincoln and George Mason Law School. You can learn more about Cara at www.caraputman.com and www.carasmusings.blogspot.com.

summerside
PRESS™

Soul-stirring romance...
set against a historical backdrop readers will love!

Summerside Press™ is pleased to announce the launch of our
fresh line of historical romance fiction—set amid the action-packed
eras of the twentieth century. Watch for a total of six new
Summerside Press™ historical romance titles to release in 2010.

Now Available in Stores

Sons of Thunder
by Susan May Warren
ISBN 978-1-935416-67-8

The Crimson Cipher
by Susan Page Davis
ISBN 978-1-60936-012-2

*Songbird Under a
German Moon*
by Tricia Goyer
ISBN 978-1-935416-68-5

Coming Soon

Exciting New Historical Romance Stories by These Great Authors—
Patricia Rushford...Lisa Harris...Melanie Dobson...and MORE!